DIY
Home

Lorraine McQueen

 FriesenPress

One Printers Way
Altona, MB R0G 0B0
Canada

www.friesenpress.com

Copyright © 2024 by Lorraine McQueen
First Edition — 2024

ISBN
978-1-03-831812-1 (Hardcover)
978-1-03-831811-4 (Paperback)
978-1-03-831813-8 (eBook)

1. FICTION, CONTEMPORARY WOMEN

Distributed to the trade by The Ingram Book Company

DEDICATION

To my Hantsport friends who make this
community my safe home.

Acknowledgements

My special thanks to

Lisa Zanyk who provided endless encouragement,
technical and editorial support and never gave
up on finding a happy ending.

and to

The members of the Writer's Circle at the Hantsport Public
Library who have helped me lay the foundation, build up
the walls and finally put the roof on this story. I am deeply
grateful that I did not have to do it all my myself.

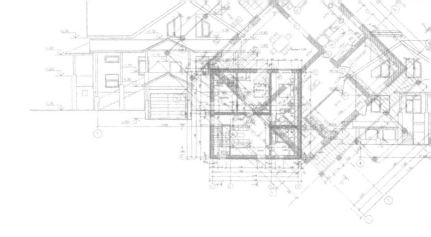

One

G EORGIE MACLEAN WRENCHED open the warped front door and welcomed her best friend Anne into her home.

"Hurry up, Anne. It's almost 2:00. Everything's ready." She led Anne to the kitchen for their annual pre-birthday party ritual. The tiny kitchen table was covered with a starched white cloth. A crystal decanter filled with a pale gold liquid stood on a silver tray with two crystal wine glasses. A small plate covered with a white cloth napkin completed the table setting.

Anne studied the table for a moment then laughed out loud. "Georgie! This looks a lot like a communion table. We should take a selfie with it and put it on social media. We could title it, *The Secret Life of Unholy Housewives*. It would go viral. Where did you get the decanter? It's epic, especially filled with our traditional apple juice."

"Stop laughing, Anne. I thought my fiftieth birthday

party deserved a bit of polish. I found the decanter in the Amigos thrift shop in Windsor. Isn't it great? It doesn't have a stopper anymore, but we don't need to store anything. It's perfect!"

Anne smiled and sat at the table. "Do you realize how long we've been indulging in this childhood ritual? Thirty-four years. Unbelievable."

"Can something be both unbelievable and important? I hope so. This annual ceremony means a lot. Thanks for sharing it with me, Anne."

"Well, I sure understood the need for the first one. You deserved to celebrate your teenage liberation. You were sixteen before your mother finally let you stay overnight at my house. Man, she was tough."

"Tough and unforgiving. If you broke the rules there was a punishment. Detention was her favourite. I was OK with it until I learned she was a liar. Then, I didn't trust any of her rules. I never felt safe in that house again."

Anne sighed. "Yeah, that Santa Claus secret Helen Carter dumped on you sure messed you up, but it's time to get over it. Both your parents are gone, and you finally have a family and a home of your own. You're safe now."

"That's just it, Anne. I still don't feel safe. Helen is still haunting me and poisoning Emily against me. Angus seems to have forgotten I live here. And I think this house hates me because I won't help it. I apologize to it all the time, especially the kitchen. I never thought I would hate anyone or anything, but I've started to hate this house. I'm sure the house feels my hostility."

"Oh, Georgie, It's not that bad. In my expert real estate opinion, you just need extensive updating, a total gut of this kitchen, and some serious exterior upgrades to give it some curb appeal. It's not about to fall down – is it?"

"Who knows what it might do. I'm the only one who ever thinks about it, and I don't do anything for it. One day its patience might just snap."

"Ha! Now I think you're talking about yourself not the house. Let's look at our box, have our treats and cheer ourselves up."

Georgie reached into the cupboard above the ancient fridge and reverently handed Anne a large red box tied with a tattered yellowed ribbon. "Don't yank on that ribbon. It's about to disintegrate. I guess it deserves to. It was tied around that box when I was sixteen. That's a long time to have to hold things together."

Georgie sat at the table and carefully removed the fragile ribbon and opened the box to reveal a plain black three-ring binder. A white label boldly announced, *My House Plans*. The two friends regarded it thoughtfully for a moment. Anne broke the silence.

"Georgie, we've been looking at this binder forever. I can't believe you still don't have a home you're happy with. I think you have to tell Angus how you feel, kick Emily out, fix up this house, and enjoy your life."

"Sure. I'll do that tomorrow right after I organize world peace."

"OK. I admit it was a rather large to-do list. But Georgie, you have to do something. You deserve to be happy."

"First, I want to look at my plans." Georgie opened the binder to reveal a crude pencil sketch of a small one room house. The interior was empty except for sketch of a bed against one wall and a large desk against another. A separate

3

sketch showed the front exterior with a central door and two tiny windows. The steeply pitched roof did not have a chimney.

Anne's giggles were as loud this year as they were when Georgie had first shown her these plans. "Oh my, goodness, Georgie. I can't help laughing. Remember how determined you were to have your own home."

"Laugh away, Anne. It's pretty funny. You know, every time I look at this, I feel my fierce teenage desire to escape my parent's house. It's amusing to see what I thought was important at sixteen: a place to sleep and a place to do homework. Turn the page."

The next drawing was a traditional house plan. It depicted a one-storey dwelling with a separate bathroom and bedroom. The rest of the floor plan showed a kitchen open to the living room. "Can you believe I was only twenty and at university when I did this?"

Anne nodded as she glanced at the plan. "Yes, very modern. You did good, Georgie. That was a tough time when your mum died and you left university to look after your dad. And then he died. Such a shock."

Georgie felt that shock again as she recalled her father's sudden death. Who knew his house belonged to the church and she would lose her father and her home at the same time? She sighed as she remembered her panic of being homeless and the gratitude she felt when the church secretary suggested she apply to be a housemother in a group home.

Georgie sighed again and smiled at Anne. "Well, it all turned out alright. I loved looking after those so-called disabled people. They were a joy and they helped me too. I had a roof over my head, useful work, a modest income, and I was able to finish my degree part-time. Those were good years. Turn the page."

The next drawing was a two-page spread of a plan for a very unusual octagon shaped house. The design was professionally drawn and depicted eight bedrooms all with private baths and a central core housing the kitchen and utility rooms.

"Wow. I'm amazed every time I see this plan," Anne said. "This was the first one I helped you with and we worked on it the whole time you were at the group home."

"I knew there had to be a better way of looking after people with mobility and intellectual issues than packing them into old houses with so many space limitations. No one listened to me though, did they? Turn the page."

The last plan was folded into a bulky envelope. Georgie carefully pulled it out and spread it on the tiny table.

"This plan always makes me so sad," Georgie said. "I had it drawn up by an architect who was staying at the women's shelter when I worked there. I wanted to build a better home for the shelter. You remember, Anne, I came and talked to you about possible properties in Wolfville."

"Oh, I remember alright. You hounded Walker Real Estate for the entire three years you worked there. There was never anything in Town your volunteer board could afford."

Georgie carefully folded the plan and put it back in its envelope and closed the binder. "What a crazy keep-sake box. There's a house plan to improve every home I've ever lived in. Let's have our ritual bread and water and toast the new birthday year."

"Just a minute, birthday girl. There's still no plan for this house. I thought you decided to make this your final resting place."

"Yeah, I 'm resting but not comfortably, that's for sure. You know why. When I first moved in and suggested changes the MacLean family court met and determined that I was engaged in criminal intent and sentenced me to eternal conflict until I agreed to endure in silence."

"Oh Georgie, Emily was just a confused kid and Angus, well, he never sees the need for change. I didn't realize you were still so unhappy about the house."

"Believe it! I've given up hope and so has the house." Georgie poured apple juice from the crystal decanter into the wine glasses and lifted the napkin off the plate of graham crackers. "Let's forget all that. It's time to do our chant and then we can indulge in these silly childhood treats. I love this part!"

The two friends raised their glasses smiled at each other and chanted together as they had done since Georgie was sixteen years old.

Friends together, Friends forever, Friends without end,
Forever and ever, Amen

Anne laughed and took a long drink from her wine glass. "Boy, you sure were a churchy one back then. You should have felt safe. Don't they always say, 'Safe as a church'?"

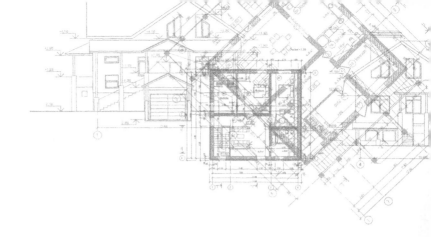

Two

I T WAS BIRTHDAY eve. Georgie stood alone in her kitchen trying to ignore how she was feeling. It should have been easy. A lifetime of self-denial had given her lots of practice, but this morning her feelings seemed to be affecting her whole body. She looked around searching for something positive to distract her. That didn't help. There was nothing positive in this miserable kitchen. She gave in to temptation and thought about herself. She wasn't sick, but she didn't feel well. She placed a limp hand on her forehead. It was cool. She didn't have a fever, but she felt hot and bothered. She considered her GI tract. It wasn't rumbling, but her customary intestinal fortitude was missing. It seemed her whole body was rebelling against today's demands and obligations.

A weak mind creates a weak body, she thought. Time to regain control. She squared her shoulders and fixed the cluttered kitchen with a determined eye. In this lonely place she created miracles, and the multitudes were fed. She was prepared to do it again. Every surface in her small kitchen was covered with freshly washed baking pans, serving dishes and orderly rows of special ingredients. She studied the familiar preparations for a moment then sat down heavily at the tiny kitchen table.

She longed to put her head down and rest, but there was no room. She leaned against the kitchen wall and closed her eyes. Her fiftieth birthday party would happen tomorrow. She needed to cook. She opened her eyes and stared at the ancient oven. "Well, I hope you last for one more birthday. You've got to get me get through this." She stood quickly and grabbed a mixing bowl. *Now, I'm talking to the oven,* she thought. *Bad enough that I've been talking out loud to this kitchen for years. What next?*

She added ingredients to the bowl and considered her future. What next, indeed. She vigorously beat her cake batter as her thoughts turned again to herself. *I'm not feeling angry,* she thought. *That would be pointless. I'm not unhappy. That would be ungrateful.* She wiped a drop of moisture from her cheek. She was crying? This was uncalled for and highly unproductive. She needed to get busy. People were counting on her. She scraped her cake batter into the pans, prayed for a good outcome and thrust it into the oven. Ten people were invited to the birthday dinner. She was expected to provide a variety of dishes for her family and guests. She stared at the crowded counter. What if she just cooked what she liked this time. "You know, Kitchen, I don't want to cook for anyone. I just want to bake my birthday cake."

OK, now she knew what she was feeling. Selfish. Unacceptable! She wiped another tear away and grabbed her phone. It was time to call for support. She called Anne.

"Anne, I need help."

"Of course, you do, Georgie, but you never accept it. What's up?"

"It's birthday eve and I have tons of things to do, but I don't want to do any of them. I'm feeling very strange. I think I might just quit."

"Quit? That's a new one. You never quit. You're always taking on the next great cause. Quit what?"

"For starters, the birthday. Why celebrate my fiftieth birthday when my whole life is worthless."

"Yeah. Yeah. Yeah. Tell me a new one. I've heard that story since you were a kid. It's time to change the narrative, develop a new plot, anticipate a happy ending."

"Very funny. My life isn't one of your precious romance novels. I can't see a happy tomorrow let alone a happy ending. Half my life is over, and I've been left alone in this god-forsaken house."

"Alone? That's rich. You're surrounded by more grateful people than you can count. Angus is the most devoted husband on earth and your doting stepdaughter still lives at home. Then there are legions of the downtrodden and needy you help every day of the week. Alone? Get a grip!"

"See what I mean? Even my life-long best friend doesn't get it. I've been abandoned. Angus and Emily hardly notice I'm still here and the downtrodden and needy don't care who I am. Anne, I'm so tired of being helpful. I don't want to do anything for anyone anymore."

"Wow! This is new and I like it, but your timing sucks. Get this birthday party over and then we can create the self-indulgent happy Georgie I've been waiting years to meet."

"I don't think I inherited the happy gene. My parents only had self-sacrifice in their DNA."

"Oh, Georgie. Stop being a lamb and learn to be a lion. You are woman. Let me hear you roar."

Georgie snorted with laughter. "Anne, pay attention. I'm limp, weepy and confused. The most noise I can make is a whine. Do I cancel the party? My cake is in the oven."

"Ah, The Cake. We can't waste that annual treat. Let's get this birthday party over and then we can work on your jungle moves. Just do what you always do when you're feeling blue. Get busy. Look after people. Cook for everyone. We all love you and we'll be with you tomorrow evening. You are cooking my special cauliflower dish this year again, aren't you?"

"In return for this great advice and all your support?"

"Yeah, you can always count on me. Start cooking! We'll be there tomorrow. You. Alone. What a laugh. Bye, Georgie."

Georgie disconnected and looked around her dreary kitchen. She was alone. How had this happened? Never mind. It was time to cook.

"All I want is a room somewhere," Georgie sang the next morning as she put the finishing touches on her birthday cake. She smiled at the two-tiered chocolate cake piled high with billowy white Italian meringue. She swirled it into a lovely drift of snowy goodness and smiled at her creation. She was feeling better, but there was much more cooking to do.

The landline phone rang, demanding attention like everything else in Georgie's life. No one called her on the landline these days. Their demands were always cell phone urgent.

"Hello?"

"Am I speaking with Mrs. Georgina MacLean?" a deep male voice questioned.

"Yes, you are."

"Mrs. MacLean, this is Simon Peters from Peters, Peters and Peters in Toronto. I understand that our junior partner Mr. Alexander Peters has already talked to you about the distribution of your Great Aunt Beryl's estate."

"Oh yes, we had a lovely conversation. He was very considerate, not at all what one would expect from a busy Toronto lawyer. He said someone would be in touch."

"Mrs. MacLean, we need to talk about your inheritance. Your aunt left a considerable estate, and you are her sole beneficiary. We need to discuss…"

"Well, my goodness, Mr. Peters, I know all this already and I expected you to send me a cheque, I would cash it and that would be that. I'm quite busy today. What is there to discuss?"

"Our firm is prepared to offer investment and other financial advice in such cases as yours. The acquisition of such large sums sometimes overwhelms people who are unused to managing a portfolio as complicated as your Aunt Beryl's."

"Investments? What on earth are you talking about? Aunt Beryl wasn't rich. I should know, I had to send her care packages all the time. She was always a very needy woman."

"Mrs. MacLean, your aunt left an estate in excess of five hundred thousand dollars."

Georgie hung up the phone, sat down at the kitchen table and pulled the icing bowl into her lap. She ran her finger around the rim and licked off the wonderful soft icing. Once a year she iced her birthday cake with her favourite icing. She deserved Italian meringue and a little peace.

The phone rang again. She went to the sink and washed and dried her hands. The irritating ringing finally stopped.

She unplugged the landline from the phone jack and threw it in the kitchen junk drawer. Then she put the cake in the fridge and rinsed out the icing bowl in case she was tempted to lick the bottom clean.

Georgie sighed as her thoughts circled back to Aunt Beryl. "Mercy, Kitchen, now look what that deceitful old dear has done. An estate in excess of five hundred thousand dollars. What a burden! I thought when she died, I'd be finished looking after her." Georgie had sent the last care package to her long-term care home at Christmas. "Well, I guess she finally decided to pay for all that postage. The old tightwad! I refuse to think about her anymore today. I have too much to do."

She grabbed her car keys and her shopping list, climbed into the car and backed out of the garage. Safely on Main Street she burst into song and headed for the Wolfville Farmers' Market.

"All I want is a room somewhere, Far away from the cold night air, With one enormous chair, Oh, wouldn't it be loverly?"

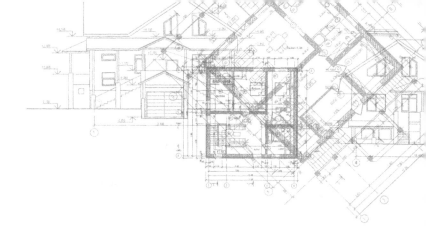

Three

G EORGIE STOPPED SINGING as she pulled into a parking spot at the market. She sat quietly in the car and practiced deep breathing which was supposed to bring calm. It wasn't working. The day was sunny, but she sensed dark clouds on the horizon. Why did her birthday have to be in January when the world was dark and there was a darker and stormier month ahead? Her body felt too heavy to move. Singing usually cheered her up, but that old song just brought feelings of lost hope and impending doom. Was she the only one who could hear the painful longing in those verses? Was she the only one who knew there were people suffering without a room of their own, even in comfortable Wolfville?

Tears blurred her vision as she thought about all the people who were longing for better living conditions. People living in unsafe, violent, or substandard homes and all the people with disabilities trapped in institutions or dysfunctional group homes. A small sob escaped her throat. Some people went through their whole lives without ever feeling safe and having a place to call home. Now she felt like one of them. She couldn't help herself. She couldn't help anyone, but her parents would expect her to keep trying. Her father's earnest reminders to take care of others and her mother's demands to do good every day were a heavy burden. She pounded the steering wheel in frustration. Both her parents were dead but their constant presence in her mind was a powerful argument to believe in eternal life. She searched for something positive to lift her spirits. She was a good person, wasn't she?

She'd spent fifty years helping others, being good, doing the right thing, following her parents' rules. Now, over half her life was gone and despite all her good works she couldn't find any joy in her heart. Well, joyless or not, she had to provide for her guests. It was time to fake it. She was good at that.

She left the car and strode purposefully toward the market. *Blast it!* Anne was standing at the entrance talking to Helen Carter. Georgie hastily wiped her eyes and put on her habitual enigmatic smile. *A lifetime of hiding your true feelings comes in handy*, she thought. *Maybe I'll send an e-mail to CISIS offering to train new Canadian spies based on my fifty years of subversive living.*

Helen saw her coming and hurried away. Good! Whenever they met, Georgie was unfailingly polite, and Helen, unfailingly snide. They had never been friends, but since Georgie's marriage Helen couldn't even maintain a polite facade. Worse yet, Helen was her stepdaughter's aunt and had encouraged Emily to make Georgie's marriage as difficult as possible.

"Georgie!" Anne called. "Happy Birthday! Did the cake turn out? Is your birthday suit washed and pressed?" Anne's loud laughter at her own joke made the market shoppers of Wolfville smile as they passed.

"Very witty, Anne. Yes, the cake looks perfect and almost everything's ready. We'll be ten this year, some old and some new—same as usual."

"Who are the strangers this year?" Anne asked.

"Angus is bringing one of his grad students, Emily invited two clients and I've invited the young couple who just moved in on Pleasant Street. I met them at the Newcomers Club."

"Sounds interesting. See, you won't be alone. I'll be there too and there's no one who loves you more, especially when you cook my favourite food."

Georgie sighed and reassured Anne that she would get her troublesome cauliflower dish, which had to be done at the last minute, and took up much needed oven space. Really! Cauliflower in January. It was so annoying. She said a hasty goodbye and finished her shopping.

SATURDAY AFTERNOON GEORGIE stood in her dull kitchen and reviewed the party menu, a complex meal of family favourites and thoughtful options for the invited strangers.

This tradition had started the year she married Angus. Emily, her then fifteen-year-old stepdaughter, had demanded to know her age. When Georgie replied she would be thirty-four on her next birthday, Emily laughed and told her, "Well, don't expect a birthday party here. We don't do that kind of thing."

Recognizing Emily's challenge, Georgie didn't respond. Her personal experience with birthday parties was very limited. Her parents didn't believe in them. They told her they were happy she'd been born, but not to use the gift of her life as an excuse to ask for presents. Well, her parents were gone now, and she had a new family. She questioned Angus.

"Angus, why don't you have birthday parties here?"

"Birthday parties? Oh, we tried that when Em was small, but somehow, they never went over well. I missed a lot of them, and she was always so angry. We thought it best not to keep upsetting her and just give her a present without a party."

Understanding dawned. Georgie determined to celebrate a family birthday with Angus in attendance. She would use the occasion to invite strangers to share the feast. Of course, she would insist no one bring cards or presents. Her father would be pleased she was thinking of others and asking nothing for herself. She remembered his earnest instruction.

"Practice JOY every day, Georgina. Remember; Jesus first, then Others and then You – JOY. That's the way to a life of perfect peace and abundant riches."

A sharp pang of conscience reminded her of her recent hang-up on poor Mr. Peters who was simply offering her those long-promised abundant riches. It wasn't like her to be rude, but lately her well-guarded tongue was slipping past its usual restraints.

"Whoever guards his mouth preserves his life: he who opens wide his lips comes to ruin," she recited. Ah, yes, her thorough religious upbringing had provided enough spiritual one-liners to guide several lost people through life. She certainly qualified as lost. She no longer went to church. She hadn't trusted her father's God since Grade Four when Helen Carter pulled her behind the cloak room door and gleefully

told her there was no Santa Claus.

Georgie had blurted out the shocking story to Anne as they walked home. Anne already knew and had laughed at her.

"You're mad at your mother and father for lying about Santa Claus? Don't be silly. All parents do that. They think it's fun to fool little kids. Just let on you still believe them. You'll still get Christmas presents."

"Parents shouldn't lie. They always talk about telling the truth and being a good person and stuff. I'm not going to live with them. If they can lie about Santa Claus, they can lie about anything—maybe even God. I'm going to fix up my tree house and move in there."

"Don't be a dummy, Georgie. You can't live alone when you're ten. Your mother would lock you in your room and your father would preach about you in church. Hey, that would be really funny."

Georgie knew Anne was right. She resigned herself to living with her righteous parents. They would not allow rebellion. Her mother, Margaret, had resigned her position as a high school principal in Ottawa when she had unexpectedly and inconveniently become pregnant. Her father, the Reverend George Shaw, accepted the call to become the minister at the Wolfville United Church and her parents devoted themselves to raising their child in the wholesome and supportive environment of a small university town.

The pregnancy and move had not thrown Margaret off stride. She believed in the old adage, *When life gives you lemons, make lemonade.* Georgie understood early that her mother's tart instructions, rules and warnings were focused on making very good lemonade from an inconvenient lemon.

Georgie stared for a long thoughtful moment at her small, dreary kitchen. "Well, my parents were sure they had all the answers. I've tried to live a life they would celebrate, but now I'm fifty and things aren't working out. What went wrong?"

She waited a moment hoping for a revelation. The kitchen was silent. She sighed and opened her birthday recipe box. *"This is the day the Lord hath made. Let us rejoice and get on with it,"* she misquoted to the gloomy kitchen. There really wasn't time to review her entire life. She opened the vintage fridge and took out a large cauliflower and studied it.

"Okay, Anne," she said. "I'll cook your stupid cauliflower dish one more time." Georgie sighed heavily. I'm still trying to make everyone happy. There doesn't seem to be a moment's peace. Where in the devil is that 'peace that passes all understanding' my father was always talking about?

Hours later, she reviewed her dinner preparations. Angus's favourite Beef Wellington was prepped, and several vegetarian dishes were cooked waiting for those who couldn't or wouldn't eat meat. The vegetables were prepped except for Anne's demanding cauliflower dish. A fresh fruit salad was ready for those who couldn't or wouldn't eat her birthday cake. She checked her cupboard to be sure she had a variety of herbal teas for those who couldn't or wouldn't drink fair-trade coffee, either regular or decaffeinated. She looked around the kitchen and remembered the landline phone now lying dead in her junk drawer. *Rest in peace*, she prayed and left it there.

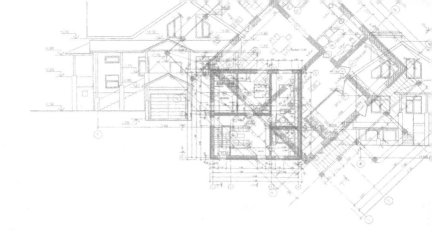

Four

No phones were ringing at the Walker Real Estate office. It was closing time on Saturday night. The thriving Wolfville business of Anne and Terry Walker was strategically situated on Main Street not far from Tim Horton's and the pub. Emily tided her desk and glanced at the office clock. It was only 5:30. She had lots of time to pick up her new client and bring him to the birthday party. Yup. Another weird Stepma birthday party.

Carrie bounced into the room, make-up freshly applied and every shining hair in place. Her latest fashion statement revealed more of her trim body than Emily thought fitting in the Walker Real Estate office.

She studied her friend and fellow real estate agent for a moment. "Is that a dress or a nightgown? No, forget I asked. I wouldn't even wear it to bed. And may I remind you, this is January? Cover up!"

"Fashion knows no season and stop looking at me like

that, you prude," Carrie twirled, sending her barely-there, spaghetti strap mini-dress swirling about her. "Henri likes fashionable women."

"At least you'll be having fun tonight. I'll be hanging out with my parents and yours. It's The Birthday."

"Oh, lucky you. You'll get to eat The Cake. Don't whine. You love Georgie and her crazy birthday parties. Not everyone has a parent who organizes her own birthdays. You don't have to do anything, as usual. Just show up."

"Yeah, lucky me. Before Georgie, Dad never remembered anyone's birthday, including his own. Now, we get an annual ritual and share it with a bunch of strangers. That's my Stepma."

Carrie studied her reflection in the front window with obvious satisfaction. "Right, Georgie's a super Stepma. If it weren't for the poison your Aunt Helen drips in your ear, you would have realized it a lot sooner."

"Yeah, Aunt Helen and Georgie have a weird war going on. I don't really know why. Georgie never says anything bad about people. It's one of her rules. The only thing she's ever said about Aunt Helen is, 'Never trust that woman with a secret'. It's probably something from high school. You know how that stuff hangs on."

Carrie gave Emily an intent look and rolled her eyes. "Oh, yeah. I remember all your teenage shit. You were a weirdo then and you're even weirder now. I don't know how Georgie puts up with you and all your nonsense. You still live at home and let Georgie do everything for you."

"Ha! Don't feel sorry for Georgie. She needs to be needed more than anything. Sometimes it's exhausting just keeping her busy."

"Yeah, sure. No one does my laundry, picks up my dry cleaning, keeps my apartment clean and fills my fridge with good food."

"Carrie, sometimes she drives me crazy. I wish Anne were my mother instead of yours. Anne lets you live your private, adult life free from caring eyes and concerned, helpful hands. You and Henri wouldn't last a week in my apartment."

"Carrie giggled and managed to look smug at the same time. "You'll break out one of these days when you find a good reason. Maybe you'll meet a perfect one at the birthday party tonight. There are always new people. Who are you taking this year?"

"Two recent clients. Mrs. Levy is coming and I'm picking up Ross Saunders. He's having a hard time finding a starter home in town and had to take a sub-let for now, but we're still looking.

"Yeah, housing in town is getting tighter and tighter. No new construction, and the prices of older homes are ridiculous. Mum and Dad said everyone at a real estate meeting in Halifax was talking about a looming housing shortage."

"Tell me about it! Stepma and her affordable housing cult have been whining about this for ages."

"Your stepma's awesome. Mum says she never gives up fighting to help other people. She's a warrior."

"Hmmm. You know, Ross may have to look outside of town. I'm thinking I might show him something in Hantsport. It's a surprising little community."

"Good idea. See if he'll be happy in the Wolfville suburbs. Oh, there's Henri. Where's my coat? Au revoir!"

Emily moved through the empty office checking that everything was in order before she locked up for the night.

She felt a moment of guilt over complaining about Georgie.

She sighed as she remembered the trouble she had caused when Georgie and her dad married. Aunt Helen had urged her to be mean and encouraged all her bad tricks. Her dad had been no help. Emily sighed again as she recalled her father's useless advice.

"Em, don't fuss. I know you're used to my parents looking after both of us since you were born. Now, they're moving to Tideways to be with their friends and enjoy Mum's retirement. Give Georgie a chance. She loves looking after people and she'll take great care of us." Clearly, he didn't understand that being "looked after" was the last thing she wanted. She had wanted to be left alone, but it was not to be. Emily's grandparents moved out, Georgie moved in, and Emily's life was suddenly overwhelmed with intrusive kindness.

She was saved from complete rebellion by Carrie. In the beginning, Emily and Carrie had escaped to Emily's room and plotted passive resistance while Georgie and Anne spent hours in the kitchen discussing how to renovate and improve Emily's cherished childhood home. The house was always a very explosive topic.

"What right does she have to move in here and change anything? She looks at everything with that holier-than-thou expression and I know she has schemes. She's always talking renovation plans with your mother. This is my house. I hate her!"

"Mum says she and Georgie have been planning and renovating imaginary houses since they were kids."

"Well, that's just stupid. How can you renovate an imaginary house? Georgie told me herself she's always wanted a home of her own, but she's never had one. Now she's moved into mine. What a loser."

Remembering her adolescent resentment of Georgie still had the power to make Emily blush in embarrassment. So, OK, Georgie turned out to be a winner. She was wise enough to leave Emily's home mostly unchanged and accepted her assigned role as unpaid housekeeper until Emily was old enough to accept her as a friend. Emily locked up and left to pick up Ross. She would do her duty and attend another obligatory January family birthday party.

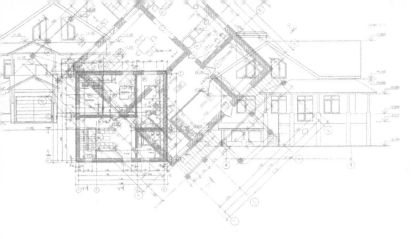

Five

THE PARTY WAS in its traditional pre-dinner waiting stage when Emily and Ross arrived. Georgie welcomed them warmly, made the necessary introductions, and gave the standard yearly apology. "I'm afraid dinner will be a bit delayed as we are still waiting for Angus to arrive. He goes to the university every afternoon, even on Saturdays. Sometimes he's a bit late getting home. Emily, please see that Ross has something to drink while I rescue things in the kitchen."

As they waited, Emily entertained Ross with stories about her childhood home. "My grandfather built this house himself. He was a musician, and this living room was designed to double as a rehearsal hall for his band. He and Nana moved out a few years ago, but we don't feel the need to change anything."

Ross smiled. "It's an impressive space. Will there be line-dancing after dinner?"

"It would serve you right, but I can't imagine my dad keeping in step with anyone. He only dances to the tunes in his head."

Thirty minutes later a relaxed Angus arrived. He smiled benignly at the assembled guests, kissed Georgie's cheek, and surveyed the room. "Good evening, everyone. Is dinner ready? I'm starving."

Georgie presented her unapologetic husband with his usual pre-dinner Scotch, and urged everyone to the table, and the annual birthday party began. The meal was served family style as there were dishes for all food preferences and tastes. As platters and bowls were passed, Georgie anxiously recited the ingredients in every dish. Fortunately, Georgie's birthday menu hadn't changed significantly in the last ten years so Emily could simply help herself and relax. Unfortunately, it took no time at all for Anne and Terry, the owners of Walker Real Estate, to begin educating the strangers on the wonders of Wolfville and the surrounding Annapolis Valley.

Anne started the discussion. "Did you know we have wonderful local wineries. There's a dozen within easy reach of town. You should take one of the wine tours."

Emily had heard it all before. She worked in real estate, but she wasn't interested in selling all the time. She tuned out as the real estate moguls and the newcomers entertained each other. Next year, she silently vowed, I am preparing a guidebook entitled, *Birthday Party Advice*. I'll distribute it before dinner so we can dispense with all this earnest instruction about how to get the most out of your new life in Wonderful Wolfville. Then, perhaps we could have a spirited conversation about politics, religion, or maybe even sex.

She suddenly became aware of Ross Saunders looking at

her across the table. He caught her glance and smiled. *Yes, definitely sex*, she thought.

She enjoyed a few moments of quiet study of her new client. He was a very attractive man. This conversation must be making his already curly hair curl tighter. He was a local boy who had grown up in Wolfville, graduated from Acadia with a business degree, then worked for several years in a large financial services company in Toronto. He had returned recently to work in a local firm. He didn't need the sales pitch.

Still, he managed to convey an air of polite interest even though Emily was certain he was completely bored. She smiled at him in sympathetic understanding. He raised his fork in an irreverent salute and winked. Whew! Stepma must have put a ton of pepper in this casserole. Emily could feel the heat flush her face. She turned her attention back to the table.

Georgie was not eating and was not doing her usual routine of urging others to try every dish. She was sitting quietly, her hands folded on her lap, gazing down the table at Angus. It was not a loving look. Her dad was busily eating his meal and taking no part in this annual recitation of local attractions. His mind was undoubtedly elsewhere, probably working on a math problem. It had taken Emily years of frustrated attention-seeking to learn that her father could not be trusted to hear or remember her most earnest request. He was the very definition of an absent-minded professor. She had finally concluded that the university existed primarily so people like her dad could earn a living.

What was wrong with Georgie? Perhaps the years of patient, loving concern for her exasperating husband were wearing thin. Emily sent an earnest, silent plea to Georgie and the heavens. *For God's sake, don't lose your patience now, Stepma. I'm counting on you to be here for the long-haul. I'm ready to leave the nest. You can have Dad and the house with my blessing.* No, that couldn't be the problem. Georgie lived to look after people. Perhaps now that she was fifty, she was having some hormonal imbalance. Dad better pay attention.

"Hey, Dad. How's the Beef Wellington? You seem to be enjoying it. Georgie's a fantastic cook, isn't she?"

Angus gave a slight start at hearing his daughter ask him a direct question. "What? Oh yes, of course. Wonderful," he said. The strangers wouldn't notice but both Georgie and Emily recognized the standard Angus cover-up. Angus would politely agree to anything, confident in his ability to later deny any recall of the conversation.

She cast an irritated frown at her father and glanced again at Georgie. Georgie had not moved and was now looking at Angus with tight-lipped disapproval. Something was definitely wrong. Why couldn't Dad rise to the occasion and be in the moment once in awhile? He was so irritating! What if Georgie gave up on him? *Hang in there, Stepma*, she urged silently. *Dad needs you and I am desperate to move into my own home and stop worrying about you both.*

She stole a quick glance at Ross. Her face flushed again. She moved the spicy casserole to the side of her plate and helped herself to a large portion of her favourite Duchess Potatoes that Georgie cooked every birthday—just for her.

Georgie was not enjoying this birthday dinner. Patience was a virtue, she well knew, but virtue was not always possible or rewarding. She fought an urge to shout at Angus. He was his usual non-attentive self. He was enjoying his special birthday dish and no doubt thinking great thoughts that had nothing to do with her. *He's left me alone too long. I'm waking that man up before I have another birthday*, she vowed.

She watched Anne scoop a large spoonful of roasted cauliflower onto her already loaded plate. *I'm not cooking that mess next year*, she decided. She looked down the table to see everyone had plates loaded with colourful and abundant food. She noted Terry tentatively tasting the lamb and yogurt stew placed before him.

"If you would prefer a vegetarian dish, Terry, please try my Mushroom Wellington. I think I remember you enjoyed it last year." She watched as he put a slice of the mushroom dense dish on his plate only to regard it with caution. *I'm not cooking that again either*, Georgie thought.

The meal dragged on with Angus, as usual, contributing nothing to the dinner conversation, which always ended up with Walker Real Estate and the newcomers dominating the table. Georgie realized with a start that she was really, really annoyed.

"Wolfville is not the only good place to live," she said, as she stood up and started clearing the table. "I like Berwick, I like Lunenburg, I like Musquodoboit Harbour, for heaven's sake. Is everyone ready for birthday cake?"

Angus continued to chew thoughtfully. He was always the last to finish. Georgie stared at him for a long moment then, without a word, grabbed his plate and marched to the kitchen. Emily and Anne exchanged significant looks.

"I'll go," Anne said.

"What's up, Georgie?" Anne asked as she started loading the ancient dishwasher. Georgie was standing in front of the vintage fridge with her birthday cake balanced on one hand while she studied it carefully.

"I'm trying to remember why I got married," she said. "I know! It was all your fault. You set me up! I was happy working as the housekeeper at The Granary when you demanded that I come to your annual February Blahs party. Remember?"

"Of course, I remember. It was a brilliant move on my part. You were so depressed you needed a little jolt."

"Brilliant? You promised me a grand surprise. I thought you'd bought me a present."

"Yeah, you got a gift that night. You thought working at the Granary and looking after all those people would make you happy, but it didn't. I had to do something. You were so unhappy."

"And what makes you think your grand surprise fixed that? Georgie snarled.

"Hey, get real! I'm proud that I got you two together. You needed to be rescued from your life of perpetual denial of your own needs."

Georgie put the cake back in the fridge, slumped into an ancient kitchen chair and burst into tears. "Anne, I'm very annoyed at Angus. I don't want to cook for him anymore and I don't want to share my birthday cake with anyone. What's happening to me?"

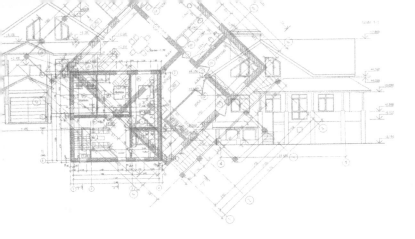

Six

E MILY BREEZED INTO the kitchen with a load of food
platters and bowls. "Dad was surprised you took his
plate, Stepma. He's eating Mushroom Wellington from the
platter. What a hoot. Hey what's going on? Are you crying?"

"No, no. Just tearing up from a good laugh with Anne. I'm
fine. Let's put this food away and serve the birthday cake.
I've been waiting a whole year to have a piece."

Together they served the fair trade regular and decaffeinated coffee and the required King Cole tea for Angus and
offered five varieties of herbal teas to the guests. The birthday cake was properly admired and shared. Finally, everyone
but Anne went home. She joined Georgie at the tiny kitchen
table and they shared the last piece of cake. Unaware and
untroubled, Angus had gone to read in the den.

Georgie was still annoyed. "You were wrong, Anne. I
wasn't unhappy at the Granary. Or at least I wasn't any more
unhappy there than I've been for years. I liked Beth and

David and the Boys. I did good work there and was always busy. I like being busy."

"Sure, you like being busy. It's your escape route in life. If you're run off your feet you don't have to think about anything except getting your to-do list finished."

"Well, at least at the Granary people appreciated me. I don't think Angus even knows I'm still here." Georgie licked that last bit of Italian Meringue of her fork and sighed heavily. "I feel so alone, Anne."

"Never say that. You have me in this life and the next. Angus just needs a little wake-up call. He woke up nicely when you got married. You can wake him up again."

"Yeah, it was good in the beginning." Georgie smiled and gave herself a hug. He's not a total disaster when he's awake."

"Hey, Angus isn't a disaster. You know you've been attracted to him since high school. You would have hooked up in grade twelve if your parents hadn't raised a sexually repressed do-gooder and that slut Julie hadn't seduced and married him."

"Anne! Language! That slut is Emily's birth mother." Georgie tried to look shocked and failed. It felt so good to have Anne on her side.

"Oh, she made me so mad—the snake!" Anne said. "She just slithered in, wrapped her coils around that poor boy's neck and woke up all those hormones you and Angus had been ignoring."

"Too true. I never thought of him as a boyfriend until Julie got to him. After graduation, I just tried to forget about him and move on, but I guess, 'What if?' was always in my mind."

"Mine too! When he dropped into Walker Real Estate and told me he needed to make some changes in his life, I immediately remembered your crush on him and I thought, why not?"

"Oh, I admit I was smitten. His attention was so flattering to a thirty-three old virgin. He was so attentive and so sweet while he calculated when to make his proposal, I had dreams of a wonderful partnership like my parents had. Silly me."

"You weren't silly. You were in love–at last."

"Oh, Anne. Where did all that love and attention go? There were hard times at the beginning with Emily being so difficult, but Angus was on my side. We were a team and I felt so important to him for three whole wonderful years until he got tenure. Now, he loves that damn university more than me."

Anne had no answers and quietly went home. Georgie poured herself another glass of left-over wine, guiltily reconnected the landline and sat at the worn and wobbly kitchen table trying to understand how her decisions had led her to this truly depressing space.

She raised her wine glass to the kitchen. "Sorry, Kitchen, but you really are a dismal excuse for the heart of the home. You look more like a cell in a women's prison."

Gosh, that was harsh, she thought, but years of solitary confinement in this 1960s handyman's kitchen had wiped out any hope of rehabilitation or early release.

When a smiling Angus had showed her his home and had explained that his draft-dodging, hippy father had built it himself in 1967 with the help of his back-to-the-land friends, Georgie had laughed with innocent pleasure. She completely missed that Angus was smiling with pride, not sheepish embarrassment.

The house was what was known in Nova Scotia as a storey

and a half. Its high-pitched roof created a loft that ran the length of the house with two small windows at either end. When Angus married Julie, his enterprising father had created a loft retreat for them. He had added some additional space for a bathroom by raising a section of the roof and adding a small dormer at one end. From the street it always looked to Georgie as if the house understood how unbalanced and lop-sided it looked and was winking at you inviting you to share the joke.

On the ground floor a central hall ran from one end of the house to the other with an outside door at each end. At the front, an ill-fitting front door opened directly into the living room. In the back, a narrow wooden door gave access to the back yard through the kitchen.

The house had an exit door on every side, but after years of incarceration Georgie knew there was no escape. The combined force of a hysterical, hostile teenage stepdaughter and the inertia of a contented spouse ensured that nothing short of a prison riot would open the gates of change. The house came with Angus and Angus came with the house. Forever and ever, Amen.

Georgie drank the last of her wine and apologized again to the kitchen. "Sorry, Kitchen. It's not your fault I'm miserable. I should have been paying closer attention at that fateful February Blahs party. I knew February was a treacherous month."

Angus had been seriously paying attention then. It seemed his parents' decision to move out had focused his mind on self-preservation and Anne had thrown him a lifeline. A week later he invited Georgie to dinner at the Old Orchard Inn. Soon, he became a daily visitor at the Granary where she worked as a housekeeper. He often dropped in with Carol, his colleague at Acadia who was a good friend of Beth, Georgie's employer. Carol was full of cheerful advice.

"Grab him while he's awake, Georgie. He must be strongly attracted to you for him to be so attentive. He's usually oblivious to anything but academic issues. He's a good guy, but he needs a strong person like you to guide him through life."

"Smarter people than Carol have made the same mistake about me," Georgie told the patient kitchen. "They see someone who is organized, energetic and helpful and think we're strong. Anne knows the truth about me. I'm so busy because I'm so scared all the time."

After three short months, Angus had made his proposal. Georgie was equally flattered and amused. It wasn't a romantic proposal. It sounded more like a solution to a math problem.

'Georgie, I've considered the problem carefully and worked out a very elegant solution. We were meant to be together, but I screwed up as a teenager and we've both been alone too long. Let me offer a new equation. Marry me and come enjoy my comfortable home and my beautiful daughter. I'm mathematically certain we can make this work. Carol teaches sociology and she assures me people who marry later in life are statistically more likely to be successful.'

Georgie had accepted his unusual marriage proposal with hope and optimism. She looked forward to a new purposeful life caring for her highly intelligent, if somewhat perplexing, husband and his equally perplexing, independent daughter. She was determined she would make them both happy.

They were married on August 30th, a date chosen by

Georgie to be as far from February as the calendar allowed. She wanted those stars to align in that mysterious universe her boss Beth was always talking about. Marriage to a successful and respected university professor promised a level of security and safety that Georgie desperately needed. It hadn't hurt that his casual but genuine affection was waking up some long-repressed but demanding urges.

So, seventeen years ago Georgie had leapt into the marriage bed secure in the knowledge that Angus and his teenaged daughter both needed her. *Rescue the perishing, care for the dying*, Georgie thought. *That old hymn should have been written into her marriage vows.*

After three years of marriage, Georgie understood Angus's brain was so preoccupied with mathematics he was unable to function adequately on his own. She took over domestic management and enabled him to live his intellectual self-absorbed lifestyle.

And Emily! After her devoted, indulgent grandparents moved out, Emily convinced her father to let her move into the small attached student apartment at the back of the house. From that strategic outpost she waged a constant and effective war against any of Georgie's suggestions or plans for change. Angus and Anne became her willing allies.

"Give her time, Georgie. That's what I always do," Angus had advised.

"Stop trying to turn this mess of a house into the Granary," Anne had scolded. "I admit the place is depressing with no curb appeal, but you aren't trying to sell it, for goodness' sake. Relax! Emily will grow up eventually. In the meantime, enjoy those lively hormones of yours. Angus will never change, but you should be grateful for that. He's a good guy and he loves you in his own way. Patience, Georgie. Patience!"

Georgie rose from the table, carefully placed her empty wine glass in the chipped white enamelled sink and went into the family bathroom to wash her tired face.

"One year older but no wiser yet. Patience, Georgie. Patience," she told her weary image in the tiny bathroom mirror.

Seven

IT WAS A sunny Sunday morning, but Georgie was not going to church today. *"The Sabbath was made for others but not for me,"* Georgie misquoted to the disinterested kitchen which had heard it all before. She recited her Sabbath mantra every Sunday morning to justify her decision, taken when her father died, to never go to church again. She hoped Jesus would understand.

She had always valued Jesus. He liked women, helped the unfortunate, and preached the power of love. Who could be upset with that? It was God she had trouble with. God, who was reported to be watching you all the time to see if you were wicked or good. That sounded very much like another being she once believed in. She had decided to ignore the God story and just live her life trusting that her good works would be rewarded.

Sunday morning was now her own to enjoy with her family. When she first married and had influence in her husband's household, as long as she didn't change anything, she had established a Sunday morning family brunch. This Sunday, like every post-birthday party morning, was given over to a birthday party review.

"You had a great idea when you decided to have your birthday party on the third Saturday in January, Stepma," Emily said. "By now we're all over Christmas and ready for another feast. And I love being able to re-hash the event on Sunday morning. Did this one bother you for some reason? You didn't seem happy."

Angus looked up from his second stack of blueberry pancakes. "I thought it was a bit unusual too, Georgie, I never got to finish my Beef Wellington."

"I suppose I might as well warn you both. I may be having a bit of a mid-life crisis. Turning fifty seems to have awakened long-buried needs," Georgie said, as she poured a large amount of low-calorie syrup over her skimpy pancake.

"Emily erupted in laughter. "Wow! Dad, you've been warned. Pay attention or get swept away by the tide. It's time to man the lifeboats. Here comes the Change!"

Angus bestowed his sweetest smile on his daughter and took Georgie's hand in his own. "I'm sure any change Georgie goes through will be as kind and considerate as she has been her whole life. She's my lighthouse to a safe harbour. We'll sail those stormy seas together, eh Georgie?"

"I'll save you a life jacket, Angus, but you'll have to remember to get in the boat."

"Remembering things has always given me trouble, but I never forget how much I love you two," Angus declared. Satisfied that he had avoided a sudden squall, he took another large forkful of pancake and, chewed thoughtfully.

"And now he's gone," Emily said. "You have to admit when he pays attention, he does some good work."

"Oh, he is the most exasperating man alive." Georgie smiled at a now oblivious Angus. "I love him dearly but sometimes I feel so alone."

"Don't give up on him, Stepma. He's fifty years old too and there's such a thing as male menopause. Perhaps he'll go through some changes himself. It could be good."

"You'd better grab a life jacket yourself, Emily. This feels like it might be quite a stormy year."

GEORGIE WOKE UP early on Monday morning. Hallelujah! A full week ahead to right wrongs and do good works. Perhaps the sun was shining out there somewhere, but never in this bedroom. Angus insisted on sleeping in total darkness, so the heavy drapes over the small bedroom window were eternally closed. The glowing numbers on her small digital clock were the only bright things in the room. Georgie threw back the duvet and slipped out of bed leaving a peacefully snoring Angus. There was no need to be quiet. Nothing would wake him for another hour or two. This was her time.

She shed her nightgown and went naked into the chilly bathroom. She turned on the hot water in the tiny shower and used the toilet. She sat there thinking positive thoughts about the day ahead until the bathroom was warm and steamy. Adjusting the shower, she stepped into its warmth and sang a rousing calypso version of *Morning has Broken*. Her years in the church choir had filled her head with countless sombre hymns. It was fun to jazz them up.

"Hey, I've still got rhythm," she told her blurred image in the steamed-up mirror as she brushed her teeth. "I love messing up those old hymns."

She had been rewriting hymns and bible verses since she was a teenager to amuse herself and share with Anne. Anne had encouraged this creative rebellion declaring a good laugh to be an effective antidote to too much religious instruction. Dear, dear Anne. Her spunky irreverence had kept Georgie sane.

Clean and self-satisfied, a cheerful Georgie left the bathroom and quickly dressed in the dark bedroom. Still smiling, she hurried into the kitchen. Its ambience hadn't improved overnight. OK. She would continue to work with what she had. She sang a churchy version of *Morning has Broken*, as she made her morning porridge.

"Still singing, Stepma?" Emily rushed into the kitchen with her empty travel mug in her hand. She filled it from the coffee pot Georgie had programmed to be ready for her. "You're always so cheerful in the morning, but that song sounded more like a dirge. I didn't catch the words, just the tune. I remember it from Sunday school. Thanks for the coffee. Gotta run."

"Sell lots of houses," Georgie called to her stepdaughter's departing back. "And buy one for yourself," she added as she heard the side door slam.

"Oh, Kitchen, that was unkind. I guess the raging hormones and the loose tongue are still with me. I'd better have a big bowl of calming porridge before I talk with poor Mr. Peters in Toronto."

She finished her breakfast and reorganized the overburdened fridge, wrapping and freezing birthday leftovers and planning what to serve for dinner that evening.

She heard the shower go on in the bathroom and began

to cook bacon and eggs. She always prepared a substantial breakfast for Angus as he never ate lunch. This meal would be his last until hunger drove him home for dinner.

Some time later, Angus arrived in the kitchen and sat at the table. He smiled at Georgie as she put a mug of strong coffee before him. "Breakfast smells good, Georgie."

She didn't bother answering him. He was already reading the academic journal he had brought to the table. *He was probably reading that in the shower,* she thought.

She put his plate of bacon and eggs and two slices of toast in front of him and took the journal out of his hand. "I'll just hold this for you until you finish your breakfast, OK?"

"Thanks, Georgie. I'm going to have to write a letter to the editor about this Erlichman article. The solution proposed is totally inadequate. I don't understand peer review anymore. Where do they find these peers?"

"Angus! Stop!' She reached over and moved the sugar bowl. He looked up in some surprise. 'I always have sugar in my coffee, Georgie."

"Yes, dear. But four teaspoons are enough sugar for one cup of coffee. You wouldn't want to ruin that boyish figure of yours." He still did look very much like the teenage boy she was once too repressed to make a move on. Thankfully, they had enjoyed lots of moves when they were first married. It seemed so long ago. *Oh Angus,* she prayed, *please wake up and love me again. I'm so lonely.*

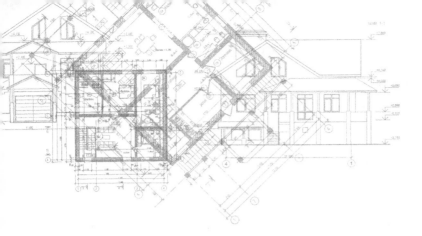

Eight

ANGUS QUICKLY FINISHED his breakfast, picked up the journal and his coffee, and went into his office.

Alone again in her dreary kitchen, a resigned Georgie refilled her coffee mug and settled at the kitchen table with her weekly planner. Good works would distract her all week. This week included Tuesday's Town Council meeting when she would present her latest appeal for affordable housing. She didn't have to work on that speech. She had been giving it for years.

Her mind reviewed her morning with Angus. How had she let him slip away? Early in her marriage Georgie had realized Angus was not just preoccupied with intellectual matters, he was consumed by them. She reminded herself that he was a kind, generous man when he was told of the need. That certainly counted as a very large pro on any wife's pro and con list.

It's a good marriage, Georgie reassured herself. It had

certainly been fun in the beginning as a thirty-three-year-old virgin and a self-described born-again husband explored the delights of the marriage bed. What Angus claimed to have forgotten about sex resurrected itself quite naturally. Georgie revelled in letting go of the control she had previously imposed on her body and let it enjoy itself without restraint. She finally understood why her parents were so afraid of sex. It was wicked fun and wildly addictive.

Slowly, Angus and Georgie found a way to share a harmonious and peaceful union in this tired, old house with a willful, resentful teenager. There were no more children, of course. Angus had had a vasectomy years ago. "I was determined I wouldn't be responsible for another woman's death," he confessed to Georgie before their marriage.

Georgie gradually took over the routine maintenance of their daily life and became a stalwart community volunteer. Her life was full and full of purpose. Many people depended on her. They still did. Why did she feel so alone? A sudden spurt of rebellion interrupted Georgie's calm appraisal of her married life. "I don't want to do anything for anyone today. I'm going shopping," she announced angrily to the innocent kitchen.

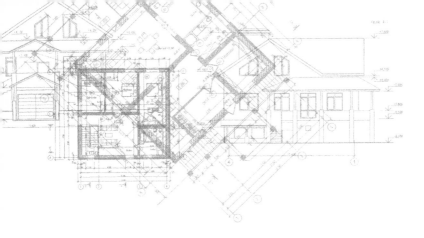

Nine

T HAT NIGHT, A guilty Georgie served Angus leftover casserole and reheated birthday party veggies. He didn't notice the leftovers or her inner turmoil.

"Angus, have you heard the phrase, 'retail therapy'?" she asked.

"I think Em may have mentioned it a few times," he said, "but I've never really understood it."

"Well, it might work for teenagers, but it doesn't work for a middle-aged woman. I went to the city today and visited every box store and every second-hand outlet I could find. It made me miserable."

"Box store?"

"Oh, never mind. I'm going to call Anne." She left Angus at the dining room table and went into the kitchen. She picked up the landline and saw a 'new message' notice. She quickly hung up and grabbed her cell.

"Anne, I need help."

"I know Georgie. I saw the agenda for the Town Council meeting tomorrow night. I see you're scheduled to make another presentation. How long are you and that rabble rousing group of housing activists going to harass Town Council? You know municipal governments don't control the housing market."

"Well, of course I know that, but they can set policies and restrictions that ensure there are affordable units included in every new development. Even that small change would help."

"Oh Georgie, you know that isn't a viable solution, but you never give up. Well, I'll be there tomorrow ensuring a voice of quiet reason to counter your unrealistic demands. You can't change the entire real estate market overnight, you know."

"Overnight? Jesus wept! I've been working for decent affordable housing for the past 25 years. Twenty-five years of watching successive governments do nothing while my housing advocate groups faced years of disinterest and hostility for trying to establish adequate housing as a basic human right. I'm so tired. Forget real estate. I'm in other serious trouble."

"Hey! Glad to hear it. It's time you did something sinful. Let me guess. You bought two new pairs of socks and you only needed one. Avarice."

"Anne!"

"Not spending money on yourself? I know. You were supposed to take cookies to that old lady you check on every week and you forgot. Elder neglect."

"Anne, stop!"

"No, no. I get three guesses. I know. You were helping that boy you tutor to get ready for a math test and he failed. You were always terrible with math, but you thought you could help. Vanity."

"Anne Walker, stop right now. I need help and I'm not the problem. It's my Aunt Beryl who's committed the sin. You remember her, my mother's oldest sister who moved to Toronto years ago and has been plaguing me ever since."

"Sure, the one you're always sending care packages to? What's she done now? The old girl must be in her nineties. It can't be that bad."

"You think? Well, after years of urgent phone calls every two or three months for items she could not live without, she up and died. I just sent her a box at Christmas full of dulce, Nova Scotia maple syrup, King Cole tea, Purity ginger cookies, and Milk Lunch crackers supplemented by my own baking. She had to have my gingerbread, orange and raisin cake, and oatcakes every Christmas."

"God almighty, Georgie. Not much wonder she died. What were you thinking?" Anne laughed and then sobered. "Oh, sorry, but that was a very funny list. What happened?"

"She died of a massive stroke, so it might have been glut-tony that took her away."

"Gluttony? Oh, you and your seven deadly sins! Stop worrying. If she ate a big piece of your gingerbread, I'm sure she died happy."

"Just listen, Anne! I got a call from her lawyer saying I am the sole beneficiary of her estate, and she left me a lot of money."

"OK. Now I get it. This is that deadly sin called avarice you talk about all the time. You're opposed to accumulating worldly goods and you don't want to have to decide what to do with the money. No worries. Just give it to one of your causes like you always do."

"Well, perhaps, but this is a little more complicated than a tax refund cheque. She left me over a half a million dollars."

There was an unusual silence on the phone line. Georgie waited patiently until Anne had regained the power of speech. It didn't take long.

"Hold on a minute! Don't do anything rash. I know you. You're going to tell that lawyer to keep the money. Georgie, you need to think carefully about this. Don't make any hasty decisions."

"I'm trying to stay calm, but it was an awful shock. Who needs that kind of responsibility? The lawyer called me on my birthday. I was busy icing my cake and I hung up on him. I should have called him back today. I had good intentions this morning, but then I couldn't face it, so I went to the city and avoided the phone all day. I'm on the road to hell."

"Oh, that preacher father of yours. You are the most guilt-ridden non-believer I know. Lighten up. It's too late to call Toronto now. It's OK to sleep on this for another night or two. Lawyers are never in a hurry. Don't do anything stupid. Take your time. Promise you'll talk to me before you make any decisions. Promise!"

"OK. OK. I promise. I'll talk to you before I make any decisions." Georgie ended the call with relief. There was no hurry. Mr. Peters could wait. She and Anne would talk this through. Anne lived in what she always referred to as 'the real world'. Georgie wasn't certain buying and selling were more real than giving and receiving, but they certainly were more popular.

"*Tomorrow, tomorrow, I love ya tomorrow,*" Georgie sang, as she got ready for bed. "I love that song. Things always look better in the morning."

ANGUS DID NOT appreciate mornings, but they were not usually so confusing. This Tuesday morning, as he walked down the hill to his university office, he realized his thoughts were unsettled by the morning's events. He recalled Georgie's surprising mood and demanding questions.

'Angus. Hurry up. I need to clean up this inadequate house and make some important telephone calls. Can't you read that journal at the university?'

'Angus, I'm going to cancel the landline. No one ever uses it except nuisance callers. Emily can't object to that, can she?'

'Remember, I won't be home for dinner tonight. My Citizens for Affordable Housing group is making a presentation to Town Council and then we'll go to the pub. I'll leave you a cheese sandwich and program the coffee maker for 6:00. Can you be home by then?'

Angus knew Georgie didn't expect answers to all those questions. After seventeen years of marriage, she understood he couldn't respond to demands in the morning. He left as quickly as he could and sought the safety of his ordered, academic life. No one expected immediate answers to any questions at Acadia. They understood intellectual considerations took time.

He stopped for coffee at the student union kiosk and saw Greydon, Carol's husband. "Hey, Greydon. Heard your new research project got funded. Congratulations. By the way, does Carol ask questions at breakfast?"

"Thanks, Angus. It's an important project. We hope we'll be able to influence environmental protection policy. Carol? Questions? Never. But she does tell me a lot sometimes."

"Never, eh? It's a real bonus to be married to another professor. Georgie is a wonderful woman, but she doesn't appreciate some aspects of the academic life. Sometimes she just wants action, not careful consideration."

"She has my sympathy being married to a pure mathematician. You theoretical guys never reach a conclusion. Greydon laughed and strode off to the certain world of applied science leaving a bemused Angus standing helplessly in the great divide between pure and applied research.

"Well, Erlichman thinks he's reached a conclusion," Angus told Greydon's departing back. "But when he reads my letter to the editor about his latest paper, he'll see how far off the mark he is. Conclusions in mathematics are always subject to criticism and improvement. That's the beauty of real intellectual endeavour."

Satisfied with his defence of his beloved mathematics, Angus put morning confusion behind him and entered his comforting office. The Math Department was housed in the basement of the science building. It was fitting, he thought, that mathematicians should be on the bottom floor.

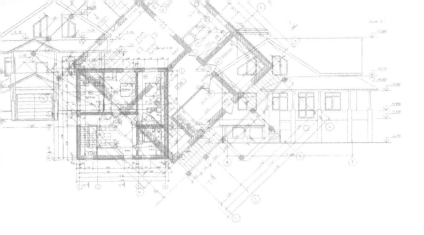

Ten

STILL TRAPPED IN the house, Georgie said a little prayer of forgiveness for her unkind treatment of Angus and turned her thoughts to housework. *Work for the night is coming,* she sang as she dragged the ancient upright vacuum from the cubby hole under the loft stairs. Unkind thoughts surfaced again as she surveyed the living room's worn carpet. It wasn't improving with age. "Nothing I do makes any difference around here, she thought. But Tuesday we vacuum, so vacuum we must.

She paused to study the dining room table which still had its birthday decoration in place. It looked worn and depressing without the cover of birthday food. *Why didn't I buy a new birthday tablecloth?* All these tired decorations are so shabby, just like the rest of this house. *Why am I always making do? I want to buy some new things. I want...*

"Selfish, selfish, selfish," she chanted as she forcefully yanked off the offending tablecloth. She decided to buy a beautiful new one the next time she was in a box store. Most of the time she didn't know what would make her happy, but today she was certain. She wanted to be surrounded by beautiful things. A wave of guilt arrived right on cue. *Selfish, selfish, selfish.* It was her personal mantra whenever she dared to think about what she wanted for herself.

Her cell phone rang in the back pocket of her jeans. *I want a beautiful room with a large bookcase and no telephone,* she thought. *Oh, wouldn't it be loverly.*

She checked caller ID. It was Emily. "Hi, Emily. Did you forget something?"

"I just called to remind you about the dry cleaning. I'll need my suit tomorrow. Can you pick it up today?"

"No problem, sweetie. I'll have time this afternoon. Remember, tonight, I'll be at Town Council. I'll leave your suit in your apartment. OK?"

"Thanks, Stepma. You're the best. Bye."

Tuesday morning housework done, and unselfish purpose restored, Georgie packed away the birthday debris, put the tired vacuum back in its place and left for the dry cleaners. Later, there would be time enough to make that important, difficult telephone call to Toronto.

Stepping reluctantly into the pungent interior of the dry cleaners, Georgie tried to remain calm. The rows of hanging clothes always evoked the memory of that hated elementary school cloakroom. The place where she lost her childhood faith in Santa Claus, her parents and God.

The memory was still vivid and still felt like an open wound. Anne had never understood the power this secret had on a child who had been raised to be honest and do good every day. Georgie had tried to explain.

"Anne, my parents lied about Santa. They took away my trust in adults. I felt betrayed and completely on my own. They didn't even love me enough to tell me the truth. I knew I would have to look after myself from then on."

She sighed heavily as she handed the dry-cleaning ticket to the friendly lady behind the counter. The clerk regarded her closely and asked. "Havin' a bad day?"

" It's not your fault," Georgie told her. "But this place always reminds me of a very unhappy childhood memory."

"Tough, I have a few of those myself. Childhood ain't all it's cracked up to be. That'll be $34.95 including tax. There's another bad memory for you."

Georgie tried to ignore the lady's amused chuckle as she swiped her credit card, carefully draped the expensive wool suit over her arm, and headed out the door.

"Have a nice day, dear," floated out behind her on the chemical laden air.

"You too, smarty pants," Georgie muttered as she started the car. She tried to regain her composure and not think anymore about cloakrooms, Santa, and wise cracking clerks. "Have a little sympathy, Georgie," she told herself. The poor woman would probably have to retire early with chemical induced lung problems or terminal guilt from causing her customers bad memories.

She felt her optimism returning as she self-righteously passed each New Minas fast food establishment and turned carefully into her favourite lunch time haunt, Edible Art- wholesome local food artistically presented. She would have a sandwich and buy one of their excellent soups to leave in Emily's fridge when she dropped off her suit.

That would count as a good deed. *Some of my childhood*

memories are good, she thought as she munched her delicious turkey melt. Father was right about so many things. There's nothing so uplifting as doing a kind deed. She smiled as she remembered how her father's church had become her good deed training ground. In her early years she folded church bulletins, dusted pews, and helped tidy Sunday school classrooms. As a teenager she babysat in the nursery, taught Sunday school, and sang in the youth choir. Oh yeah, and worked with Angus at the local food bank. That was good.

Doing good had become her way of life, but it was strange how it never felt as though she had done enough. No matter how many people told her she was wonderful, she was always sure her father would want her to do more and be more. Poor Father, he never felt he had done enough to save the world. Now, the sins of the father were visited upon the next generation. Well, at least he never learned that her good works had become her personal atonement for losing her faith rather than proving her devotion to it.

RETURNING HOME, GEORGIE delivered Emily's suit and supper to her private apartment. The apartment was the one building project in this hippy-built house that Georgie appreciated. Emily's Grandfather, William Robert MacLean, AKA BillyBob to his Alabama family and BB Gun to his fans, had created much needed student housing when he enclosed the long porch on the back of the house. He built an outside entry, a tiny galley kitchen with a breakfast bar, a modest living room, a three-piece bath, and a small cozy bedroom. A convenient connecting door had been added between the apartment bedroom and the house kitchen when Emily moved in as a teen-ager.

Georgie moved through the apartment tidying as she went and entered the house through the kitchen door. She remembered again her shabby treatment of Angus at breakfast. She would make amends by putting his favourite lamb shank recipe in the slow cooker. *I wonder how many sticky notes I need to lead him to his dinner*, she thought. One on the coffee pot, one on the fridge door, one on the cupboard with the dinner plates and one on the cutlery drawer should do it.

She shared a sudden thought with her unresponsive kitchen. "You know, Kitchen, I am a great consumer of sticky notes. I could use some of Aunt Beryl's money to buy stock in the sticky note company. Of course, I haven't decided yet how to manage Aunt Beryl's legacy. I don't believe in investing in the stock market, and I don't have a clue who makes sticky notes. Stupid me! Stupid money!"

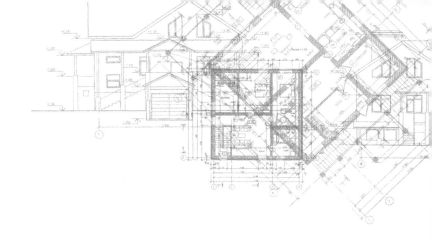

Eleven

GEORGIE CONSIDERED HER wardrobe as she considered how to dress for her presentation to Town Council. She wanted to look forceful but not pushy. *Why did women have to worry about their clothes all the time?* She had never paid any attention to fashion trends, but she did care about making a good impression. Professional competence was a difficult look to pull off with her selection of jeans, tee-shirts, and bulky sweaters. *Maybe I should borrow one of Emily's suits,* she thought. *OK. Perhaps not the best look for someone who doesn't own panty hose or a shoe with a heel. I'll go as myself – again.*

She was getting tired of talking to Town Council. This was her third presentation in the past two years. Her committee had lobbied hard to have the latest Wolfville housing development include affordable rental units. Now that the project was complete, it was clear the people she represented would not be renters. Tonight, she was expecting significant frustration on all sides. Helen would be there sending snide looks and bad karma. Sometimes Georgie regretted her childhood vow not to use nasty swear words. Anne used all those words anytime she felt like it. Georgie smiled as she remembered Anne calling Helen a 'stupid bitch' in high school. That was a fun day.

The poor and Helen are always with us, she misquoted as she dressed in appropriate basic black and left the house.

Georgie largely approved of Wolfville Town Council and its charismatic Mayor. It was a quirky body that made wildly newsworthy by-laws. Hailed as a progressive and bold governing body, it had distinguished itself by establishing Wolfville as Nova Scotia's first nuclear-free zone. Georgie still remembered the pithy comments in her father's congregation about how safe they felt now that Russian submarines would be banned from the Wolfville harbour.

Why couldn't there be a by-law against homelessness, she wondered. Unfortunately, homelessness was a concept widely recognized by the general population as apt punishment for 'those people'. The wayward, uncontrollable teenagers, drunks, drug addicts and others who obviously deserved what happened to them. Society was generally content to let people die on the street every winter. Many were comforted by their conclusion that the dead were victims of their own irresponsible life choices.

Georgie knew better. She knew many people were homeless because the only home available to them was unsafe. This was especially true for women and children. Others suffered from mental health problems that made the regimented and restrictive rules in social housing impossible for them. Over the past twenty-five years Georgie had worked to improve shelters, manage soup kitchens, organize winter clothing drives, and push for affordable housing. It was not enough.

Sometimes it seemed a hopeless struggle, however, "the times they were a changin'", as Bob Dylan sang. About ten years ago there was a serious economic recession affecting mortgages and home ownership. Now, the advent of Airbnb and upward pressure on the housing market was beginning to change public perception. The media were reporting relentlessly on the need for affordable housing and the public was becoming aware that house purchase and rental costs were rising to a point of crisis. Suddenly, it seemed even 'good people' were finding it hard to find an affordable home.

Tonight, as Georgie and her group arrived for another presentation, she was hoping to appeal to the self interest and self preservation of the middle class. She noted that Helen was in attendance. She was talking earnestly with Stan Keddy, a local builder. He didn't look pleased with her attention. *I wonder what poison secrets she's whispering in his ear.* Georgie thought and then forgot about Helen as the Mayor called the meeting to order and her presentation began.

In this year of 2018, affordable housing is no longer the problem of the poor and disadvantaged. It has become an economic reality for many of our fellow citizens. The current real estate market is driving the cost of rental accommodation and available homes out of reach even for those with steady employment. We understand this is a national problem partly caused by global events. It is entirely possible that some new unforeseen economic crisis or other world-wide event will potentially create an even more serious housing shortage. We need to be prepared. We need action now.

"THEY MIGHT AS well have told us not to come back," Harold growled, as he wheeled up to the table. The presentation over, Georgie and her fellow committee members had moved to the pub. Georgie didn't drink alcohol in public. Her mother might be dead, but her dictates were not forgotten. She joined the others and despondently sipped her mineral water.

"I know, Harold. It's very disappointing and I think we may have to look elsewhere for solutions. It seems Town Council is not going to help us. Perhaps we need to appeal to the Provincial government. I'll do some investigating. When we meet again in March, we may have some other ideas to explore."

"That's too long. March is too far away. Oh, I forgot. We don't meet in February," Isobel said. She looked at the floor as she spoke. Her self-confidence had improved since she joined the group, but years of being called stupid had left her with scars. She still couldn't give her opinion without expecting ridicule.

Georgie hastened to reassure her. "That's true, Isobel. It does seem like a long time before we meet again, but some of us have trouble getting to the meetings in winter and February is always a bad month. I'll check in with you next week. You always have good ideas to share." A shy smile lit up Isobel's face.

The frustrated conversation about their latest failure continued around her as Georgie sipped her drink and observed her loyal soldiers. She had just led them into another defeat. That wasn't fair. These were wounded people who had suffered so many defeats in their lives. Anne had told her the Council couldn't help, but she had insisted on trying again.

Good Heavens. Her actions were a perfect example of sinful pride. It was a sobering insight. Self-awareness and a sense of shame at her own shortcomings almost overwhelmed her. *I need to revise my plans, my leadership role, and maybe my whole life,* she thought.

She sat at the table nodding and smiling and feeling a new understanding and appreciation of Angus. Sometimes, it was a good thing not to be entirely engaged in a conversation while you considered startling new thoughts.

She decided to use these last days of January for some serious self-reflection. Another bible verse came to mind. St. Luke had some good advice.

> *For which of you, desiring to build a tower, does not first sit down and count the cost, whether he has enough to complete it?*

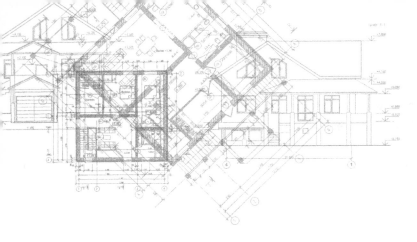

Twelve

FEBRUARY ARRIVED RIGHT on schedule and Georgie
was miserable. Again. February was a month of
frozen thought and stormy emotions. A month to endure.
Remembering her mother's stern voice demanding that
she, 'snap out of it!' didn't help. Georgie tried to keep a low
profile until the longest month of the year for her came to
an end. Experience had proven it was impossible to control
February events.

It didn't help that this February's miseries were augmented
with a burden of guilt. She still had no more insights for her
housing group, had not talked to Anne about her legacy, nor
called Mr. Peters. The last days of January had melted away
on a slippery slope of defeat and avoidance. She finally sent a
message to Mr. Peters telling him she would not be prepared
to speak with him until March.

February! Before she could control it, her February
worry list took over her thoughts. February was African

Heritage month in Nova Scotia. The media reminded her daily of the suffering, oppression, and injustice her black friends and their ancestors suffered for over a hundred years of dark Februarys. As if that weren't enough, remembered death dogged February. Her mother had died suddenly of a massive stroke on February 2nd. Georgie then left university to look after her father and only a year later, on February 21st, he had a heart attack and died on the way to the hospital.

And, how could anyone forget February 14th, St. Valentine's Day? Georgie knew, despite all the media hype, this was often a miserable day for children and adults. Charlie Brown's experience of Valentine's Day was a truer reflection of the day for her and many of the disadvantaged and isolated people she knew. They never received any loving recognition from anyone. Her own Valentine's Day neglect had not changed with her marriage to her calendar-challenged husband. February14th! Bah! Humbug!

Anne understood Georgie's irrational fears of February and the general February malaise Nova Scotians felt as the uncertain winter wore on. She hosted an annual February Blahs party on the Saturday after February 14th, a party where everyone could put aside their Valentine's Day disappointments, their weariness with winter, and celebrate that the month was now more than half over. Guests were encouraged to bring favourite comedy clips to share, play games, sing Karaoke or just eat, drink and be merry. Georgie had reluctantly attended every year, but had yet to feel merry.

Anne had already called several times to ensure that Georgie would come to her party this year. Tonight. Georgie decided she would rather live with her blues than endure another night of Anne's idea of fun. It was late in the evening, but she called Anne anyway.

Anne answered immediately. "Georgie! I was just about to call you. I have the best news. Carrie tells me Emily and Ross, that attractive young man she brought to your birthday party, have been seeing each other almost every day. Carrie says Emily is really interested in him. If she gets lucky then so will you. This may be the start of her needing a place of her own."

"Oh Anne. Emily has 'gotten lucky' before, but she never even thought of moving out. She just went on a lot of weekend trips. I don't think she wants to depend on a man."

Anne was sympathetic. "You can't blame her, Georgie. She's lived too long with Angus to think of men as useful."

"Sad but true. I've given up hope," Georgie said.

"You always give up hope in February. Listen up! Today is Valentine's Day. I know you didn't notice, but the party's this Saturday. Emily and Ross will be here and so will Carrie and Henri. We need them to start making marriage plans. Good-bye blues, hello grandchildren! Then we can work on world peace. Don't come without Angus. He needs to see them together too."

"I'll think about it. I'm going to bed. Bye."

GEORGIE ENTERED THE dim bedroom in a very irritated mood. Once again Angus had not noticed it was Valentine's Day. Thoughtless, neglectful man! Oh, she had to get a grip on these raging hormones. She learned early in life that anger was counter productive. Her childhood anger was met with instant punishment by her mother and bewildered, wounded hurt by her father. Anne had always laughed at her.

Angus followed Georgie into the bedroom fully prepared

to launch into his nightly routine of reporting on the exasperating world of academic publishing. However, tonight, Georgie was going to set the agenda. She spoke sharply before he could begin.

"Angus! Pay attention please. You need to hear this. Anne tells me there's a new man in Emily's life. Apparently, she's seeing a lot of that nice looking young man she brought to the birthday party. Perhaps there will be some changes here. She may want to move out."

Angus stared at the cracked ceiling thoughtfully for a few moments. "Oh, I wouldn't think so, Georgie. Em's been interested in men before, but she always remembers her place is with her family."

"Angus! That's absolutely gothic! This is 2018 not 1818. You can't be serious. You daughter is thirty-two years old and needs a family and home of her own."

"This is her home, Georgie. It was our agreement when we married. In fairness to you and your need for security, I put your name on the deed. In fairness to Em we both left the house to her in our wills. She loves this house as much as I do. I promised her when you moved in that you wouldn't change it and she would inherit it one day. I can't see her giving that up for a man. We can always expand the apartment if necessary." Distracted from his normal routine he crawled into bed and turned off his reading lamp throwing the room into irritating darkness. "Sweet dreams, Georgie. Don't worry about Em."

Georgie gave up on another fruitless discussion with Angus. OK, let's face it. She always gave up. Conflict wasn't any more productive than anger. Unfortunately, her childhood family had not given her any training in the execution of either. In her home she had been taught that love was the answer. So far, she didn't see it working in the world, or in her own life. She had been pouring love into Angus for years without effecting any change. *I need to learn how to live with a little conflict in my life*, she thought. Could you have conflict without anger? Maybe you had to have both to make things change. *That's just wrong*, she thought. *I need to hold on to Father's belief in the power of love. Trust in your Father with all you heart*, she misquoted to her pillow and began to relax.

She welcomed the next peaceful hour when she was free to dream before she fell asleep. Imaginary house building had been her bedtime relaxation exercise since she had lost her sense of safety in her childhood home.

Tonight, she was dreaming of building a rather elaborate house suitable for a mature woman with a substantial personal fortune. The design was very modern with huge windows and sharp angles. She imagined the unusual house built with a sturdy concrete foundation on a steep hillside overlooking the Bay of Fundy. It was a satisfying project. Georgie snuggled into her pillow, comforted again as she created a home of her own.

Emily and Ross interrupted her thoughts. What if they really were seriously interested in each other? Surely, Emily was old enough and wise enough not to cling to this old house. Perhaps someone should warn Ross about Emily's fixation and encourage him to help her get over it.

Tomorrow she would call Anne and promise to drag Angus to the Saturday night party. Perhaps there would be an opportunity to give Ross a subtle hint and do her part to encourage grandchildren and world peace.

EMILY AND ROSS were having a Valentine's Day dinner at a newly discovered restaurant in Hantsport. Hantsport was a compact community off Highway 101 between Windsor and Wolfville. Emily had discovered it through a recent real estate listing. The local restaurant, Surf, provided the perfect spot for a wholesome lunch and a moment of relaxation not possible in a Wolfville restaurant full of people who habitually eavesdropped.

Ross was frowning "I'm not sure I should have come back to Wolfville to try to establish myself here. There was no way I could afford a house in Toronto, but I was sure I could afford one in Wolfville. I never expected such high house prices in Nova Scotia. Some financial planner I turned out to be."

"Hey, don't be so hard on yourself. These high prices are new. You couldn't have known. You have a great down payment and a good income. I'll find you a great house. At least you aren't desperate and living in your car."

"Emily! Don't even joke about that. Imagine my clients learning their financial advisor was living in his Honda. I'm having a hard enough time establishing myself as it is. Thank God, Bruce offered me a sub-let on his Railtown condo until September."

"Sorry. Hang in there, Ross. Wolfville is tough to break into, but you're a good old boy and an Acadia grad so you'll do OK. It'll just take a little time. Patience, patience, patience as my Stepma is always saying."

"Oh yeah, your Stepmother. Did you know she called me? I'm not sure why. She asked what kind of financial services I offered and asked for an appointment for March 1st. Do you think she has a financial problem or is she just checking up on me because I'm courting her daughter?"

Emily smiled and sipped her tea. "Are you courting?" she asked.

"You bet! Haven't you noticed?" He reached for her hand and held it for a moment. "Emily, I'm in deep water here. I just met you in November, but now I want to see you every day. I don't have any experience with a serious relationship, but I'm feeling serious."

"Don't worry, Ross, I'm feeling rather serious myself. I'll take care of you and if I don't, you can count on my Stepma. She lives to take care of people. I wonder what she wants. It's probably something to do with all those community boards she manages."

She smiled at Ross. "I think she will test your professional expertise. She doesn't believe in making or keeping money. She's a life-long do-gooder and a dedicated community activist. Don't be fooled by her appearance. She looks like a middle-aged, contented person but she's relentless when she has a mission, believe me."

"Ah, were you one of her missions?"

"Yeah, I was a fifteen-year-old jerk when my dad married her. I made her life as miserable as I could, but she never fought back. She was so nice it was exhausting. I finally gave up and decided to get along with her. Now, I love her."

"Ah, were you boy crazy when you were fifteen?"

"It wasn't boys we fought about. It was my house. My grandfather built it and it's famous in Wolfville. It's unique, but she wanted to change everything. We fought until she stopped talking about changing it."

"I was in your house. I don't remember it being exceptional."

"You were there on a dark January evening. I'll take you

on a tour in the daylight and point out the really clever things my Poppa and his friends did with salvaged materials. It's fascinating."

"OK, it must be exceptionally good if a real estate agent of your stature is in love with it. Hey, we've been invited to a February Blahs party filled with real estate professionals. Maybe the Walkers will have some good advice."

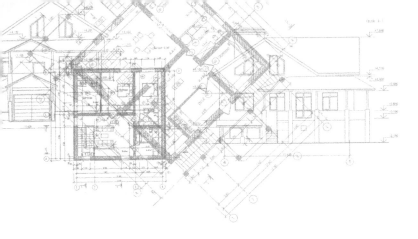

Thirteen

THE FEBRUARY BLAHS party was in full swing when Angus and Georgie arrived at the Walker homestead. Anne and Terry had been early investors in Woodman's Grove, one of the most exclusive neighbourhoods in Wolfville. It was a well-planned subdivision with up-scale houses. They had bought a very large two-storey on a pleasant tree-lined street.

Woodman's Grove was tucked between Main Street and another equally famous Wolfville development, the co-op seniors' complex, Tideways. It had the reputation of being a socially and politically active community. Anne laughed at the cheek-by-jowl location of the two developments. "Well, Georgie, when we are tired of living in wicked, privileged contentment in our little subdivision, we won't have far to move to join the crème de la crème of Wolfville progressive society and be saved."

Georgie was not amused. She had argued with Anne

68

and lobbied Town Council as both developments were established. Neither had met her high expectations for sustainable, affordable housing. However, as she and Angus drove through Woodman's Grove, she had to admit she never visited Anne without feeling a disconcerting jolt of house envy.

Terry, the happy host, ushered them in. "Welcome! Welcome! It's chaos here as usual. Angus, I'll get your Scotch and you can relax. I've already started without you. It's the only way to get through the karaoke. Anne is in the kitchen, Georgie."

Georgie made her way through the spacious, tastefully decorated living room filled with a noisy, cheering crowd of karaoke participants and supporters. She slowly made her way past the loaded dining room table surrounded by the eat drink and be merry crowd who were chasing away the blues with gusto.

Reaching the kitchen, she paused for a moment to admire the bright, modern space which stretched across the entire back of the house. Were there enough brilliant adjectives to adequately describe this incredible space? Were there enough words in her vocabulary to convey the depth of her lust? *Thou shall not covet thy neighbour's kitchen,* she misquoted to herself. She summoned up a smile for her best friend, and nodded to the ten or more guests who littered the kitchen. They were offering advice and gossip and getting in the way as usual.

Anne called to her. "Georgie! Here. Take this cheese tray into the den. The kids are in there dancing to some automated dance thing. I'll be right there with some drinks. Let's break the February curse!"

Later that evening as two weary fifty-year-olds crawled into bed, Angus patted Georgie on the arm and reassured her. "I know you worry about bad things happening in February, Georgie, but Em is OK. That young man seemed to be more interested in real estate than romance. He was talking a lot to Terry."

Georgie sighed in frustration. Angus had never moved out of his living room chair. He hadn't seen the dancing in the den. Ross and Emily were more than connected at the hip. She would be grateful when February was over. She had a feeling good things might be happening in March.

MARCH CAME IN like a lion with the typical mess of Maritime weather designed by Mother Nature to provide lively conversation for all to enjoy.

"Hell of a day, eh?" a sympathetic stranger greeted Georgie as she cautiously stepped out of her car in the parking lot across from Railtown.

"A little snow, a little freezing rain, and a bitter northeast wind. Sounds like March to me," Georgie replied. "At least February is over," she added as she pulled up her hood and waved a cold goodbye.

She crossed the street and paused for a moment admiring again the determination of the developers of Railtown.

The proposed mixed development of condos and retail space was built on the land between the defunct rail line and the Minas Basin. Pundits pointed out this was a flood plain protected by dykes which had failed with disastrous consequences in the 1950's. However, despite community concerns, financial problems, and false starts the project was finished and the first residents moved in.

Condo owners had a choice of second floor units. They could choose a condo on the north side of the building and enjoy the spectacular view of Minas Basin, or they could choose the south side and live in the sunshine. Unfortunately, their sunlit view was of the busy parking lot behind the commercial buildings on Main Street.

Anne had sold the first condo in the building to a retired couple who chose to live without the sun. She had no guilt selling them into perpetual darkness. "Stop fussing, Georgie, they have a cottage. When they need sunshine, they can always go there." Georgie gave up. Real estate agents always had ready excuses when closing a deal or justifying themselves.

Georgie made her way carefully through the slippery parking lot, crossed the street and entered the posh financial offices where Ross awaited her.

"Mrs. MacLean, come in. Heck of a day, eh?" Ross took her damp coat and hung it on a very modern coat rack. It went with the well-appointed office and the stylish young man who now gazed curiously at her. This whole environment was far too polished and too youthful. It made Georgie anxious. How could someone so young help her sort out her financial burden and deliver world peace and grandchildren?

She smiled through her doubts and took a seat in front of the steel and glass desk. "Please call me Georgie. Yes, a real March Lion kind of day."

Ross sat down on his high-tech office chair which seemed to have enough knobs and levers to launch a career. He was obviously a modern young man. *Perhaps he could help,* she thought. He leaned forward, put his expensively clad forearms on the desk and waited. *Was that a silk suit?* He regarded her earnestly. "How can I help you, Georgie?" he innocently asked.

Georgie considered him thoughtfully for a moment. He really was a very attractive young man. A vision of a curly-haired grandchild filled her mind. "Is your hair naturally curly?" she said.

Ross sat up straight, burst into laughter and flung himself back in his very supportive and highly flexible chair. Georgie took a moment to enjoy his good humour at her inappropriate question. His laugh was as attractive as his earlier earnest persona. And he obviously had taken very good care of his teeth.

"Oh, yes. It's naturally curly and I'm stuck with it until I go bald like my dad. That should only be another few years if he's any example. It gave me a lot of grief in high school, but no one seems to notice it now."

"Well, I like it. It suits you. However, I'm embarrassed about the personal question. Sorry about that." Georgie said. "Can we start again?"

"Of course. No need to be embarrassed. Why did you want to see me?"

"I hardly know how to begin. I have a very complex problem which is worrying me considerably, but for the time being I don't want my family to know. I realize you and Emily are friends. Will that be a problem for you? Emily knows I'm coming to see you today."

"Not at all. Emily and I are seeing each other, but we are both professional people. We understand the absolute need for client confidentially. Trust me on that."

"Thank you. I don't want to talk to Angus and Emily until I have some sense of peace about the mess I'm in, and what my options may be."

"OK. Since you came to see me, I assume this is a financial problem. Are you in debt? Sometimes people take chances with their financial resources that lead to disaster. Have you been gambling? I'll do my best to help you."

"Gambling! Oh, goodness! No! You completely misunderstand, but then how could you understand unless you know me a little better. My father, a wonderful man, was a United Church minister. He disapproved of all forms of gambling. You know, those schemes designed to take your money by promising false hope of prizes and riches. Money that could better be spent on the needs of your family or others. No, I would never gamble.

"My religious upbringing has informed my decisions all my life. I find I am still trying to make my parents, especially my father, proud of me. He had very strong opinions about money and many other things."

Ross nodded and remained silent.

"I don't really believe in the old teaching that, 'Money is the root of all evil', but I have a great deal of respect for the corrupting power of riches. I am convinced that the pursuit and obsessive protection of money leads to much misery in the world. I've tried to avoid the problem by living frugally and contributing any excess above my basic needs to others."

"Hmm. So how have you gotten in trouble?"

"It wasn't me! It was my Aunt Beryl. I haven't had a close relationship with her since my mother died, but I've kept looking after her, thinking she was poverty stricken. She lived in Toronto and she was always asking me to send her care packages. I've been baking a Christmas box for her for ages. I think the last one killed her, but that's another story."

"Oh!" Ross said as he did his best to preserve his

professional demeanor. "So, what did Aunt Beryl do? Did she leave you debts to pay?" Ross raised an attractive eyebrow and invited Georgie to continue.

"Well, I heard about her death from a nice lawyer from Toronto who called me in December shortly after she died. He said I was the sole beneficiary in her will. Then, on my birthday, a man who said he was a senior partner of the firm called to offer me assistance in managing Aunt Beryl's estate. I'm afraid I was a bit rude when he told me the amount she left. I panicked and hung up. I haven't talked to him since. I wanted to consult someone who had my best interests in mind before I did anything."

"I see. So, I'm guessing Aunt Beryl wasn't as destitute as you thought, and she left you more money than you're comfortable with. Is that the problem?"

"Oh Ross, the lawyer said, and I quote, 'Mrs. MacLean, your aunt left an estate in excess of five hundred thousand dollars.' I just feel sick every time I think of it. What am I going to do?"

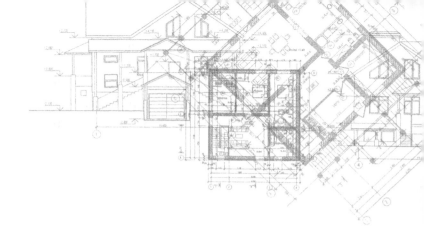

Fourteen

EMILY DIDN'T KNOW what to do about her persistent, irritating best friend and fellow employee. The attacks were becoming more frequent. Carrie was relentless and getting on her nerves. She was being harassed in the workplace and it was driving her crazy.

"Carrie! Stop or I swear I'll tell your mother on you."

"Ha! That's a good one. She would cheer me on and you know it. Emily, it's time you grew up and moved out of that closet you've been hiding in. Why on earth do you think you have to stay there? It's totally insane."

"Wow! Insane? Ross called me fatally stubborn, but it took my best friend to lay it on the line. Thanks for diagnosis."

"You're entirely welcome. You're so sick. Ross asked you to move in with him. How long are you going to keep him waiting? What do you think Georgie will do if you move out? She's not the wicked witch. And you aren't the teenager who wanted to rush home every day to throw water on her and make her melt. She isn't going to tear the house down after all these years. Although come to think of it, that's not a bad idea. Besides, she's devoted to Angus. It's time for you to leave them in peace. Fatally stubborn, eh?"

"Yeah. I took him for a tour of the house and showed him all the clever things Poppa had done. He wasn't impressed. He thought I'd be much happier with him at the condo. Oh, he made me so mad."

"Don't tell me. Let me guess. He noticed the dreary student digs you put up with and the shabby condition of the main house. Men are sometimes quite practical. Henri thinks you should move."

"Ross just missed the point. It's not supposed to be practical. It's art. Poppa was an artist who saw beauty everywhere."

Carrie couldn't contain her laughter. "Oh, Emily. You live in the ugliest house in Wolfville. Let's face it. Your grandad didn't see beauty. He saw the bottom line. He was a cheapskate and I heard he picked up every bit of junk in Wolfville while he was building that house. Mum told me he was a legend. Town Council discussed nominating him for a landfill reduction award. You gotta laugh."

"Carrie. Back off! That so-called ugly house has been my sanctuary since my mother died and Poppa and Nana looked after us. I might never have grown up if they had left me and dad on our own."

"Too true, you owe them a lot. But you don't owe them your happiness in exchange for the misguided protection of a bad real estate investment. I bet they don't even care about that monstrosity anymore. It's served its purpose, and now they live in Tideways and half the year in Alabama. They've moved on and so should you. It's March already. Go out like a lion and make a move on Ross."

MARCH WAS FINALLY over. It was April. Spring had officially arrived on March 21st and Georgie supposed the hibernating animals had ventured out on schedule. Poor dumb animals. Warm weather and good food would not be here for weeks.

Easter Sunday fell on April 1st this year causing lots of conflict for Nova Scotians who loved their jokes and pranks on April Fool's Day. There was no levity in the MacLean house. There was no family Sunday morning brunch. Emily was absent again. Angus complained to Georgie as he dined on Easter lamb. "Why didn't you invite Ross here for Easter dinner? Then Em would be here too. Where is she?"

"I don't know, Angus. She said they were spending the weekend together and I didn't ask questions. I told you they had plans."

The day was long, and Easter Monday seemed endless. Georgie practiced her patience until the Easter holiday was over and Ross was back at work. *A fool and her money are soon parted*, Georgie prayed as she stepped into Ross's office to hear about his progress with her troublesome legacy. He had been working on it for a whole month.

She had signed what felt like a thousand pages of financial legalese to authorize Ross to transfer and manage Aunt Beryl's estate. Today, Ross was going to tell her exactly what he had found. She pulled her invisible cloak of righteousness around her and prepared herself to hear the worst.

Ross welcomed her with a very attractive smile. "Georgie, don't look so worried. It's all good news. We can sort this out and decide how you want to proceed. First, I should tell you that the book value of the estate today is $728,450.00. Your

Aunt Beryl seems to have been a very astute investor. She left an estate with an excellent mix of mutual funds, stocks, bonds, and GICs with only $85,000.00 in cash. She probably had plans about reinvesting the cash but didn't have time to do it. We can take care of that. All in all, you have a very sound investment portfolio to work with. Congratulations."

"Stocks? Stocks in the stock market? Stocks in companies that are destroying the planet? Oh, Ross, this is awful."

"No, no, Georgie. The stocks are in very good, stable companies. I've prepared a detailed list for you so you can review the whole portfolio. It's quite good reading." He smiled broadly as he placed an expensive looking binder embossed with gold lettering on the edge of the desk within her reach.

"You told me you have no experience with investing, so I put the information in very plain language," Ross said. "You should have no trouble seeing how your investments are working for you. We can go over it today if you like, or you can take it home and we can meet again. After your review, we can discuss what you would like to change or move and what you would like to do with the cash."

Georgie looked at the binder with horror and pushed it back toward Ross. "I can't take this home. I don't want to review it. I want it gone!"

"Gone? Oh, have you already decided on how you want to disburse the funds? I didn't realize..."

"Disburse? Like give it away?" Georgie interrupted. "No, I can't do that until Anne and I talk. I promised her."

"I see. Georgie, there's no hurry about any of this. The portfolio needs some management, but I can do that. Take your time. You've given me all the authorization I need to keep things on track until you know what you want to do."

"Time," Georgie groaned. "I used to think I had all the time in the world, but since my fiftieth birthday I feel so anxious." She reached into her pocket, pulled out a handful of crumpled tissues and burst into tears. "I want a safe house to live in. I want world peace. I want grandchildren, but all I have is money. I don't understand why this is happening to me."

Ross rose slowly to his feet and cautiously came around the desk to envelope Georgie in a comforting hug. "Let's go to lunch. I know a quiet place where we can talk privately about more important things than money. Come on."

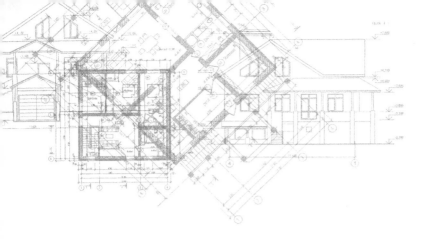

Fifteen

A NGUS FELT CONFUSED. He slowly reread the letter from Professor Erlichman. Clearly, he had understood it the first time. Professor Erlichman was writing, as Head of the Mathematics Department at the University of Toronto, to invite him, Professor Angus MacLean of Acadia University, to work with his research group. He was invited to lead a graduate seminar for the upcoming summer session beginning June 1st and ending August 15th. Professor Erlichman was impressed with the comments Professor MacLean had made on his latest paper and would like the opportunity to work collaboratively on this most intriguing math problem. A stipend and accommodation would be provided. A prompt reply would be appreciated.

"He wants a prompt reply? What month is this anyway?" Angus consulted his trusty computer. He was reassured when it told him it was the first week of April. Ah, no need to make hasty decisions. Lots of time to think and consider the problem. Lots of time to expand his argument about the foundation of Erlichman's research. He tucked the letter in the journal he was reading and smiled as he imagined the intellectual fireworks he could ignite in Toronto.

Late that afternoon, Angus left his office to walk the long uphill trek home. He glanced over at the administration building and paused to consider again how lucky he was not to work there. Research was the real work of the university. He could never understand how professors could give it up to become a dean, or worse yet, a university president.

Satisfied again with his choice in life, he set off with energy wondering what dinner Georgie had prepared this evening. He was rather hungry and the long uphill climb in the fresh air always increased his appetite. He recalled his disappointment last evening when he arrived home to find Georgie had gone to another meeting. Perhaps there was leftover lamb for supper. He quickened his pace.

Arriving home, he struggled with the side door. It seemed to be sticking more than usual. Entering, he threw his jacket on the chair in his office, took his journal out of his briefcase and made his way to the kitchen. Ah, good. Georgie was there and she was cooking something.

"Angus! You're home early. I'm glad. Emily and Ross are coming for dinner. Isn't that wonderful?"

Angus lifted the cover off a pot on the stove and sniffed the rising steam. "Oh, chicken. I was hoping for lamb." He turned from the stove and gave Georgie a perfunctory kiss on the cheek before settling at the kitchen table with his journal.

"Don't be a glutton, Angus. You have lamb frequently. Here's your Scotch. I've made your favourite pineapple upside-down cake for dessert. Cope with the chicken. You'll be happy by the end of dinner."

I wonder if I will ever be happy, Georgie thought as she took salad ingredients from the fridge. She glanced at her absorbed husband who was absently sipping his drink while reading yet another academic journal. How could his brain absorb any more intellectual input? Didn't he know enough already? Suddenly, Georgie was furious. She was finished with being slow to anger, as her father always advised. Even Jesus lost his temper. She marched the five short steps to the kitchen table and snatched the journal from Angus's hands.

"Angus! Pay attention! I'm having a mid-life crisis. Emily and Ross are getting serious about one another. This house is beginning to fight back. I heard you struggling with the side door. I have to struggle with it all the time. Angus! Things are happening. Wake up! Stop reading these everlasting journals!"

She was so angry. It felt good to yell and see the startled expression on his face. She shook the journal and threw it as hard as she could at the back door. "Leave your darn journals at the office and start paying attention around here! Your wife and your house are falling apart."

The kitchen door opened to reveal Emily and Ross who had obviously heard every word Georgie had flung at Angus. They crowded into the emotion-packed kitchen and stood looking very unsure of their welcome.

"Oh, for Heaven's sake," Georgie said. "Come in. I just lost my temper. I'm entitled to do that once every seventeen years. "Angus, take Ross into the living room and give him a drink. Emily, you can finish putting the salad together. I'm going to wash my face and regain my composure. Dinner will be ready in half an hour." A fully back-in-charge Georgie left the room on a rather shaky high note.

A SOMEWHAT TENSE dinner was finally over. Ross had gone home. Angus was in his office reading again, and the women were cleaning up.

"You doin' OK, Stepma?" Emily asked as she dried a bright yellow pot and looked for a place to put it.

"Oh, I have to store that one in the oven," Georgie said. "I know better than to buy a new casserole dish, but that one was so cheerful I couldn't resist it.

"Why can't you buy a new casserole dish when you want one? Is money tight? I thought you were the world's best money manager."

Georgie stared at her stepdaughter and didn't try to hide her exasperation. "It's not a question of too few resources. It's a matter of an abundance of questionable riches," Georgie shot back. "You should already know this. Your beloved childhood juice glasses take up half a shelf in these miniscule cabinets. There's absolutely no room for anything new in this shrine to all things past."

"Whoa, Stepma! What are you talking about? I don't use those juice glasses. I thought you wanted to keep them."

"Me? When did what I want ever matter in this house? Perhaps you don't remember the weeping and wailing and gnashing of teeth that greeted me every time I made a suggestion about changing something here, but I certainly do."

"What the hell? I was a kid. I admit I was a pain in the ass, but I thought we got over that years ago."

"Oh, yeah. We got over it when I promised your father I wouldn't make any changes here until you moved out. But, of course, at the time I didn't realize he was certain you were never going to leave."

"Holy shit!" Emily plopped into a kitchen chair and started to laugh. "This is fantastic and not in a good way. It's a freaking circus. You think you can't change anything. Dad thinks I'm never moving out and I'm exhausted trying to hang on here for you two when all I want to do is start living my own life."

Georgie wasn't laughing as she sat at the ugly kitchen table and studied her stepdaughter. "Emily, is this true? You think you have to stay here because of us? You think we don't want you to have your own home and family?"

"Oh yeah. I got it straight from the horse's mouth. About a year ago I wanted to buy a cute little house in Berwick. It was a steal and I've always loved Berwick. I told dad and I got a lecture worthy of a university professor. You know the kind. One of those lectures where there is only one way to look at things–his way. He said you didn't have family pride in the house and he was depending on me to stay here and protect it. He said it's my heritage, and my responsibility."

"Emily, this makes me so angry. We've both been played. That man has gone too far. He's been manipulating both of us so he can remain undisturbed in his cave. It's time he was booted out of his life-long hibernation. Leave him to me. I'm the one to deliver the wake-up kick."

Silence fell on the gloomy kitchen as both women sat and adjusted to a new reality. Georgie roused herself first and rose to pour them a restorative dram of Angus's Scotch. "I'm going to do it, Emily. I'm going to free us both," Georgie vowed.

With tearful understanding reached and mutual support

pledged, Emily left to be with Ross. Georgie wiped her tears and rose to clear the table. As she pushed in Emily's chair, the leg caught on a white envelope. She picked it up and saw it had been opened. From U of T? It must have fallen from Angus's journal when she threw it at the door. What was this all about? She read the letter with growing glee. "Time to drag you out of your den, Angus. Yahoo for spring!" A song burst forth in the quiet of the patient kitchen.

Here comes the sun, Here comes the sun, and I say, It's all right, Little kitchen...

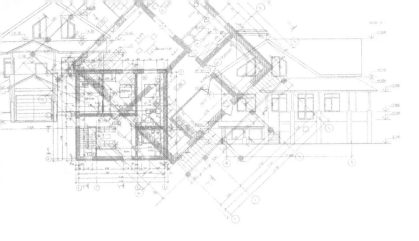

Sixteen

"I LOVE THIS KITCHEN," Georgie gushed as she perched on a very comfortable stool at Anne's enormous kitchen island. "Do you mind if I make mine just like it?"

"Georgie! Stop! I can't keep laughing while I'm trying to drink coffee. I haven't been able to swallow a drop since you arrived. I've never seen you in such a positive mood. I can't believe this is you; the down-trodden, defeated, long-suffering martyr that I know and love. What's up?"

"What's up is why I'm here. You've helped me with every plot I've ever hatched, and I've got a big one to work on now. But first, we need to talk about money. I promised I wouldn't do anything with Aunt Beryl's legacy until we talked. I need to tell you what I've done."

"Oh, Georgie. Have you already given it all away? You said you wouldn't. Oh, I'm so upset!"

"Calm down! I haven't given anything away. I promised I would talk to you first, but I did go see Ross and hired him as a financial advisor. He took over the management of the estate from the firm in Toronto. Now, I can make some decisions."

"Ah, Ross. Yes, that was a good idea. Does Emily know?"

"She knows I'm consulting him, but she thinks it's about my Citizens for Affordable Housing group. I haven't told her or Angus about Aunt Beryl yet. I needed to talk to you first and get my head clear. It's worse than I thought, Anne. The estate is worth almost 800K and because she had lots of investments it just keeps growing. It's a nightmare!"

"Tough! Listen. Don't put off telling Angus and Emily too long. Secrets are never a good thing in families. Now, the bottom line. Do not give all this money away. You must know by now that you can pour all the money you have into those causes you support, but nothing will change until there is political will to fix the system. Hey, now that you 're independently wealthy you could run for public office. That's what bored, rich people do."

"I don't think I'll be rich long enough for a political career. First, I have to clean up this money. I don't like investments in mutual funds or the stock market if the companies are raping the earth, destroying indigenous lands, exploiting desperate people or otherwise acting like corporate pirates. As a first step, I'm going to get Ross to move everything he can to ethical investments. I've been reading up on it."

"OK. Fine. No selling. Just moving. That's good."

"Yes, and as much as I fear and loathe riches, I might have need for a lot of it. I may not be able to arrange world peace, but I think some personal liberation may be in the works. Perhaps, even some grandchildren. Wait till you hear what I found out from Emily and uncovered about Angus. This tale will make you laugh and cry, and you'll be very afraid for both of them. I'm calling a family conference where all secrets will be revealed, and liberation will be initiated. I may have to create a new Liberation Ceremony." Georgie smiled broadly at Anne and rose to pour her stunned best friend some hot coffee.

HOURS LATER, GEORGIE returned home armed with a new path forward and righteous determination. She paused in front of the house and studied it carefully for the first time in years. She noticed spring growth near the curb. Crocus! They were tucked in around the large heap of stones piled haphazardly on the lawn by BillyBob, Emily's grandfather. They were leftovers from the rock foundation he had used to secure the house to the side of the hill. Angus had pointed out the stones with pride. "Dad knew the old ways were best, Georgie. Rock foundations were used by the early Acadians and still exist today." Georgie sighed at the memory and drove into the gloomy garage. Why they still called it a garage was beyond her. Years ago, the sagging doors had been removed and it now looked more like a shaky carport. She paused by the side door and bent to pat the widening crack in the wall beside it. She was certain the foundation rocks were slowly sinking into to the earth from whence they came. *Ashes to ashes and all that,* she thought, as she stepped on the sinking doorstep. "Hang on, House. Help is coming."

She threw her shoulder against the sticky side door and entered the house. There was no coat closet, of course, just hooks on the wall. "So practical, Georgie," Angus had explained. She hung up her coat and glanced at Angus's home office. The small room had served as Angus's bedroom, then Emily's until she moved into the apartment and Angus reclaimed the space. The next room was the troublesome bathroom. BillyBob had provided for a guest bathroom and an ensuite by creating a bathroom with both a hall and a bedroom door. Family stories were abundant about the mishaps caused by his hippy-dippy design.

Thoughtfully, Georgie continued her review of the tired house. The steep stairs to the loft rose on the left. The hallway ended there as the very large living room took over all the available space. "See, Georgie. Open concept living. Dad was very modern in his ideas."

Devoted to the old ways and very modern. Clearly Angus's admiration of his father's cleverness was not diminished by contradiction. Certainly, the large living/dining room could be described as modern, but Georgie was convinced the design was merely utilitarian. It allowed maximum practice space for BillyBob's succession of folk, hillbilly-rock, and hard-rock bands. The need for a rehearsal hall had ended twenty years ago and yet the living room still looked under-furnished and shabby enough to welcome a punk band.

She was at the first crossroad in the Liberation Road Map. Safe transportation needed to be arranged. Road signs needed to be posted. Major resources would need to be in place, However, before construction started there would need to be a few roadblocks removed and some detour signs posted. She was ready for the journey and the passing scenery would be its own reward. She moved to the front window and studied the weedy front lawn. She smiled as she quoted to the cavernous living room, *The desert and the parched land will be glad; the wilderness will rejoice and blossom. Like the crocus*

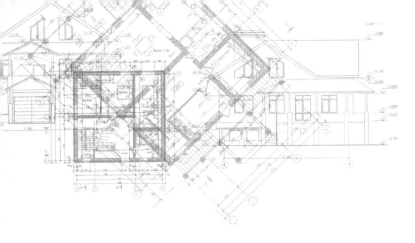

Seventeen

Emily kissed ross again and turned to gaze at the view from the condo's large window. "I'm glad your friend Bruce chose a condo on the Minas Basin side. I love the changing view. Of course, the view inside this condo is pretty good too."

"I'll say," Ross agreed as he admired Emily's warm naked body. "Do you have to leave? I can make some eggs for us here. You've missed dinner at home."

"You don't know my Stepma. If I miss dinner, she always makes up a plate and leaves it in my fridge. She's been doing that for years."

"Man. She sets a high standard. How am I going to convince you to let me look after you? I hardly ever cook."

"Do you want to look after me? That's awesome. I want to look after you too. We did OK looking after each other this evening. I'm very satisfied." She ran her hand lightly up Ross's chest to pat his cheek and then playfully ruffled his hair. "I love these curls," she said.

"Yeah?" So does Georgie. I'm basking in female admiration these days."

"Oh, does she? I've never heard her remark on anyone's physical characteristics before. When I was a teenager, she regularly gave me lectures on society's vulgar, discriminatory, and harmful emphasis on outward appearance. She said people needed to focus on finding the inner beauty in others."

"Ha! I think we explored some of that this evening too. You're beautiful inside and out. Let's explore some more." Ross pulled a willing Emily to him and demanded her full attention.

"Have you ever noticed that a second helping is just as satisfying as the main meal?' Emily asked later as she rested on top of Ross's limp body.

"Oh yeah, I seem to be hungry all the time these days," he said. Did you know that Georgie wants grandchildren?"

"What? Grandchildren? You discussed grandchildren?"

"She certainly did. I took her to Surf for lunch the other day after our meeting and she spilled the beans. She's very unhappy with the house and wants to make some big changes. She may want to include room for a day care."

Ross noticed the look on Emily's face and laughed. "Just kidding, Hon. But she's ready for the next phase of her life. I thought turning sixteen was the shiftiest time in life, but middle age seems harder. Poor old Georgie."

GEORGIE WAS SITTING at her kitchen table feeling like her energetic twenty-five-year-old self. Perhaps menopause was behind her. Anne had recalled Dolly Parton's famous saying, "If you don't like the road you're walking, start paving another one." Together they had created a road map to middle age liberation.

Some would willingly set out on this journey, but others would be searching for every rest stop. Georgie smiled as she imagined herself as a skilled tour guide introducing her passengers to the delights along the road to their final destination. She would start by building a few bridges. She called BillyBob and Miriam in Alabama.

BB was his usual charming self. "Well, hello there, little lady. Everyone in fine spirits in chilly Wolfville?"

"Oh yes, we're all fine. Are you two doing well?"

"I'm still not quite used to the pace in Alabama," Miriam said, "but I'm learning how to mosey along and stop to talk a lot."

Georgie studied their smiling faces on her phone and crossed the first tricky divide. "There have been a few new developments here and I need to ask you an important question. How do you feel about me making some changes and renovations to the house? I know you built it yourself BB, and I wouldn't want to make any major changes without your knowledge and permission."

"Oh, my land, Georgie," BB said. "You are one in a million. I suppose Angus has been talking his nonsense that the house is perfect so there's no need for change. He's been like that all his life, but bless my soul, girl. Don't listen to him. He's so conservative I can hardly believe he's mine." BB's laughter abruptly stopped as Miriam whacked him on the shoulder.

"Shame on you, BB. You know that crazy boy is ours. Georgie, we don't care what you do to that house," Miriam said. "It served its purpose, and you do what you want. Pay no attention to Angus. He hates change. Unfortunately, he's smart enough to find ways to avoid it whenever he can. You make your changes. He'll learn to love them like he loves you."

"Thanks so much, you two. Oh, Emily told me you've decided to stay in the States longer this year, perhaps until September. Do you plan to stay in Alabama? I thought you didn't like all that heat."

"So true, dear," Miriam said. We thought we might take our old camper van on the road and visit our friends in California before we head back north. Don't worry. We'll stay in touch through the internet."

"We're gonna travel a little and enjoy ourselves. Life is wonderful when you're with the right people." BB bestowed a familiar sweet smile on his wife. *Oh yeah, he was Angus's father alright.* Georgie expressed her thanks and closed her phone.

They were in favour of her plan to renovate! *"Your word is a lamp to my feet and a light to my path,"* Georgie quoted to the dark kitchen.

TODAY'S SUNDAY BRUNCH was being served in the dining room. It was a carefully chosen menu designed to offer the most comfort to those facing unpleasant road trips and uncertain futures. It started with a generous Mimosa made with freshly squeezed orange juice and an excellent sparkling wine recommended by Anne.

"Have a drink yourself, Georgie," she had advised." They don't call it fake courage for nothing. Good luck!"

Georgie watched Emily enjoy her favourite bacon, egg, and spinach pizza as Angus helped himself to his third slice of goat cheese and asparagus tart. Comfort food was being consumed. Pain killer was being drunk. She decided to announce the upcoming trip before anyone asked for sobering coffee.

"Listen up, family, I have some news to share with you and some plans to discuss. First, I've inherited a rather large sum of money from Aunt Beryl. You know how anxious I feel about having too much money, but I've decided to use it to fix some long-standing problems." She took a large swallow of her Mimosa and waited for her fellow travellers' reaction.

Emily recovered first. "Wow! Stepma! That's great news. Good for you. You know, money isn't always a bad thing."

"I'm beginning to understand that. I've recently had an epiphany. I realize I can't continue to fight for safe housing for others until I get my own house in order. I've made some plans and I'm going to use the money to liberate us all. I'm calling it my Liberation Fund. You both get to benefit." She smiled a confident smile worthy of a game show host who had just announced that today's prize was a trip around the world.

"Angus smiled back at her. "Wonderful! You girls will no doubt have a great time with your retail therapy and your box stores. Enjoy yourselves." He sipped his Mimosa and prepared to serve himself the last slice of tart.

"Angus, dear. Gird your loins, pluck up your courage, and prepare to jump ship. That midlife crisis we spoke about earlier is about to sweep you out to sea."

Emily reached across the table and took his hand. "Don't look so worried, Dad. You know Stepma. She's got everything all arranged. All you need to do is grab the lifeline she's throwing you and abandon ship. I've already made my plans."

"Abandon ship? What are you talking about?" Angus suddenly looked totally present and no longer his complacent, non-attentive self. Georgie studied him carefully.

"Angus. I have decided to set you free. I've talked to your parents and they and Emily agree that your unhealthy fixation on this house must end. Consider today the first step in a family intervention. You are going to be liberated. It's essential for all of us, dear."

"Emily, you know about this? You talked to my parents, Georgie? What's going on?"

"It's simple, Dad. We're all moving out of the house for the summer and Georgie's going to manage a major renovation. I can hardly wait to see what she'll do."

Georgie sipped her drink and smiled at Angus. "The house needs help and so do we, Angus. I desperately need a safe home to live in. This house is not safe. For starters it needs a new foundation. You are the only one standing in the way. I'll help you through this, dear. Here's what I think you should do.

"You should accept the offer from U of T. Sylvia, your Math Department secretary, will help you get that all arranged. I'll help you pack what you need and arrange storage for the rest. The house will need to be completely cleared before renovations begin. You'll have an intellectually demanding summer in Toronto and won't have to think about the changes happening here."

"And I'll help the process by moving in with Ross while we search for a house for him to buy," Emily said. "It's all good, Dad."

Angus stood up slowly and stared for a long moment at his treacherous family. "I'm going to the office. Thanks for breakfast."

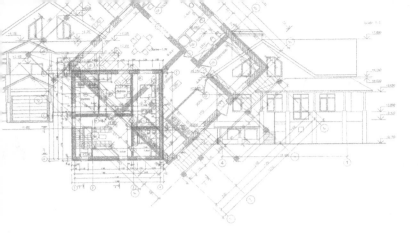

Eighteen

"IT MIGHT BE my imagination, but I think the kitchen looks more cheerful this afternoon, don't you?" Georgie poured Anne another cup of coffee and joined her at the soon to be surplus kitchen table.

"Everything looks more cheerful to a wealthy woman with a Liberation Plan. So, tell me everything. How did brunch go?"

"There were no earthquakes, but I think there is some serious underground thinking going on in that disrupted mind," Georgie said.

"Do you think he really heard you? Does he realize you've already found storage units and spoken to an architect and a contractor? His head must be spinning. Hey, that's a great image. Think of all those numbers flying around."

"Funny, Anne. No, I didn't tell him any details. It didn't seem the time to look too efficient. I was trying to be reassuring. Emily told him it would all work out for the best, but

I don't think he bought it. I remember his mother saying how smart he is in getting his own way. He won't want to be set adrift. I think he's working on a counter argument. I expect an appeal to my finer nature. Ha! Let's talk house plans."

"OK, but Georgie, I'm worried about you hiring Stan Keddy. I know he's a good contractor, but he's also done work for Helen. I see them together sometimes. It could be dangerous."

"Yeah, I know. I saw them talking at my presentation to Town Council. It's hard to find anyone in town who doesn't know her. I'll just have to trust that Stan is a professional and won't listen to her poison tongue."

"She'll be harping at Emily too. She filled Emily's head with all that heritage home nonsense when you were newly married."

"I don't understand that woman. Wasn't it enough for her to ruin my childhood? Why is she still bedeviling me?"

"I've thought about that over the years," Anne said. "She's only a year or two younger than Julie, and I wonder if she thought Angus would marry her when Julie died."

"Well, my goodness. She had years to close that deal before he proposed to me. How could that be my fault?"

"Well, you know after Julie died Angus did his grad work at Dal so he wasn't around much for a few years. Helen married that guy from Gaspereau, and lived there until her parents died and left her the house in Wolfville. Her husband had already left her. I think she's always felt like a loser. Julie was so beautiful and so popular it was a hard act to follow."

"Well, I survived Helen's spite for the last seventeen years as she did her best to get at me through Emily. I don't see how she can hurt me now. Let sleeping dogs lie. Let me show you the idea I have for a grandchildren's playroom."

Anne suddenly laughed out loud. "Angus, a grandfather. It boggles the mind."

ANGUS SETTLED INTO his university office retreat and reread the U of T letter for the umpteenth time. Toronto! He would be lost. The largest city he knew was Halifax and he hadn't really lived there. All through his grad studies at Dalhousie he was a father to a motherless child. His parents supported them both through those hard times, but he chose to live at home and commute to Dal so he could have breakfast with Em every day and remind her he was her father.

Now, he was questioning all that sacrifice. How could she abandon him and the house? True, he had made some mistakes in his day that shocked his parents, but he had been seventeen. Em was in her thirties. She was well past teenage rebellion. It was very confusing.

Actually, this whole situation was confusing and unsettling. His parents had agreed to let Georgie destroy the house? He had been steadfast in his support of it since they had left him and Emily alone there. They should be grateful for his efforts and support him.

He suddenly recalled it was an unexpected legacy from his Alabama grandparents that had caused his parents to leave him. His mother had looked at their augmented bank account, resigned her job, and announced they were moving to Tideways. Obviously, legacies caused nothing but unexpected misery. "I'll protect Emily," he announced to his steadfast office. "I'll leave all my money to Acadia."

His thoughts turned to Georgie. Sweet, kind, comforting Georgie. She had seemed quite calm as she declared she was renovating his house and his life. It was clear her legacy had the same dire effect on her as his dad's had on his mother. He now understood Georgie's long-standing aversion to having too much money. She couldn't handle it. He would have to look after her. She had always taken care of him, and now he would do the same for her. He would help her dispose of this burden.

After several restful moments of profound thought, a solution made itself known. He smiled as he considered his inspired idea. They would establish a mathematics scholarship, perhaps two, if the legacy were large enough. It would be called the *Angus and Georgina MacLean Scholarship*. He enjoyed a pleasant hour developing a compelling argument concerning the importance of encouraging young people to study pure mathematics. Georgie liked to help people. She was just overwhelmed by this disastrous legacy. Best to get rid of it quickly, then they could be comfortable again. Poor Georgie, she was very confused. He certainly would not be moving to Toronto, even temporarily.

Toronto! Erlichman's offer was very flattering. Perhaps he could arrange to work remotely with him. Acadia was well-known for being a high-tech university. U of T surely couldn't be too far behind. He would send off a message to Erlichman tomorrow when Sylvia was back at work and could help him. He would stay in Wolfville. He would help Georgie. He would save his home. He would continue to love his wayward daughter. QED.

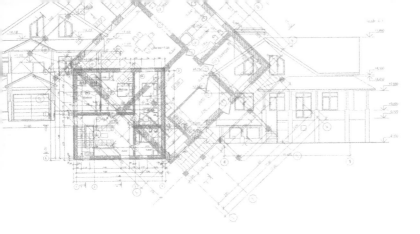

Nineteen

"EMILY! THIS BUILDING is a church! I can't believe you brought me to Hantsport to consider buying a church. What were you thinking?"

Emily smiled her most reassuring smile at her astonished client and launched into her prepared sales pitch. "Ross, just consider. This used to be a church, but now it's the deal of the year. Hantsport is a great community. Property prices are easily fifteen percent lower than in Wolfville, but that will no doubt change as Hantsport is discovered by people who are commuting to Halifax. It's only fifteen minutes from Wolfville and an hour to the city. It has great amenities.

"Yeah, OK. But Emily…"

"Try to work with me, Ross. This property is a bargain for someone with energy and a little imagination. Wait till you see inside."

"OK, already. We agreed earlier that Hantsport was a reasonable place to look for a house, but…It still has a steeple for God's sake." Ross got out of the car and studied the building. "Well, it's a stubby steeple, but really Emily. A church?"

"This church is unique. Most people are afraid of renovating a church because they often have nasty basements. This church is built on the side of a hill so most of the basement is above ground level. Think of the high ceilings, the large spaces, and the thrill of cashing in on a property that has been on the market for over six months. I know there is negotiating room on this deal. Hey, just look at this beautiful, landscaped lot and all those wonderful trees."

"Hmm, I will admit that I would have lots of room for my friends to party. It's not every property that comes with a parking lot for twenty cars."

"Ha! Have your fun, but I think you'll be surprised. The woodwork is outstanding, and the west window is spectacular. Here's another bonus. Stepma will be very pleased with you if you buy a church."

GEORGIE WAS IN her patient kitchen preparing a comforting dinner for Angus. Thank goodness, Emily and Ross were house hunting. They would not be here tonight to witness the battle of wills that would surely take place. She had spent a peaceful and energetic afternoon packing two huge suitcases for herself and Angus. They needed enough clothes to last the summer. The house renovations would not be finished until September.

She didn't pack anything in Angus's office. She would suggest that he spend Monday and Tuesday sorting out what he wanted to take to Toronto and what he could store in his university office or put in storage. She had yet to tell him the movers were coming to clear the house on Wednesday.

The ancient oven timer wheezed its feeble signal, and she removed the shepherd's pie made with lamb and sweet potato topping from the tiny oven. His favourite brownies were already baked and waiting for the required scoop of vanilla ice cream.

If your enemy is hungry, feed him; and if he is thirsty, give him something to drink. In doing this, you will heap burning coals on his head.

Poor Angus. He was his own worst enemy. His stubborn resistance to change had led to this confrontation, but he was going to lose this battle. She smiled at the worn white enamel kitchen sink and told it, "Not long now, my chipped friend. Everything will be renewed, including you and Angus."

Suddenly, her father's voice echoed in her head. *Do not gloat when your enemy falls; when they stumble, do not let your heart rejoice...*

"Oh, my goodness, Kitchen! I must remember to be gracious. Angus isn't my enemy. He'll need my help and support. I'll be patient, kind, and comforting. I won't pile burning coals on his head. I will pour loving kindness on him until his unhealthy house obsession melts away. Of course, it helps that he'll be in Toronto and won't see the destruction before the reconstruction begins. I'll only let him see what he can handle. I'll take good care of him."

Her cell phone interrupted her plans for Angus. It was Anne.

"Georgie, how are you doing? You haven't given up, have you? You said he didn't fight back this morning, but I'm sure he's been sitting in his stupid office all day planning how to stop you. He's a master practitioner of passive resistance. I'm so worried you'll lose heart and let him change your mind."

"Ha! Not a chance, Anne. He's not the only one who's been thinking this afternoon. Tonight, I'm softening him up with his favourite comfort food and over dinner I'll tell him the movers are coming on Wednesday. I'll be firm but kind. After all, it's practically his last supper.

"Oh God, Georgie, you and your religious references. Be careful. You know what came after the Last Supper."

"Anne, don't be silly. It's not that serious. I'm sure Angus will overcome his resistance and make the best of it. I intend to help him. I'm going to change his mind with the power of love. I'll help him see the pain and suffering that his self-absorbed attitude is imposing on all of us, including this long-suffering house."

"Oh, I wish I could be there tonight. Be strong. Be crafty. Beware! Call me when the dust settles. Love you."

THAT EVENING, TWO determined, thoughtful people sat down to dinner in the spacious, open concept living/dining room. Angus noticed Georgie had a far-away look in her eyes and seemed very distracted. Poor Georgie. He was determined to be positively attentive. There were no academic journals in sight. He leaned forward in his chair and regarded her intently.

"A truly wonderful dinner, Georgie. I think that casserole is one of my all-time favourites. And this brownie is delicious."

"Thank you, dear. I knew you'd be hungry." Georgie glanced at the living room carpet and smiled at the thought of golden oak hardwood flooring.

Angus scooped up the last of his dessert and reached for

her hand. "I was sorry to hear about your Aunt Beryl's legacy. I'm sure receiving that money caused you great stress, but you don't have to bear this burden alone."

Georgie squeezed his hand and then withdrew hers. "Oh no. Ross has been very helpful," she said. She studied the narrow living room windows. When the heavy drapes were removed, she was sure the windows would be revealed to be slightly different sizes. *So provoking. Perhaps a large bay window...*

"Georgie, my love. There is no need to worry about the money. I will help you through this. You can count on my complete support," Angus said.

Georgie frowned in concentration. "Oh yes, thank you Angus. Support, of course." *Certainly, support would have to be taken care of first. A new foundation was essential.* She smiled at Angus. "Thank you, dear. So kind. Have you noticed the living room drapes? I think they aren't quite the same size, or else it's the windows."

"Georgie, never mind the drapes. I'm sure you agree it's important to get rid of the legacy as quickly as possible. Legacies cause nothing but chaos and disruption. It was a legacy from my grandparents that caused my mother to quit her job and move to Tideways leaving Em and me alone."

"Yes, it does seem chaos and disruptions are sure to follow. Don't worry. I'll help you cope." She leaned back in her chair and reviewed her afternoon's packing. "I'm sure I packed enough shirts, but you might need to buy some short pants. Summers are much hotter in Toronto."

"Toronto? Georgie, I'm not going to Toronto. I intend to stay right here with you and Em."

Georgie frowned again as she continued to study the

irritating window wall. "I've never been very fond of intentions, Angus. You may want to review yours. Emily and I won't be here. How do you feel about bay windows?"

Angus abruptly stood up and gazed wildly around the room. "I hate bay windows. What the hell!" He stood staring for a moment at the familiar comforting living room then slowly sat down again. "Georgie! Of course, you'll be here. We'll all be together like always. I'm not leaving. I'm staying here to help you get rid of that oppressive money. I have a brilliant idea. Wait until you hear what I've decided."

Georgie's gaze rested on the living room wall. Perhaps a bay window would not be wise. The house was long and desperately needed symmetry. *Four large windows across the front would probably be best,* she thought. She looked at Angus. "This whole plan will need careful thought."

"Exactly, Georgie." Angus relaxed again. "Careful thinking is what I've done. We could start by talking to your friend Beth. She set up a scholarship fund for Greydon. She'll be able to help us create one in pure mathematics with Aunt Beryl's money."

Georgie stared at Angus in disbelief. This was his plan? The sudden heat in her face was very confusing. Was she having a hot flash or was she about to explode? She stared at him and considered her options. Perhaps she could plead hormonal imbalance or justifiable homicide. With a great effort she gained some self-control and dumped a metaphorical load of burning coals on her husband's head. "Don't be ridiculous, Angus. There will be no scholarship. You cannot stay here. Moving men will arrive on Wednesday to clear out the house. Your self-absorbed lifestyle and selfish protection of your own comfort is at an end. I'm saving you and this house!"

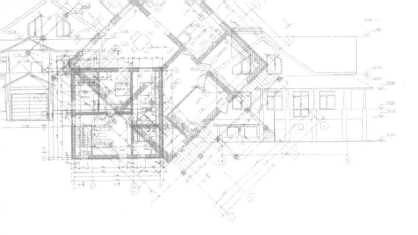

Twenty

EMILY'S EXCITED VOICE echoed in the empty church. "I'm beginning to understand Georgie's passion for renovation. This church needs to be saved. Let's stay awhile and soak up the atmosphere." Emily and Ross were watching the late afternoon sun set a stained-glass window on fire. They had spent the last hour inspecting, exploring, plotting and considering what needed to be done to turn the abandoned church into a modern home.

"What fun, Ross. You would need a hefty renovation budget and a good contractor, but I think it's a very sound investment.

Ross stood at the front of the old church imagining the place filled with people who truly believed. "Whoa! Look at the reflections from that window. Those godly people sure knew how to strike awe into the heart of us sinners." He sank gratefully into an uncomfortable but supportive pew. "Man, this place is so peaceful."

Emily agreed as she settled beside him. "This must be the *peace that passes all understanding* Georgie is always talking about." She was acutely aware of the strong, warm body next to her on the hard pew. She felt his calm rhythmic breathing slowly seep into her core. This must be that Pranayama yoga breathing Carrie recommended for people who didn't have a love life. Nope! That breathing was supposed to replace the sexual urge. This breathing was definitely having a different effect. *I could stay here and breathe him in for a lifetime*, she thought. "I want to stay like this forever," she said.

"Well, honey, you're the professional here, but I think we'll have to leave before then. Should I really think about buying and fixing up this place? Having a stained-glass window and a stubby steeple would be cool, I guess—maybe." He laughed and hugged her hard.

She leaned into him and kissed him with longing and just a bit too much passion for a church pew. In a few moments she sat up. "Sorry, bad timing," she said.

"Yeah, let's get out of here and neck in my twenty-car parking lot. We might as well prepare the neighbours for the new owner. Am I really going to buy this place? Good god, I think I am. I was just imagining those stained-glass reflections on your naked body. Let's go!"

CHEERFUL MORNING LIGHT was reflected on the bedroom walls when Georgie woke alone on Monday morning. Angus had not come to bed and Georgie had left the bedroom drapes wide open. She slipped out of bed and listened carefully for signs of life elsewhere in the house. All was quiet. She looked in the office to see Angus asleep on his ancient recliner.

She made her way to the bathroom and had a quick shower. There was no singing this morning in recognition of the mourning in the adjacent office. Dressing quickly, she made her way to the kitchen, started the coffee, sent a text to Emily, and called Anne.

"Georgie, you beast! You didn't call last night. I was afraid to call you. What the hell? What's going on? If you don't tell me everything right now, I'm coming over."

"I'm sorry, Anne. I knew you were waiting, but it didn't seem right to call a friend for comfort when Angus has no one to call. I wasn't very nice to him. He's not talking to me. I sent a text to Emily and asked her to come over this morning to help him."

"So, OK. What happened at dinner? Did he try to talk you out of it? Of course, he did. What did he come up with? I bet he found a way to get rid of your money so you couldn't do the house. The louse."

"Anne! That's my loving husband you're calling a louse. He was consideration itself. He had decided that he would take the burden of the legacy away from me and use it to create a math scholarship. Then we all could be happy again."

"Oh my God. I knew it. What did you say? Did you dump shepherd's pie on his head instead of loving kindness?"

"It was worse than that. I lost my temper. I told him the movers were coming on Wednesday and his life as he knew it was over. He didn't take it well. He went into his office and closed the door. He never came to bed. Guess what? I left the drapes open, and the bedroom was filled with light this morning. It was beautiful. I'm planning on a much larger window for that room."

"Yeah, that was a change. You've been waking up in the

dark since you got married. Hey, is there a life lesson there? I'll have to think about that some more."

"Oh Anne, you can always make me laugh, but I just recalled one of dad's proverbs. *Even in laughter the heart may ache, and the end of joy may be grief.* Poor Angus is really suffering, and I have to remember to be kind."

"OK. Kind but relentless. You know he has to get over this so you can both be happy. Don't give up."

"I gave up for seventeen years because of a child's feelings. Now that I know Emily wants to leave, I'll find the strength to save us all. Fear not!"

"You go, girl. Have you talked to Sylvia at the Math Department? She's part of our Plan. Will she help Angus get to Toronto?"

"Oh, he says he isn't going. I really don't care. He can bunk with me as long as exits this house."

"Hey! Don't offer to share our guest room with him. He would weep on us day and night. We don't have enough Scotch for that."

"Oh, no, I wouldn't inflict him on you and Terry. I was thinking I would rent a room in the Grand Pre Motel. They do a wonderful breakfast there and I could drive him in to Wolfville every morning."

"Bloody hell. I forgot the man hates to drive himself because he always gets lost. Rent him a car of his own. It will keep him out of your way."

"Anne! Stop it. I'll need to look after him if he doesn't go to Toronto."

"Sounds like purgatory to me. You should love it!"

"Very funny! I just heard Emily come in. Gotta go."

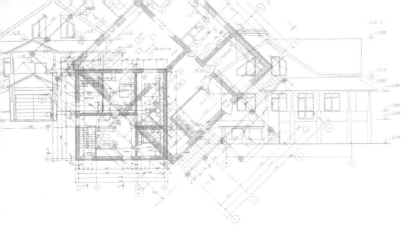

Twenty-One

WALKER REAL ESTATE was having a staff meeting. The staff was gathered in the conference room, but gossip was the only item on the agenda. Carrie had supplied carbs and caffeine. She and Anne were waiting impatiently for Emily to tell all.

"Thanks for the muffin and the coffee, Carrie." Emily slowly added another sugar packet in her large double-double.

"Stop stalling! I want to know what you decided about the church. Start talking."

Anne lost her patience. "Carrie, for God's sake forget about the church. There are more important issues here than real estate. Emily, what happened with your father this morning? Tell us every word he said." Anne was leaning so far forward in her chair she was in danger of sliding out.

"Sorry, Carrie, the boss scares me more than you ever could, so I'll start with her. It's not very comfortable being the focus of so much powerful attention." Emily smiled at

Anne and stuck out her tongue at Carrie.

"Well, you know my dad," she said. "There were no loud scenes. When I arrived, he had just finished his shower, but he had to dress in yesterday's clothes because he refused to go into the bedroom. He was packing his briefcase and was planning to leave for the university without his breakfast, so I knew he was very upset. He refused to speak to Georgie. I think he would have preferred not to talk to me too, but I just walked along with him. He doesn't know how to resist lecturing, so he gave me a lecture all the way to his office. It was really quite sad."

"I suppose he's still hoping to use you to control Georgie like he's always done," Anne said.

"Yeah, I guess so. I just listened and let him get it all out. Then I told him that I agreed with Georgie, and if he loved us, he would support Georgie's plan. At that point he did stop talking. I hope it was because he was reconsidering, but I'm not sure he's ready yet."

"Did he say anything about going to Toronto? Georgie's hoping that Sylvia at the Math Department will help him organize that," Anne said.

"He was very clear he would not leave Wolfville. I don't know if he plans to haunt the house or not. I really don't know what will happen. It's all rather worrying. However, I've decided to let the parents work this out on their own and get my own life in order." Emily sighed heavily and took a large sustaining bite of her carrot muffin.

"Aha! Now we're getting to the good stuff," Carrie swept the remainder of Emily's muffin into her lap. "Not another bite until you spill the beans about the church and your plans for the curly headed hunk."

"OK, Carrie. Your turn. Ross and I spent a long time in

the church imagining how it could be reconfigured to be a modern family home. It has some lovely features; high ceilings, great woodwork, lots of space and a stunning stained glass window facing west. It also has a very peaceful atmosphere." She sighed heavily and a slow smile spread across her face. "And there's a large parking lot. Ross and I agreed it would be a great investment."

"Well, that sounds promising. Is he going to make an offer? Is it really suitable as a family home? Is there room for lots of kids?" Anne asked.

"Wow, Mum. You are definitely back in real estate mode, or is that godparent mode?" Carrie teased with a laugh.

"Yes, he's going to make an offer." Emily said. "We drove around Hantsport and then had dinner at Surf. Hantsport's a lovely little community and I don't think Ross will miss Wolfville at all. There's a certain relief in living where everyone doesn't know all about you."

"Yadda. Yadda. Yadda. The church is fine. What about the real dirt. Are you two going to renovate a church and live in it together? Come on, Emily. Give!"

"Carrie, do you never give up? Never mind, I already know that answer. Well, over dinner Ross and I agreed that we would work together on this project. We figure by the time we collaborate on a major renovation we'll know whether we're a safe bet for the long haul. We're being somewhat cautious, but we're excited. It's going to be so much fun."

"And as the Wolfville house story unfolds, you'll be concentrating on Hantsport. Good thinking, girl!" Carrie jumped up to give Emily back her muffin and execute a jubilant high-five. Wait 'till I tell Henri. You and Ross are building a future."

GEORGIE CLEARED THE dining room table and set up her laptop. This project was going to be demanding. Thank goodness she had gone to Acadia, worked on administrative positions and was computer literate. She set up a spreadsheet and listed as many parts of the project as she could imagine.

Stan Kirby would be here this morning to talk in general terms about her house plans. She would get his advice on project management. Of course, he would be most responsible as the general contractor, but she had waited too long for this adventure to simply sit back and watch others work. She was going to be involved.

Her thoughts turned again to Angus. He hadn't spoken to her since dinner last night. Thank goodness Emily had come this morning and walked to the university with him. He was hurting and he needed a friend. Poor Angus. He was so stubborn and so dependent on his family. Over the years he had let most of his early friendships wither and die. Perhaps Sylvia could help him. He was such a good man in so many ways but...

There was a sudden loud pounding on the front door. She glanced out the front window to see Stan's large white truck at the curb. She hurried to the door and struggled to open it. Finally, it gave up its sticky resistance and she yanked it open.

"Good morning, Georgie. That's a fine front door. No one's going to sneak in here, that's certain."

Darn! Stan was already enjoying himself at the poor house's expense. She would have to set him straight. "Good morning, Stan. Thanks for agreeing to take on this huge project. Come in. Come in. I need to tell you a few things before we discuss business. Would you like coffee?"

"No thanks." He moved to the dining room table and sat

looking curiously around him. "You know, I haven't been in here since old BB Gun gave up his last band. He was a real personality in his day. He built this house himself, you know. I see it hasn't changed much."

"No, and that's something we need to discuss. Angus feels strongly that the house his father built shouldn't be changed. I checked with all members of the family including his father, and we all agree that major repairs and a renovation are necessary. I'm a joint owner and I'm prepared to go ahead with the project. However, Angus is not entirely happy. Do you have any problem with that?"

"Well, this is a small town, Georgie. I think everyone already knows this house desperately needs some work. Angus is an intelligent man. I'm sure he'll come 'round. Besides, if I sign a contract with you, then you and I have a contract. I won't be dealing directly with Angus. If he's a problem, he'll be your problem."

"Excellent. There's just one more thing. For the sake of Angus's feelings and his father's memory, could we treat the house with respect? I don't mean not to change it. I just think we shouldn't encourage too much talk about how awful it is. It's easy to poke fun at it, but I don't want to make this any harder for Angus than it already is."

"No problem. I've dealt with lots of old houses that are almost as quirky as this one. Let's take a tour and see what you have in mind."

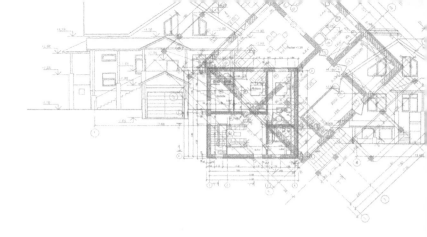

Twenty-Two

Ross and Emily were in the Walker conference room and had just finished agreeing on the details of the offer for the church. "I feel giddy with anticipation," Ross said. "Kiss me so I can anticipate some more."

Emily glanced at the open conference room door and then complied with enthusiasm.

"Emily Julia MacLean! I never thought I would see this kind of behaviour in my niece. This is a place of business and not that kind of business."

Ross nodded at the intruder, kissed Emily a very businesslike farewell and left.

"Hi, Aunt Helen. What's up? You usually don't come into the office. I was just finishing up some business with Ross Saunders. You might remember him. He's a Wolfville boy and he's just putting an offer in on a property."

"I know the family, but Emily, you surely don't carry on like that in the office, do you?"

"He's kind of special, Aunt Helen. Did you want something?"

"I wouldn't come in here unless I felt it was critical. We need to talk. Can you come to my house for lunch?"

"Sure, give me a half-hour to put in this offer and I'll come along."

Moments later Carrie stuck her head in the door and said, "She's gone. She never comes in here. What was that all about?"

"I don't know, but she wants me to come to her house for lunch. That's distressing. She lives for gossip and if she doesn't want to talk in public something big must be on her mind."

"You don't have to go, you know. I've been telling you for years she doesn't like Georgie and she's lives to cause trouble."

"Yeah, I know, Carrie. But she's my mother's sister and the only connection I have with that side of the family. She lives in the old family home. When I visit, I can imagine my mother there. We often get out the family album and talk about her. Dad never tells me anything about her at all. It's as if he didn't really know her."

"I can believe that. He was only eighteen when she died. What eighteen-year-old guy knows anything? OK, go to lunch, but be careful."

Emily put in the low-ball offer, crossed her fingers it would be accepted and walked the short distance to her aunt's house. It was close to the university and Aunt Helen supplemented her income by renting rooms to students.

As she walked up the front steps Aunt Helen opened the door. "Emily, hurry up. Didn't I tell you this was serious?"

Emily's anxiety rose to a new level. "Serious? Are you ill?

What's wrong?"

"It's not me who's sick. It's that stepmother of yours. Do you know she asked Stan Kirby about doing a major renovation on your home? That Miss Goody-two-shoes puts up a good front, but I've never trusted her. I knew she was up to no good when she moved in. Angus must be completely devastated. She probably didn't even tell you about it. She knows how much you love that house your Poppa built. Don't worry, darling. It's not too late to stop her. I'll help you. Let's get down to business."

STAN'S TOUR WAS over, and Georgie was alone again in her condemned kitchen, "I was very impressed with Stan's restraint, Kitchen. I asked him to treat the house with respect and he did a great job. I don't doubt that he'll have a good laugh with his wife over dinner, but he held himself together here. All he said about you was, 'That's quite a kitchen.' I like him."

Georgie took her coffee and a sandwich into the dining room and ate a late lunch while she added to her project spreadsheet. She and Stan had established some rough guidelines, and he was going to come back tomorrow to do some proper measurements. Georgie made a list of what they had already agreed upon:

- Remove garage and apartment/addition
- Put in new foundation
- Upgrade basement - move laundry upstairs
- Add full second storey with symmetrical dormers
- New windows—energy efficient—same size
- New siding—consistent on all sides

- Bring all plumbing, electrical and insulation up to code
- Install central heat pump and external generator (to be ready for climate change)
- Expand master bedroom and bathroom
- Reduce size of 'open concept' living/dining room
- Create a modern kitchen with large island
- Harwood floors throughout
- Be kind to Angus

She finished her list and called Anne. "Stan came this morning, and we got a solid start. I think it's going to be a good working relationship. I asked him not to be unkind to the house and he didn't even laugh at the kitchen. I'm glad I called him. He's coming back tomorrow to take some measurements and make further suggestions. Anne, I'm so happy. Things are moving. Now, if only Angus loved me as much as he loves this house."

"Georgie Shaw MacLean! That's terrible. Of course, he loves you more than the house. He just wants everything to stay the same. That's as understandable as it is stupid. Did Emily call you today by any chance?"

"No, she went off with Angus this morning and I haven't talked with her since. I expect I'll hear from her this evening. She knew Stan was coming and she'll want a full report."

"Hmmm. Little Helen Carter came in here at noon today and took Emily to lunch. She may be trying to cause trouble."

"Well, she's good at that, but I'm not worried. Emily's not fifteen anymore. Besides, there's no cloakroom door to sneak behind. There's nothing she can do to hurt me now."

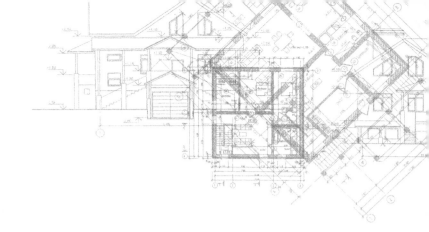

Twenty-Three

"*One more cupboard and that's the bathroom cupboard, One more cupboard. One more cupboard to clear...*"

Georgie was singing lustily as she cleaned out the loft bathroom. A large garbage bag was almost full of expired drugstore products that were probably hazardous and didn't deserve to take up space in expensive temporary storage. On Wednesday the movers would come, and she could start to create a beautiful home. Then she and Angus would live the rest of their lives in safety and comfort and prepare to nurture grandchildren. Her strong voice filled the loft.

"*One more cupboard...*"

Her solo concert was interrupted by her cell phone. It was a number she didn't recognize. What now? Well, it was a local number and not another shocking call from Toronto. She decided to answer.

"Georgie, this is Sylvia from the Math Department. I

need to talk to you. Could I come over right now?"

"Of course, Sylvia. I'm expecting Angus home for dinner any minute, but you are certainly welcome. Come to the garage door. It's much easier."

She slipped her cell phone back in her jeans and wondered what Sylvia could want at this hour. They had often met at university functions and commiserated about absent minded math profs. She was a patient, kind den mother to the assorted denizens of the math department. Perhaps she had convinced Angus to go to Toronto. Hallelujah!

She had just filled the coffee maker when she heard Sylvia pull into the driveway. She opened the door and faced a frazzled and frantic Sylvia. "Georgie, I don't have much time. I've left Angus with my husband and they're drinking Scotch and staring at one another. My husband doesn't understand why Angus is at our house."

"Well, neither do I, Sylvia. I expected him to come home for dinner tonight."

"He said he won't come back here until you change your mind. I reminded him about the great offer from U of T but he wouldn't consider that either. He said he was sure you would soon give up your plans and then things could get back to normal."

"Sylvia, I'm so sorry. Should I come back with you and pick him up?"

"I don't think it would work Georgie. I've never seen him like this. He was going to stay in the office all night, but I just couldn't leave him there. I brought him home and I'll feed him supper. You know he never eats lunch. He can stay in our son's room tonight, but he'll have to leave tomorrow. My husband doesn't like professors much. He hears too many stories from me, I guess."

"Thank you for taking him in, Sylvia. That's very kind of you. Please keep him tonight and I'll come to the office tomorrow morning to talk to him."

"Thanks so much, Georgie. I didn't want to try to explain this over the phone, and I thought I might pick up an overnight bag for him."

"Of course. How thoughtful. Give me a minute and I'll pack one."

EMILY AND ROSS were enjoying a pizza at the condo. Anticipation had been replaced by action and both were feeling satisfied and hungry.

Emily chewed thoughtfully and smiled at Ross. "I gave the church agent twenty-four hours to respond to your offer. By this time tomorrow we'll have an answer. If only all problems had a closing deadline, life would be easier. I'm worried about my family."

"Yeah, Georgie called me to say she's ready to hire a contractor. I think she intends to sign a contract tomorrow. I take it your dad is still not on board."

"Right, he's more like a massive anchor. He's not my only worry. My Aunt Helen, my birth-mother's sister, wants to round up a fleet of warships to blockade the ship at dock or possibly scuttle it."

"Interesting. What's her angle?"

"Oh, she says it's on my behalf, but there's some long-standing feud between her and Georgie that I don't understand. She wants me to fight Georgie on this. I told her no way. I want to move out of the house. That didn't go over well. She finally stopped trying to win me over, but I think she's planning to cause trouble."

"I wouldn't worry about her too much. Georgie has the resources and the legal right to make renovations. I suppose Angus could take her to court, but I don't see that happening, do you?"

"God, no. He's stubborn and unhappy, but not crazy. I guess my big worry is Wolfville itself. I don't want my family to be the source of the best gossip in Town. You know how people talk."

"Yes, I do and there's a great song about that. Ross swallowed the last of his pizza and pulled her from the table. "Let's give them something to talk about," he sang as he danced her back to the bedroom.

Hunger and worry forgotten, Emily welcomed the strength and comfort Ross provided. She needed to give something back. "Ross, I want to look after you like you look after me. I'm going to get you a church and your very own stained-glass window to light up your life."

Ross laughed into her breast where he was applying himself to great effect. "Yeah, you go, hon. I love it when you talk churchy!"

Emily stopped trying to talk and gave herself over to feeling. *I've had sex before,* she thought, *but this is so much more.* She pulled Ross up for a heartfelt kiss. "Ross," she murmured, "I think this is what they call making love."

"You bet! You make me so happy. I see great things in our future. Don't worry about your family. They'll work things out, and in the meantime, we have each other. Life is good. What do you think about expanding that church parking lot?"

Laughter and love filled the darkening condo as evening came and the lovers finally dozed.

It was fully night when Ross stirred sleepily and sat up. "Man, I'm famished. Let's finish that cold pizza and then we can have dessert." He grinned at Emily and pulled her from the bed.

They made their way to the dinette and Emily grabbed her discarded slice of cold pizza and put it down again. "Ross. I'm so happy. I can't eat because I can't stop smiling. Along with multiple orgasms I think I've just had an epiphany. You know, I told Georgie to tear down the apartment. I think she was going to make a new one on the second floor, but Ross, I just realized I never have to go back there. I can live where I want. Hey, here's some more churchy talk for you. Thank the Lord. I'm free at last!"

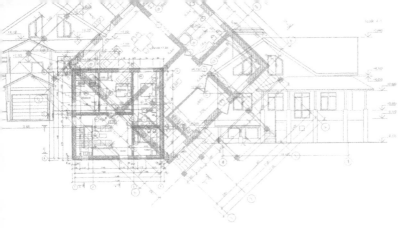

Twenty-Four

MORNING HAD BROKEN and the soft light of a spring dawn flooded the bedroom, but Georgie didn't feel like singing. Last night Angus had not come home. He was not going to Toronto. She would see him later today and offer to be with him at the Grande Pre Motel for the summer. The silly, stubborn man.

It was early, but Georgie hurried to dress and eat a quick breakfast. She loaded two huge suitcases and several boxes of perishables from the kitchen into her car and drove to Anne's.

Anne and Terry were not home. She let herself into the house, put the food in the fridge, and settled at the kitchen counter with her laptop. It was too early to call Emily. She reviewed her renovation list for her meeting with Stan later this morning. Anne's kitchen was bright and peaceful. She vowed she would have a kitchen like this by September. It would give Angus lots of morning light to focus his attention.

Anne threw open the kitchen door. "Georgie! We saw your car in the driveway." Terry bent to give her a quick kiss on her cheek and poured himself a large glass of orange juice. "The dyke was fantastic this morning. You should join us while you're here. There's nothing as invigorating as a morning walk on the dyke."

"Thanks, Terry. I'm not sure if I'll be here or not. I intend to see Angus today and offer to bunk with him in Grande Pre. The movers will be taking everything to storage tomorrow, but I may want to bring some precious things here for the duration."

"No problem, sweetie. How is the old man?" Terry asked and then caught the look in Anne's eye. "OK, then. I'll push off and oversee the real estate world while you two plot. You're very welcome here, Georgie. I'm sure things will work out."

"What a good guy you have, Anne. You two work and live together, but never seem to be tired of each other."

"Yeah, yeah, yeah. Never mind us. What happened when Angus got home last night?"

"Well, our Plan didn't take into account how stubborn Angus could be. He refused to come home, and poor Sylvia had to take him home with her for the night. I'm going to talk to him today, but I can't do it until later. Stan is due in about a half an hour, and I want to get that contract signed before I talk to Angus."

"Yeah, do that, kiddo. All Angus would have to do at this point is let a tear fall and you'd be stuck in that mess of a house forever."

"I know. I'm already wavering. Perhaps, it would be enough to just fix the foundation. Then, the house wouldn't be sliding down the hill and the doors would work. I could cope with the rest like I've been doing. I'm positive my father would approve if I compromised."

"Georgie! Stop it. You deserve to live in a safe, comfortable house that you love. We talked about all this. You knew there would be a tough period while Angus tried his best to maintain the *status quo*. That house needs substantial help. You sign that contract and let the *fait accompli* and the *status quo* fight it out."

"That's just it, Anne. I have never learned how to fight. I'm really scared that Angus will hate me."

"Rubbish. You don't know how great a good fight can be. Terry and I have some real loud ones. Making up is one of the best parts of a happy marriage. Have courage. You wanted to wake Angus up. This should do it. I'm dying to see what happens next."

EMILY WAS HAUNTING the office fax machine. It was almost noon, and she was waiting impatiently for the response to her church offer. The agent had called and told her a counteroffer would be coming by the deadline.

Carrie breezed in wearing minimal clothes and an irritated frown. "I don't know why we're still doing business by fax. When you and I take over things will be much more fashionable." She twirled around so Emily could see the back of her dress. "Like it?"

"How does it stay up? And what's it supposed to cover? It's missing some parts."

"It's a Bandeau dress, Prudie. It's got a lot of Spandex in it and it knows how to cling. Henri loves it."

"Hmmm. I'm sure. Where the hell is that counteroffer. I want this property!"

"Ah, passion! I've waited a long time to see this. You go, girl!" Carrie twirled beck to her office and left Emily free to daydream about life in a church. Ross was right. Her family could sort themselves out while she and Ross were busy in Hantsport. She glared at the fax. "Spit it out, you useless piece of outmoded technical junk!"

"Hey, do not abuse the office machinery. It can fight back." Ross bent to kiss her cheek. "Where's your aunt? I'm on my best behaviour today. I've come to hear about our offer and take you to lunch. What's happening?"

Before she could answer her cell phone rang. It was Georgie. What now? "Hi, Stepma. What's up? Sorry I didn't call last night but I fell asleep. Did you and dad have a good talk?"

"Not yet, dear. I went to the Math Department this morning after I finished with Stan. It was just about noon, but I didn't worry because you know your father never eats lunch. He wasn't there. Sylvia hadn't seen him leave, but one of the other profs said a woman he didn't recognize came by and Angus left with her. I thought it might be you."

"Nope, I haven't talked to him since I walked him to the office yesterday morning. He probably had to do something in the admin office. I'm sure you'll find him. He's a creature of habit."

"Well, he seems to be behaving somewhat out of character at the moment. I won't keep you, Emily. Hope you're not finding all these changes too hard on you. I love you dearly, you know."

The fax machine finally rattled to life. "Gotta go, Stepma. You keep going with your plans. Dad will adjust and I want you to have a home you love. I think I'm going to get one too. Bye."

She grabbed the offer, and they went to her office to consult. "Ross, they only countered 5K. I think that's a clear indication they are anxious to sell. I suggest we counter and raise our offer by 2.5K and move up the closing date to the end of this month. I'm practically certain the church will be yours."

"Seal the deal, Babe. Then I'll take you to lunch. I've been working too. I've made a list of church essentials. I'm going to Canadian Tire after work to buy a good air mattress, a bar fridge and a microwave. I'm going to establish our own summer church camp."

A smiling Emily faxed off the counteroffer and they decided to follow Carrie who had just left for lunch at the pub. They were heading out when Carrie burst back through the front door.

"Emily. Ross. Don't go out! We have to think! Oh my God! What are we going to do?"

"Carrie, calm down," Emily said. "Whatever it is it's not the end of the world. Did someone bar you from the pub until you put on some clothes?"

"Emily! This is no time for jokes. Your father and your Aunt Helen are sitting in the front window of the pub eating lunch and drinking beer! I think Armageddon has finally arrived!"

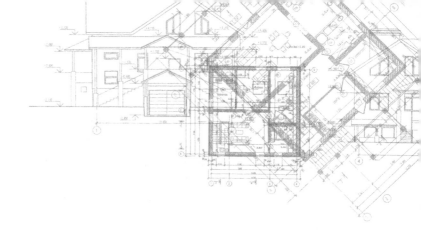

Twenty-Five

G EORGIE MADE A tour of the campus but didn't find her stubborn mate. He obviously had gone to ground somewhere. Oh well, he couldn't avoid her forever. If he wasn't going to Toronto, he would have to share a room with her-somewhere. She decided to stop looking for him. She still had things to pack including his office.

She would put everything in one storage unit so he could find all his important papers in one place. She went to Wolfville Home Hardware to pick up more packing boxes and returned to the house to find Stan standing in the garage with an older man in a buffalo plaid shirt and oversize work boots. His baggy jeans were covered in mud.

Stan greeted her. "Hi Georgie, this is Earl Preston, one of the best foundation men in the business. We're just looking over the job."

"I was telling Stan here that I well remember when old BB Gun put this place together. He hauled these rocks from an old foundation out Port Williams way. He was a real good scrounger."

"I'm pleased to meet you Mr. Preston. Do you think you can put the house on a strong foundation? I've been worried about it for some time. It seems to be slipping away."

"You call me Earl and we'll get along real good. The first thing is to jack up the house and then we'll see how the sills are and just how much trouble we're in, but I've seen worse. We'll replace old BB Gun's rocks with some good concrete and this old house will be good to go for a hundred years."

"Thank you. Earl. My father-in-law is in favour of the renovation. He told me he had to make do when he built the house but he's happy we can fix it up now." She noted with satisfaction the look that passed between the two men. It didn't hurt to let them know the legendary BB Gun approved of her plans.

"We'll be starting on Thursday morning early, Georgie. Can the house be empty by then?" Stan asked. We'll be taking down the garage and the back porch apartment, so Earl just has the main house to jack up."

"No problem. The movers are coming tomorrow to put everything in storage. Emily has already moved out and Angus and I will be moving in with friends or something until the project is finished. I'll leave you men to your talk and finish my packing."

WHERE WAS ANGUS? How long did he think he could avoid her? He must know they had to talk. Stubborn old coot! She stood in his small office doorway and considered her task. All this needed was a plan. Three filing cabinets could go as is. No need to pack their contents. There were four unpainted bookshelves with five warped shelves each. They could go to the dump! She would pack the contents of each shelf in a separate box and label them clearly. The desk drawers could stay packed but the stacks of papers and journals on top would have to have their own box. The recliner and lamp could go as is but the stack of books, journals and papers beside the recliner would have to have its own box and label. Piece of cake! She began to fold and tape packing boxes.

By 4:30 she was hot, dusty, and cranky. Where was that man? He should be doing this packing himself. Oh well, the job was done and whatever she didn't get packed in the rest of the house the movers could deal with. She was wiped.

She went to the bathroom and had just finished her shower when she heard the outside door open. Finally! "Angus. I'm in the shower. I'll be right out."

"It's just Ross and me, Stepma. We'll wait in the living room. Take your time."

GEORGIE WAS VERY, very angry. Ross and Emily had delivered the news that Angus had gone over to the enemy camp. War had been declared. It was now past midnight, The war council over dinner at Anne's didn't offer any solutions. Carrie repeated her fear that Armageddon was upon them. Henri googled the unfamiliar term. *Armageddon: the last battle between good and evil before the Day of Judgement.* Everyone solemnly agreed it was a fitting description.

Georgie glanced at her watch. 1:00am. The young people had gone home. Terry had gone to bed and Anne was sitting in her favourite rocking chair watching Georgie pace. "I don't think it's quite as beneficial as a walk on the dyke in fresh air, but you are getting some good exercise there. I love watching you get riled up."

Georgie flung herself on the coach and stared angrily at Anne. "I'm still mad. I didn't know anger could last so long and feel so right. I'm so damned fed up with that woman."

"Oh, my goodness, gracious, me. Was that a naughty word? Think of your reputation. Think of your poor parents. Imagine how good Helen of Troy would feel knowing she'd brought you this low."

"Yeah, I know. I should turn my thoughts in another direction. I think I can understand Helen's motive. She lives to cause me trouble, but Angus must have lost his mind."

"I agree. It sure wasn't her beauty that lured him to move in with her and start a war. Of course, she offered him a port in a storm. Oh, I don't like where this story is going. You'd better rescue him before she lures him from her spare room onto the rocks."

"Well, Anne, you just lost any admiration I had for your positive thought expertise. What a horrible image." Georgie jumped up and began pacing again. "No, I can't believe he would betray me like that. Of course, he might not notice until it was too late. Oh, I'm so angry at both of them."

"Stick to the Plan. The renovation contract is signed. The movers will clear the house tomorrow. Stan and the foundation guy will start work on Thursday. No matter where Angus hangs his hat it won't be in his daddy's old house. That's progress. Let's go to bed."

Georgie went to her room and crawled into the comfortable empty bed. Angus was in Helen's house, in his own empty bed, she reassured herself. Perhaps he would move in here with her tomorrow when he realized the scandal he'd caused. She was too angry to sleep. She tried to calm herself by dreaming of the safe, beautiful home she was creating for them both. It didn't work. Instead, she spent a pleasant hour counting foundation stones as they flew from BB Gun's basement to land on Helen's fragile roof.

ON WEDNESDAY MORNING the movers arrived at 11:00, only two hours later than their appointment time. It didn't matter. Georgie had lots to do. Sylvia had texted her at 8:00 to say that Angus had arranged for a temporary office at the university and would like her to send the entire contents of his home office there. Georgie's anger had fueled a furious round of relabeling every single box and every item of furniture in the office, including four poorly built, flimsy bookcases and the ratty venetian blind on the window.

The storage unit she had designated for Angus's office would now be her very own. She loaded her car with some things she might want over the summer and a few special items she wanted to move into the renovated house. Emily had already packed the special family keepsakes she valued.

Georgie smiled as she carefully placed the bright yellow casserole dish in her car. "I'll find you your very own open shelf," she told it. It would be a bright reminder of Emily's confession and the beginning of the Liberation Plan.

The Plan had to work. She had known the decisions she was making and the changes to come could lead to anger and conflict. She and Anne had considered the cost. At the time, Georgie was convinced that Angus would eventually recognize her overwhelming need and approve of her choices.

Eventually! In the meantime, little Helen Carter had her hooks into him. A sudden surge of pain almost overwhelmed her. He had fallen under the spell of another Carter many years ago. His sudden intense interest in Julie had ended their teenage friendship and Georgie had lost him for years. She was surprised how much it still hurt. Helen had been gleeful at the time, and it had taken all Georgie's resolve to never admit to anyone how much his loss had affected her.

Helen! If I were writing the story of my life and recording the most traumatic incidents of my youth, Helen Carter would be right in the middle of them. Well, I lost Santa Claus forever and Angus once, but I am not losing him again. We are anchored together for the rest of our lives. We both know that. Pay attention. Angus! Back off, Helen!

Georgie noticed the movers were very efficient once they got going. They were dealing with a lot of stuff. She had not packed the contents of many cabinets and cupboards. Almost everything would have no place in her new home. She had decided to send it all to storage. The house furniture and contents would go into several storage units and she planned to offer the units to various non-profits so they could sort and salvage what they wanted over the summer. She stood in the kitchen doorway for a few moments watching the shelf of juice glasses being carefully wrapped and snugly packed in a sturdy box. Was that a twinge of kitchen nostalgia she felt or was it just another Angus pang?

She grabbed a kitchen chair and carried it to the corner of the living room. She would perch there until the movers were finished and had their cheque. Tonight, she had a dinner date with Ross and Emily. Life would go on. These were dark times especially with Helen throwing dirt in everyone's eyes. Wake up Angus! Her eyes blurred and her throat ached. Angus did love her. He would see the light – eventually. She looked around the desolate living room. She was alone. She began to sing quietly to herself and to her stubborn husband whom she had backed into a very dangerous corner.

"Jesus bids us shine with a pure, clear light, like a little candle burning in the night. In the world is darkness, so we must shine, you in your small corner, and I in mine."

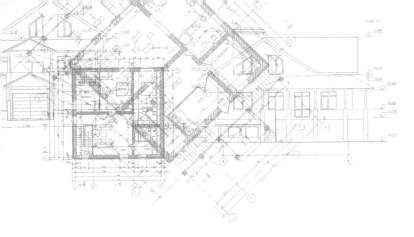

Twenty-Six

S URF RESTAURANT WAS busy, but it was a friendly busy. Everyone was relaxed and enjoying the food and the view of the Avon River. Georgie joined Emily and Ross at a table by the window. They were holding hands and looking very young and happy. "Hey, kids, what's the news? Will there be another church in my life?"

"You bet, Stepma. The deal is done, and the church is secured. They accepted the offer and even agreed to move up the closing date. Ross will have possession in ten days."

"I decided there was no need to wait when my mind was made up. I'm anxious to take possession of their generous parking lot." Ross grinned and gave Emily a wicked leer then turned a friendly face to Georgie. "How did your day go, Georgie? Any word from Angus?"

"No, nothing from Angus. I spent the day at the house and the movers have taken everything to storage except for a few things I have in my car. I must admit I was a little unnerved to see the house so empty. It's almost like seeing someone naked. All the imperfections and bulging bits are in plain sight."

Ross smiled a very seductive smile at Emily while Georgie consulted the menu. "Some of those bulging bits are quite intriguing," he whispered.

"The fish is excellent here, Stepma," Emily said while kicking Ross under the table. I told Dad I would come to his office in the morning and deliver his suitcase. I hope I can talk some sense into him. Everyone is already asking me what's going on."

"I'm sure. It wouldn't take Helen long to let everyone know she had to step in and look after Angus," Georgie said. "She always wanted to be involved in his life and certainly was in yours. But then, she is your only aunt, and she loves you. I'll say no more on that subject."

"She's certainly involved. She's texting me every hour with questions about what's going on and suggestions about what I should be doing to stop the renovation. I don't think she's going to make this project any easier." Emily said.

"No. She's never tried to make my life easier. I think I will have the fish." Georgie put down her menu and stared for a long moment at the calming view of the Avon River.

"Despite everything and everyone I'm going to move ahead with my plans," Georgie said. "Laurie Adams has drawn up some amazing house plans for me. I met her years ago. She's a very talented architect and helped me with a design when I worked at the women's shelter. She'll be working with me and Stan to make sure we bring the house up to code, and design a pleasing, modern home. By the way, I'll want your opinion as things develop."

"Hey, Hon, maybe we should get in touch with Georgie's architect too. I know you have lots of ideas, but I assume remodeling a church is tricky. We wouldn't want to offend any spirits that are still hanging around." Ross smiled a very loving and attractive smile at Emily.

Tears welled up in Georgie eyes. She bent to retrieve a tissue from her purse and give herself a moment to regain her composure. *At least one of my dear ones is safe and happy,* she thought. *Now, I just have to rescue Angus from the clutches of a wicked witch.*

THE WICKED WITCH was having another very frustrating morning with her new tenant. Tuesday evening, he had gone silently to bed and on Wednesday morning he had silently left the house not even saying when he expected to return. Now he was doing it again! She heard him leave the house without saying good morning. That was damned rude.

When she offered to take Angus in, she expected to provide him with a convenient shoulder to cry on and get the inside scoop about his troubles with Georgie, but he was ignoring her. She wasn't going to put up with this kind of behaviour. He'd better join the team, or he would find himself out in the cold.

Helen sighed. She had him under her roof, but she had to acknowledge she didn't have him under her spell. Not yet! He had accepted her invitation, but he hadn't agreed to help with anything. He said he didn't expect the situation to last more than a few days because Georgie was a very reasonable person.

Ha! Georgie reasonable? That wasn't her experience. They were buddies in elementary school until grade four when suddenly, without any reason, Georgie stopped being her friend. From then on, no matter how hard Helen had tried, Georgie cut her out. It was totally unreasonable and still hurt.

Things got more interesting in high school. She remembered Julie laughing about how stupid Georgie was, and how she didn't even know how to attract a man. Angus and Julie's marriage was a perfect humiliation for Georgie. She tried to hide her feelings, but everyone knew she had lost, and Julie had won.

Helen smiled to herself thinking of more delicious payback to come. Angus was back in the Carter family again. Georgie would hate that! It would take some time to get Emily on board, Helen mused. Georgie had wormed her way into Emily's life and now it seemed Emily was on her side. She recalled their last exchange. "Aunt Helen, having Dad stay with you looks really bad. What are people going to think?"

'They're gonna understand that your stepmother is up to no good and that your father is not standing for it. That's what. I'm just trying to help, and as Angus said himself, I'm part of the family. It's the least I could do."

This morning as she watched a silent Angus trudge down the street, she was feeling neglected and unappreciated. She decided to go for coffee and conversation.

The local Tim's was always a good spot to find a sympathetic ear and a willing listener. She entered the busy coffee shop and immediately spotted Irene and Judy, two old schoolmates who had remained friends all these years. She took her large double-double and chocolate chip muffin to their table and sat with a sigh.

"Helen! Was that Angus that came out of your house this morning? I told Judy I was sure it was him. What's going on?"

"Good God, Irene. I don't know how anyone gets away with anything in this town. Yeah, it was Angus. He moved into one of my student rooms on Tuesday. Hey, there's nothing going on so stop that silly grinning!"

"Well, my dear, something is going on. He has a wife and home of his own. Give!" Judy demanded.

"Well, Miss Goody-two-shoes has shown her true colours at last. I always told Emily that she was up to no good and I was right." Helen took a huge bite of her muffin and chewed slowly while her friends digested her words.

"I've never really liked that woman," Judy said. "She's always dragging those disabled people around town and she's so holier-than-thou. I don't think she'd say shit if she had a mouthful."

Irene burst into loud laughter. "You got that right! Her daddy was a minister. She wasn't allowed to say a naughty word."

Helen swallowed, took a restorative sip of her double-double and launched into her tale. "You know Angus and Emily live in that house at the top of University Avenue that BB MacLean built in the '60s."

"Oh yeah, crazy BB Gun built that big house out of junk. I remember my mum laughing about it," Judy said.

"Everyone knows that story," Helen agreed. "Angus and Emily love it, but when BB and Miriam moved to Tideways, Angus went a little crazy and married that sneaky Georgie. I did my best when she first moved in to see that she didn't ruin Emily's life, but lately I haven't been so involved."

Judy and Irene exchanged sly looks. Judy spoke her mind.

"We remember all that, Helen. You were just moving back to Wolfville when they got married. You didn't have much to do with Emily until then, but all of a sudden you got real interested. I always thought you might have been pissed that Angus got married again, especially to Georgie. We all know you and Georgie are like oil and water."

"How was I supposed to be involved when I was living in Gaspereau with that asshole I married? I had my hands full with that bum."

"Yeah, that was a bad choice, but then you married him when you were in shock about losing Julie. Cut yourself some slack there, Helen," Irene said giving Judy a warning frown.

"Enough with the history. How come Angus left his home and moved in with you?" Judy said.

"Well, ever since Georgie moved in, she's wanted to make changes to the house. I warned Emily to watch out or she would find herself losing her home and that's finally what's happening," Helen jammed the rest of her muffin in her mouth and enjoyed her friends' astonished reactions.

"What the hell?' Judy said. "I thought Angus had one of those high-paying jobs at Acadia. How can they be losing the house?"

"This makes no sense," Irene said. "Why now? They've been married for years. She sure took her time if you're blaming this on her."

"Well, of course I'm blaming it on her. She's already hired Stan Keddy to do a major renovation. Angus is heartbroken and Emily doesn't know what to do. I intend to help them." Helen settled back in her chair and stared intently at her friends. "And you two are going to help me. There's no time to lose."

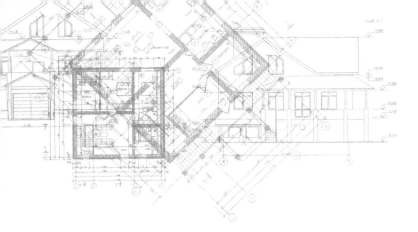

Twenty-Seven

What day is this? Georgie wondered as she opened her eyes and stared at Anne's fashionable but alien guest room. She counted slowly. Friday. It was day five without the inattentive but constant presence of Angus by her side. The rat! A surge of anger propelled her from the bed and into the guest bathroom. She stared at her middle-aged self in the handsome bathroom mirror and frowned. This state of consuming anger was new to her. She didn't like the constant turmoil that had destroyed her inner peace. She suddenly recalled a passage from Luke.

Do you think that I came to bring peace to earth? No indeed! I came to make people choose sides.

Ouch! She had destroyed her own peace and had made her family choose sides. And now, she was angry because she had lost the most important person in her life. She dressed quickly, entered the bright kitchen where coffee was brewing, and found comfort and support were on the menu.

"Good morning, sleepy head. How was your night? Terry has gone to the office, but I thought I would stay until you woke up in case you wanted to talk." Anne poured a cup of coffee and set it front of her old friend.

"Thanks, Anne. I'm still angry. It's a new experience for me. This morning I have to admit I'm even angry with myself. What a stinking mess I've made of my life."

"Hey! Stop that. Sure, it's a mess. It's called progress. You could have spent the rest of your life in a house that's slowly sliding down the hill with a trapped kid and a hibernating husband. Or you could make a mess."

"Oh Anne, I'm not sure I made the right decision. I'm afraid I've pushed Angus too far."

"Don't be ridiculous. It won't take him long to wake up when he gets uncomfortable. You've got a game plan. Stick with it. Be brave! It's good to be angry. Stay that way, but also be practical and get the job done."

"Thanks, coach. If I have to be practical, I want to start with breakfast. I was so angry last night I don't think I ate anything. Now I'm starving."

"Breakfast? Certainly, madam. Would you like our sustaining Crusading Warrior breakfast, or our popular Disrupter's Special, or perhaps the refined Daily Hero Plate?"

'I'll have it all, thanks. And give me a side order of patience," Georgie sat at the counter and prepared to take on fuel for a demanding day ahead. Breakfast finished, comfort and support consumed, she strengthened her resolve and ordered her thoughts. First, she would check on the house. Then, she would meet with Laurie to discuss more design plans. Then, she would go to the Math Department and have an adult conversation with her stubborn husband. Plans made, she got in her car and drove singing down Main Street,

Dare to be a Daniel, Dare to stand alone, Dare to have a purpose firm, Dare to make it known.

IN THE HEART of Wolfeville, the coven had finished their morning coffee but had not yet finished their plans. They left Tim's and reconvened in Helen's living room to discuss in private how best to divide and conquer.

Helen took charge. "Judy, you're a member of the Historical Society so your job is to get them involved. They should be very unhappy about what that woman is doing to an historical treasure. Irene, you organized a lot of public protests against everything. You should be able to get a group of concerned citizens to picket the house and see if they can stop the work.

"I'll go to Town Hall to make sure all the permits have been issued and complain to the mayor about the destruction of a Wolfville icon. I'll mention that reporters have been calling me. He's very protective of the town's image. He won't want to see this disaster hit the media."

Judy knew Helen well. "And I suppose you've already called the paper. You do like to spread the bad news." She grinned at her friends, "This sounds like a great project. Georgie has been a member of the Historical Society for a few years now. She's always going on about preserving historical properties to provide affordable housing. She's an almighty pain in the ass. It'll be fun to knock her on her self-righteous keister."

Irene looked thoughtful. "It's almost the weekend so I

don't think I can get a group together before next week. That should be OK though. These construction projects take a long time to get off the ground. We'll have lots of opportunity to cause a little ruckus, especially if we block University Avenue or Main Street."

Helen laughed and slapped her knee. I knew I could count on you two. Just think how grateful Angus will be when we stop that woman in her tracks. I'll talk to Stan today, so I know exactly what the renovation plan is. Then, we'll be able to print up some posters. I was thinking of an old photo of BB Gun with a rifle photo-shopped over his guitar saying, *Save my House*. Whaddya think?"

Cackles of laughter met this suggestion, and the three old friends spent another happy hour together while they plotted the spells which were about to be cast on unsuspecting Georgie.

A BLISSFULLY IGNORANT Georgie was observing progress at the house. She noted with satisfaction that Stan had already pulled down the sagging garage. She stopped to talk and learned that he had spent Thursday at Town Hall. He assured her the planning department was satisfied and the requisite permits were issued.

"They're all taken care of at Town Hall," he said. "We started work here this morning and that garage came down in about twenty minutes. I swear I heard it sigh with relief as it hit the ground. I don't know what was holding it up. I hope the rest of the house is made of stronger stuff or we might have a few surprises on our hands."

Georgie smiled and took her leave. She had no expectation of Stan finding 'stronger stuff' in his future work.

GEORGIE'S MEETING WITH Laurie lasted over an hour. Laurie was an empathetic and skilled architect who had led Georgie through a process describing in detail how she wanted to live in her home when she designed the basic house. This meeting was to sort out finishes and talk about design choices.

"Let's start in the morning. What do you want to see when you first wake up?" Laurie asked.

Angus! Georgie took a deep breath. "Angus needs a dark room to get a restful sleep, but I would love to be able to watch the dawn unfold. It's my favourite time of day. Now, I have to slink off to our small inadequate bathroom to peer out a tiny window covered in artistic sea glass. It's a frustrating way to start the day."

"You already mentioned that you wanted larger windows across the front of the house. I've designed two large windows in the dining room and living room. Then, there is a grand front door with sidelights and in the expanded master suite there are the same windows as in the dining/living room. The front of the house faces north so you won't see the sun rise but we can give you window shades or drapes with a remote so you can lie in bed and open the drapes. Would that be good?"

"And all those windows are the same size? And all are energy efficient? That sounds positively grand. I want all four of them to have the same remote shades or drapes." Georgie was sitting on the edge of her chair. "Let's do the bathroom.

"I want a large bathroom with a heated floor, a soaking tub, a walk-in shower, a double vanity with very large mirrors and lots of good lighting. Could I have a combination walk-in closet/laundry room between the bathroom and the bedroom? We don't need a huge closet, but it needs lots of drawers and shelves for my casual clothes and a space to hang Angus's suits."

"Yes, we've downsized the living room considerably to allow for the master suite expansion so there's lots of room for all that." Laurie was busily making notes.

"I'm having so much fun. Let's think about the kitchen." Georgie said a silent prayer of forgiveness as she trashed her old nemesis. "The kitchen needs to be completely gutted, but your plans keep it in the same location. It's on the Southwest corner of the house, but since Angus's father closed in the porch on the back it never gets any light. Your plan included lots of new windows so that's good, but I need a good pantry, lots of storage, and all new appliances. We can talk about those details later but make room for a double oven. That's essential.

"Between the kitchen and the dining room I want an island to seat six, I'm planning for grandchildren. You've planned for large patio doors on the west wall between the island and the dining room leading out to a new deck. The dining room will have room for a table which seats twelve. It's all fantastic."

Georgie shuddered with pleasure as she gave voice to her long-suppressed desires. A flood of warmth slowly spread throughout her whole body. Deep feelings of peace and contentment pulsed through her driving out the last of her anger and resentment. "Laurie, I'm so happy. I think I've just had a renovation orgasm!"

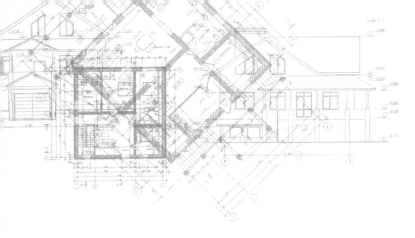

Twenty-Eight

CONSTRUCTION WAS NOT going well at the university. Angus stared at his hapless helper and demanded an explanation. "What do you mean you can't put up these shelves? They've held my books and journals for almost twenty years."

"Well, now Professor, you've put your finger right on the problem. Whoever built these shelves used ripped three-eighths' plywood and some pine boards. After all this time they're all so warped they won't go back together." Norm wiped his sweating brow and considered calling for back-up. He'd been trapped in this small office full of cardboard boxes and broken shelving for the last two hours. This prof was usually one of the quiet ones, but he looked ready to blow his cork.

They stood together in the small space they had cleared to put up the first shelving unit and stared at each other. Norm slowly picked up his tool kit and backed carefully toward the closed door.

"Don't you dare leave me with this mess," Angus shouted as Norm opened the office door.

"No, no, I'm not leaving you. I'm just going to call in and see if we can find you some better shelving. This stuff you have here is only good for firewood. I don't know why they let you use it in the first place. It's really not safe. It could have fallen on you anytime in the past twenty years."

"Stupid damn fellow," Angus muttered as he slowly sank down on a stack of packing boxes and surveyed the room. He was so tired. He seemed to have constant indigestion and he wasn't sleeping well. He looked around the room. Georgie had sent everything from his home office to this small space. His recliner was jammed in the corner under a mountain of boxes. He got up and climbed over the remains of his condemned shelving to uncover his comfortable chair.

SYLVIA WAS EATING her lunch at her desk when Georgie arrived at the Math Department. "Hello Sylvia. I'm looking for Angus. He's not in his office. Do you happen to know where he is?"

"Oh hello, Georgie. Yes, he's working with Norm from the maintenance department to get his storage room in order. I believe they were starting with putting up some shelving. I can show you where they are."

Georgie sat down with a small sigh. "Oh, please finish your lunch. I'm not in a hurry. I'm finally feeling very relaxed. Sylvia, I'm so sorry you have been dragged into this family drama. Angus is very unhappy with me at the moment. I admit I was angry with him when he moved into Helen's house, but I've had the most remarkable morning. I'm not mad at him any longer."

"Oh, I'm so glad," Sylvia said.

"How is he Sylvia? He's not used to looking after himself. I plan to talk to him today and tell him work on the renovation has already started. Hopefully, he'll give up trying to change my mind and he'll adjust."

Sylvia chewed thoughtfully for a moment and then decided to speak freely. "That would be a good thing. Frankly, Georgie, I'm quite worried about him. He's usually quiet but it's a studious quiet. He always seems to be thinking and working things out in his mind. He's really quite brilliant, you know. But this week he just seems lost. He didn't even want to answer Dr. Erlichman's invitation. He seems quite exhausted too. He said he isn't sleeping well."

"Oh Sylvia, we're both feeling lost. Everyone tells me I'm doing the right thing. There's no question the house needs to be renovated and I need a safe house to live in, but I also need Angus. Let's go find him."

Two worried women made their way to a small office in the basement of the library. There were no sounds of activity from the room. Sylvia gently pushed the door open to reveal stacks of boxes covering the floor, a pile of boards leaning upright against a wall, and a peacefully sleeping Angus stretched out almost full length on his office recliner.

EMILY WAS VISITING Ross in his office. "It's Friday, Hon. Let's do something crazy. Let's skip town for the weekend." Ross kissed Emily and pulled her on his knee. He pulled a lever, and his responsive office chair tipped them back into a very satisfying position.

Emily relaxed in his arms and returned his kiss. *Kissing this man always makes me want so much more,* she thought. She let herself fall into him absorbing his warmth and strength, then reluctantly sat up. "Sorry, Ross, I can't leave town. I have a job that gets busier on the weekends. Plus, I have a family gone to hell. Let me up before Aunt Helen bursts in here and destroys your office reputation."

"Oh, crap. Is she still on the loose? I thought someone would have locked her up by now."

"I wish that were an option, but she hasn't done anything illegal-yet. I think she's planning to cross that thin line next week. What a mess." Emily stood up and slumped into Ross's visitor's chair. "I wish I had some way to influence her. She won't listen to anything I say. She says Georgie has corrupted me and I've deserted the family. What an idiot!"

"Hmmm. I wonder if I could freeze her bank accounts and impose financial sanctions. There must me some way to put a stop to her plans for world domination." Ross said.

"OK. You.ve got a point. She's not as powerful as a foreign country, but my God, Ross, she's destroyed my peace."

"And for that I will not forgive her. I suggest an immediate text embargo, a communications blackout, and a closed office door policy."

"Tempting, but I can't close the border while I'm the only safe corridor between her and Dad. I'm also on a covert mission acting as a secret agent for Stepma. The only way I can protect Georgie is to keep up with what Aunt Helen and her wacky friends are planning. I hate this."

"It's a mystery alright. There must be more to this than opposition to a house renovation. It sounds much more personal. Why is she so opposed to Georgie? Is there any way to find out why they are such enemies?" Ross asked. "You mentioned before that this is a feud of long standing."

"That's an interesting idea. I've always wondered about them. I wouldn't call them enemies exactly. Georgie is always polite and has never tried to stop Aunt Helen from being in my life. However, Aunt Helen never says a good word about Georgie and Georgie is always warning me not to trust Aunt Helen. There are never open hostilities, but battle lines have been drawn. It's very uncomfortable, that's for sure. I wonder if Anne knows their story."

"Well, that's something for you to ferret out as you go on your clandestine rounds. I like the idea of dating a Mata Heri. Let's go buy you a trench coat and some high-tech spy equipment."

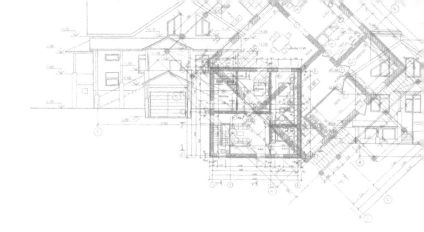

Twenty-Nine

G EORGIE OPENED HER eyes on another day. This morning was not filled with energy and purpose. Her body felt heavy and listless. Her disapproving and disappointed parents had plagued her with vivid dreams all night long. She realized their strong attack had filled her aching heart with guilt.

It was easy to see she had given them lots of ammunition to use in their assault rifles. Willfulness, selfishness, and most of the seven deadly sins were the bullets they fired. She had not only created a mess. She was a mess herself. What did they want her to do? Her saintly parents had offered condemnation but had provided no solutions. She had to ignore them. She had to stick with her plan. She was doing this for Angus as much as for herself. He needed to change. They needed to find each other again. He would forgive her. She was certain of it. Her father was always preaching about how it was never too late to be forgiven.

"So, OK," she told the bathroom mirror. "I confess. I want this renovation with all my heart. I want it even if it causes Angus pain and suffering. I want it and I know it's a good thing for all of us and for that poor, tired house. I am on the path of righteousness. So there!"

Anne knocked on the bathroom door and stuck her head in. "I heard you talking and just wanted to check to see what man you moved in last night," she teased. "We're off to the market. See you at dinner tonight."

What did a guilty but righteous person do on a weekend? Georgie found coffee and a muffin in the kitchen and called Emily. It was time to confess again.

Emily answered her phone on the first ring. Georgie launched into speech. "Emily, dear. I'm calling to confess. I still haven't talked to your father. Now it's the weekend. I don't know his plans, but I am not going to go to Helen's house to find him. I'll talk to him Monday, I promise. Can you look out for him until then?"

"Oh, I thought you went to see him at the university yesterday. What happened?"

"I found him in his new storage office where he had gone to set things up, but when Sylvia and I opened the door, he was sound asleep in his recliner. I didn't have the heart to wake him. I admit I was a bit of a coward. I didn't want to try to reason with him the minute he woke up. You know how long it takes him to become reasonable in the morning."

"Right. I get that, but it means he still hasn't faced the fact that the renovation is already started, and you're firm about getting the job done. In the meantime, Aunt Helen is telling him she knows how to stop you, and he believes her. I just don't know what to do."

"Emily, are you OK with my plan? I don't think I could carry on if I thought you'd changed your mind."

"Oh God, no, Stepma. I haven't changed my mind. I support you all the way. I tell both Aunt Helen and dad constantly that I agree with you. You keep going. Somehow, this will all work out. At least that's what Ross tells me."

"Ah, Ross. What a comfort he is. I'm glad you've found him a good place to set down roots. He's a keeper."

"You bet, Stepma. I have to go to a showing in a few minutes, but I'll keep an eye on the deadly duo for the weekend. I'll tell Dad he absolutely must talk to you on Monday. OK?"

Georgie closed her phone and considered her day. If she couldn't have resolution of her problems she would opt for diversion. There was nothing she could do about Angus until Monday.

HELEN WAS WAITING for Angus when he finally came downstairs. How could someone stay in bed until 11:00 on a Saturday morning?

"Good morning, Angus. I've made coffee and would like to talk to you this morning. You need to know what the plans are for Monday."

Angus looked startled to see her. *Doesn't he remember I live here?* She thought. He was a strange one that's for sure.

"Oh, good morning, Helen. Thanks for the offer but I'm on my way to meet Emily this morning. She's waiting for me now." He made his way to the front door and was gone before Helen could offer to go with him. She had every right to invite herself. After all, she was part of the family. Irritating man!

She decided to visit Stan and tell him he was backing the wrong horse, and all bets were off. That should be fun. She would have lots to report when she met with Irene and Judy after church tomorrow.

STAN WASN'T HOME but his wife curtly informed Helen he was at the MacLean house. Excellent! She drove up to the house and was startled to see the garage was gone. It had never looked right after BB took off the doors, but that didn't mean they had to tear it down.

She found Stan and a crew at the back of the house systematically dismantling Emily's apartment. "What in the hell are you doing, Stan? That's Emily's home you're tearing down."

"Hey, Helen. Have you come to lend a hand?" Stan grinned at her and winked at his crew.

"Don't get smart with me, Stan Keddy. You're in hot water and it's going to warm up a lot more on Monday. Just you wait!"

'Now, Helen. You just calm down and think about this situation. This house needs to be repaired and strengthened from the ground up. We're just getting the job done before the Town has to come up here and condemn it. There's no cause for you to be making trouble."

"Me? The trouble here has always been that woman who moved in here and wasn't satisfied with everything she had. I warned the family what would happen if she had her way. She's always been sneaky while she pretends to care about everybody."

"Well, I don't know about that, but she tells me old BB Gun and Miriam are on board with this renovation and so is Emily," Stan said.

"Angus isn't on board. The poor man is so upset I had to take him in until we can stop this mess and get him back in the home he loves."

"Listen, Helen, you know Angus as well as I do, and you know he wouldn't make a change until the house fell down around him. You leave old Angus alone. He'll figure out what's in his best interest-eventually."

"I'm warning you, Stan. There're more people than me who are going to protect this house and Angus too. Miss Holier-than-thou is not going to get her way this time and nether are you – you – home wrecker!" Helen yelled as a large section of the back wall of Emily's apartment fell to the ground.

Stan stared at her for a long moment. "Helen, I know you like to stir things up, but remember this. I might wreck a home, but I always have a plan to make it better. Butt the hell out of this."

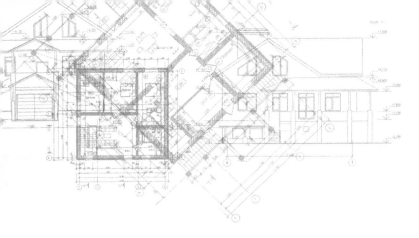

Thirty

A N ANCIENT SUNDAY school hymn rang out in Georgie's car as she drove back from a very satisfying day in the city.

"If at first you don't succeed, Try, try, try again. 'Tis a lesson you should heed, Try, try, try again."

This time retail therapy worked like a distraction charm. She had made the rounds of every retail outlet selling the latest in modern appliances and had compiled a list of essential features she hadn't even known existed. Many of those outlets also sold furniture and she had spent several hours imagining farmhouse tables, comfortable dining chairs, luxurious sofas and king size beds in her new home.

The Grand Pre exit brought her song to an end. The smell of roasting coffee from Just Us Coffee greeted her. No time to stop today. She glanced at the Grand Pre Motel and its charming old-fashioned restaurant as she drove back to

Wolfville and reality. Anxiety broke through her distraction barrier. Thank heavens it was dinner time. Anne and Terry would be home. Their steady friendship would soothe her fears.

She had time for one more fantasy before she had to face reality. Perhaps Emily had talked to Angus, and he had realized the folly of staying at Helen's. Perhaps he would be at Anne's house for dinner. Dream on!

She pulled into the Walker's driveway and wonder of wonders Ross's sporty little Honda was there. Perhaps some fantasies do come true. Perhaps Emily had convinced Angus to leave the witch's den and he was hers again.

She hurried into the house to find an atmosphere of gloom. Angus was not present among the solemn people in the living room. Terry was dispensing drinks. Emily and Ross were huddled together on the sofa while Anne was standing staring at a paper in her hand and looking unusually grim. She looked up as Georgie entered.

"Georgie! Oh, you're back. Well, I guess it can't be helped."

"What can't be helped? Georgie demanded. "What's going on?"

Emily stood up and gave her a hug. "Better sit down, Stepma. There have been some developments while you've been gone. Aunt Helen and her minions have been busy. She called me late this afternoon to ask me to help her post a few posters around town. I don't think she really expected me to help. She just couldn't wait to show me her diabolical work."

Georgie sat and Anne handed her the paper she had been studying. "I'm trying to think of something really clever to say," Anne said. "But words fail me."

Georgie stared at the poster with disbelief and dismay.

Had Angus known about this? Had he approved? She threw the poster down on the coffee table and turned to Emily. "Please tell me your father was not involved in this madness. I don't care about anything Helen does as long as Angus is not in league with her."

"Oh, God, no Stepma. He doesn't know about it yet. She told me he's always at his office or shut in his room and she hasn't had a moment to tell him. I think she'll try to get to him tomorrow morning. She thinks he's going to be so grateful. She sure doesn't know him very well. He's going to be furious."

"I hope that's true, Emily. I don't want any dinner, thank you, Anne. I need some quiet time." She gave Emily and Ross a hug and went to her room.

Ross took Emily by the hand and pulled her toward the door. "We'll shove off too. I think all of us could use some quiet time. Thanks for looking after Georgie. She's had a bit of a shock."

"Haven't we all?" Anne said as she and Terry went to the kitchen leaving the poster of the smiling local rock star BB Gun holding a rifle where his guitar should be and proclaiming in large red letters SAVE MY HOUSE.

"IT'S A GREAT poster," Irene said, as she carefully moved the pile out of harm's way. The server placed three Hot Turkey Sandwiches on the table. The three friends had gathered for a post-church lunch at Joe's on Main Street. Joe's had been their favourite hang-out for years. Today, it was a strategic campaign venue. Many fellow church goers were also here. They could see the poster and be invited to get involved.

"Yeah, it turned out great," Judy agreed. "We can use it to

advertise the march and other stuff as we get organized."

"We don't have a lot of time. I went to the house to talk to Stan and they're already tearing stuff down. That Stan was no help at all. I'm going to Town Hall on Monday morning to see what the mayor will do for us." Helen dipped a fry in a blot of gravy and pointed it at the poster. "It's great, isn't it? I can't wait to show it to Angus. He's going to be so grateful."

Irene snorted. "I haven't met a grateful man yet. Anyway, I can't put together a good protest march until Thursday or Friday. I need time to get the word out."

"As soon as you have a date let me know, Helen said. "I need to get the press and maybe the local radio station here. This will be the most newsworthy thing to hit Wolfville in years."

"Hell, if Irene does a good job, you might even get TV coverage," Judy laughed. "Wouldn't that rot Miss Goody-two-shoes's socks."

Helen moved the stack of posters closer to the edge of the table so any passing customer could see them easily. "Let's get these posted around town this afternoon. I wonder if we should put a few of them in Kentville. They have a museum and a lot of people who care about saving historic things. "

"Good idea, Helen. I can do that. I'll get our Historical Society president to talk to the Kentville people. I'm meeting her tomorrow," Judy said.

"It feels good to have a project again. I like working on something that makes the community come alive. It's been pretty dull around here for ages." Irene said as she finished the last of her sandwich.

Helen smiled at her friends. Community minded people like these two were so precious. They were her people and together they worked to keep Wolfville true to its traditional values. They were so different from Georgie who went around town telling everyone how they had to change everything to make things better.

"Let's have dessert. We need our strength," Helen called over the server and ordered three apple pies with ice cream. It was their traditional Sunday lunch meal. You did not mess with tradition.

APRIL HAD PASSED and May was turning up the heat, but Georgie felt as if she were frozen in February. This morning, she left Anne's house before anyone was awake. She drove to the Blomidon Look-Off to see if she could gain some perspective on her life. She got out of the car and stood gazing over the wide Valley and shining water of the Minas Basin. It was profoundly beautiful. Suddenly, she felt an intense longing to go to church. *I guess my sins are catching up with me*, she thought. *It's bad enough that I've messed up my own life, but I've made poor Angus so upset and now I've dragged his parents into this mess I've made.* "I'm a horrible person," she wailed and burst into tears.

"There're a lot of us around. I wouldn't be too upset if I were you. You kind of get used to it after awhile. At least that's what I've discovered."

Georgie shrieked in alarm at the unexpected voice behind her. She turned to see a man leaning on a cane. He was dressed in impeccable Nova Scotian attire with well-worn boots, jeans, and buffalo plaid jacket. His Tilley hat was the only sign he may have seen the world outside this Valley.

"Oh, I didn't see you there," she said. "I'm just a little upset today. Forgive me for disturbing the peace of this place."

"Come sit down on this bench. Let's just rest for awhile. Sometimes a little quiet is the most restorative medicine, especially here. My name is Owen and although I'm horrible too, it's only my family who suffer for it."

Georgie gingerly sat on the edge of the bench and stared into the distance. "Hello, Owen. I'm Georgie and I've always thought I was a good person, but lately I've been horrible to the person I love the most. How does that happen?"

There was no reply. Owen seemed to have sunk into a semi-doze. Georgie watched him from the corner of her eye and after several minutes began to worry that he had fallen asleep or was having some kind of medical crisis. She looked around for help, but they were alone.

She looked at him again. He didn't look in distress. Perhaps he was just tired like she was. There was no sleep in Anne's guest bed last night. Here, the sun was warm, the air fresh. The bench was hard but very supportive—just like a pew. Sometimes she missed church. She began to relax.

Owen's voice startled her again. "I think we understand the people we love and want what's best for them. The problem arises when they cause unhappiness by their actions. Then, we become the despised agents of resistance. Horrible, but essential for the good of all. At least that's how I live with it."

Georgie didn't reply. Owen sighed heavily and rose to leave. "Love is a tricky thing. Sometimes I think the very best love is uncompromising. When times are tough, I often think of that old hymn.

Must Jesus bear the cross alone, And all the world go free?

"Wait! Owen. Don't go yet. You're the first person I've ever met who quotes old hymns. I do that all the time. I would love to talk to you again. Can we exchange phone numbers?"

"Why, certainly Georgie. We can never have too many horrible friends," Owen laughed as he dug his cell phone out of his jeans pocket.

OWEN VAUGHAN, HER new friend. Georgie smiled as she drove back to town. Finding friends had never been easy for her. Preparing the guest list for her wedding had been a sobering revelation that her only close friend was Anne. She knew lots of people and many knew and were grateful to her, but none knew her heart. Her 'friends' were people who needed help or like-minded workers for the cause. Perhaps Owen would be a real friend. He didn't seem to need her help, and he did understand her already. She would tell Anne the story of how two horrible people met on a lonely hill. Anne would be amused. Thoughts of Anne reminded her of last night's missed dinner. She was starving.

Thirty-One

ANNE AND TERRY were in the kitchen. Anne pointed an accusing finger at Georgie. "Where have you been? I was so worried. Don't disappear like that again."

"Oh sorry, Anne. I just didn't think. I'm not very good at that lately, am I? I'll leave a note next time."

Terry rose from his seat. "You two take it easy today. I'm off to my golf game. See you at dinner." He bent to kiss Anne a husbandly good-bye, patted Georgie on the shoulder and left.

Anne was still annoyed. "Breakfast this morning is congealed scrambled eggs, limp toast, and cold coffee. It's the standard breakfast for people who scare me to death. I thought you had gone to confront Helen."

"That is on the dessert menu, but first I need your unappetising, cold breakfast. I deserve it. There's no family Sunday Brunch today and it's all my fault!

"Yeah, but it had to be done. Where did you go?"

"I went to the Look-Off just to think about Helen and Angus and my whole messy life. I met the most remarkable person, Owen Vaughan. Do you know him by any chance?"

"The name sounds familiar, but then there are Vaughans everywhere in the Valley. I'll ask Terry later. Now, what are you going to do about Helen?"

"My new friend Owen was talking about the crosses we bear. Well, I've borne the Helen-cross long enough. I'm going to chop that cross up into little pieces."

"My God, Georgie. I don't think I know you anymore. Where is all this aggression coming from?"

"Aggression? You bet. I'm not just crossing the border. I'm taking the whole damn country."

"OK, that does it! I'm reporting you to Martyrs' Anonymous. Come to think of it, you'll probably have to give up your Doormat Association membership as well."

"Laugh all you like. I'm going on the offensive. First, I'm going to rescue Angus and then I'm annihilating Helen. Forever and ever. Amen."

"Way to go, girl! Now you're talking."

"Dish up that cold breakfast and start thinking," Georgie demanded. We need to neutralize Helen and rescue Angus."

A very productive hour later, a Rescue Plan was in place, Georgie was on the warpath, and Anne was highly amused. "Well, Georgie, I've never seen you like this, but I must say I love it. This is inspiring. I know, I'll send in a nomination for you to the Women on a Rampage Society's annual award."

"Yeah. Keep laughing, but I'm on a serious mission. I'm ready for step one of the Plan – a call for reinforcements."

SURF WAS ITS usual ocean of flowing activity with surges of

friendly folk enjoying the faint seaside atmosphere of fried fish. In the midst of this peaceful scene was an island of tension and silence.

No one had spoken since their food had been placed before them. Emily and Ross had finished eating and had ordered coffee. Angus had ignored his meal and sat fixing a vacant stare on the Avon River. Emily studied him for a moment and considered throwing a teenage temper tantrum. Then, she recalled how her father had usually left the room during her best efforts. She decided on an adult tactic and went on the attack.

"Dad! You're driving me crazy. You've been at Aunt Helen's for a week and that's long enough for everyone at the university and in town to start speculating. I'm really mad at you both. And what in the hell do you think Georgie is thinking about all this? You've left her on her own while you've shacked up with your dead wife's sister. It's a damn soap opera and it has to stop."

Angus put down his fork which he had been using to push his fish around his plate. He stared at Emily and then at Ross. The silence continued. Emily gave Ross an encouraging nudge and he rose to the challenge.

"It does seem to be giving the town something to talk about, sir. Perhaps if you and Georgie could get together this whole problem could be solved. I understand she's willing to move with you to a motel while the house is under repair."

Angus picked up his fork and stabbed an innocent piece of fish. He looked at what he had done then turned again to stare out the large window at the peaceful Avon River. Emily and Ross waited in vain for a response. Emily tried again. Perhaps shock treatment was the only option left.

"Well, Dad. I can tell you this. If you aren't out of Aunt Helen's house by the end of this week, I will give up on both of you. I can't stand this stupid destructive behaviour." Emily burst into tears and Ross put his arm around her.

Angus pushed his mutilated dinner away and stood up. "Thank you for dinner. Would you please drive me back to the university now? I have some work to do this evening."

"STUPID, STUPID, STUBBORN man!" Emily was still raging when she and Ross reached the condo. "I've loved him all my life and I know he can be difficult, but I never thought he would wreck everyone's happiness to get his own way."

"He's certainly a master of non-engagement. I was impressed with his self-control. But, hon, his fight's with Georgie not you. Let's let them go the next round by themselves. In the meantime, we can practice a little sparring on our own." Ross grabbed Emily and threw her over his shoulder. He made his way to the bedroom, dropped her gently on the bed, and sat down beside her.

"Have faith, sweetheart. This will all work out. Next week we'll own a church. That must be a good sign. Wait until you see my camping gear!"

BREAKFAST OVER, GEORGIE tidied Anne's beautiful kitchen and considered her day. The Rescue Plan was well underway. Reinforcements would soon be here. As for Helen and her wicked plans, she would be put in her place. Just you wait, Helen Carter. Just you wait!

Her thoughts turned to Angus again. Emily and Ross had taken Angus to dinner last night. He may have already changed his mind. She would see him this morning. Surely, he would be able to stop sulking and agree to move to Grand Pre with her. She wasn't giving in. Uncompromising love was still love, wasn't it? She was sure her horrible friend Owen would approve of her plan. Even if Angus didn't see reason, he'd be out of Helen's clutches by the end of the week.

Fortified for the day, she left to meet Stan and Earl and see the progress on the house. The street was full of trucks. A large excavator was parked where the garage used to be and there was another sitting menacingly near the front door. She said a little prayer of reassurance for the house and one for herself. She was doing the right thing. She was practicing love for this old house—uncompromising love.

She found Stan and Earl consulting at the back of the house. "Good morning. Problems?" she said.

"No problems yet. We just needed a little consult before we jack up the house," Earl said. "It appears not all the sills are the same size. That old BB Gun was a hell of a builder." Earl laughed and slapped his knees. "Don't look so upset, little lady. We'll put in a good foundation for you."

Georgie nodded and said, "I hope we can be kind to my father-in-law, Earl. He did the best he could with what he had. I know he's happy that some of the problems can be fixed now. Well, I'll leave you to your work." She turned to go and Stan walked away with her.

"Georgie. Got a minute? There's something I want to show you." He led her to his truck and pulled out one of Helen's posters. "Have you seen this? Helen and her gang have posted these all over town and even in Kentville. God knows what they're planning next."

"Yeah. I've seen one, but I haven't gone into town to see

where they put them up. I did take some action though. I've been assured that Helen will cease and desist soon. I expect by the end of this week."

"Well, that's good. I'm pretty sure the house will be raised, and the new foundation poured this week. I've ordered the roof trusses, shingles, windows and doors and the new siding. We'll be in full renovation mode by the beginning of next week. It's probably a good idea for you and Laurie to decide on some design details so we can order interior finishes and fixtures. Just take care of Helen and the rest will be OK."

Stan watched Georgie drive away and went to find Earl. "She doesn't seem worried about Helen and the posters. She told me Helen would soon 'cease and desist'. That sounds like lawyer talk to me. This whole situation could get complicated. Let's get this house jacked up quick!"

Thirty-Two

ANGUS SNEAKED OUT of Helen's house before she was up. He needed to get out of here. He needed to go home. He needed to talk to Georgie and stop her nonsense. He needed coffee. His stomach rumbled and reminded him he hadn't eaten since yesterday morning. He needed breakfast. He made his way to Joe's.

"Hi there, Prof MacLean. You here for the Early Bird Special again?" The server was an Acadia student, of course. By now all the town knew he wasn't eating breakfast at home. His stomach rumbled again.

"This morning I'll have the Axemen Special, thanks. Could I have my coffee now, please?"

"Sure thing, Prof. Hey, did you lose your briefcase? You usually have something to read while you eat."

Angus looked down by his chair. She was right. He didn't have his briefcase. He thought about going back to the house and decided against it. Helen would surely catch him.

"Oh, no. No, I just left it behind this morning. Too hungry to think, I guess."

"Hey that's a funny one coming from you. You're thinking all the time. Everyone knows that!"

Angus watched her return with the coffee pot and fill his too small mug. "Do you think you could pour me another mug of coffee? I'm rather desperate this morning."

"No problem. Your breakfast won't be long. I told them it was for you."

Angus practically inhaled his first mug of coffee then tackled the second with more finesse. He was just beginning to relax when his shoulder was gripped and squeezed in what the squeezer might have considered a friendly gesture, but the squeezee deeply resented. He stood up quickly to find his attacker was Greydon.

"Greydon! What are you doing here?"

"Looking for you, Angus. Rumour has it you're here every morning these days. Carol heard that you and Georgie have split and you're shacked up with you first wife's sister. Doesn't sound like you, Old Man. But there must be something going on." Greydon laughed heartily as he sat at the table and signaled the server.

Angus slumped down in his chair and picked up his coffee mug. "That's the story, eh? Em told me people at the university were talking. Most of it is not accurate."

"Most of it? What the hell would make you move in with another woman? Georgie looks after you like a baby. She deserves more respect than this."

Fortunately, the server returned with the Axemen's Breakfast and the coffee pot. Angus concentrated on staring fixedly at the unappetising food. He was suddenly very angry.

"Please inform Carol that Georgie and I have not split, and I have not moved in with another woman. I am just temporarily staying there while I'm waiting for Georgie to get over her mid-life crisis. I am treating Georgie with all the respect she deserves at the moment."

"Angus! What the hell? What's she done to make you talk like that? She's having a mid-life crisis? It's probably menopause. Has she seen a doctor? My God, Angus, You can't just leave her on her own. Menopause is a dangerous time. Every man knows that."

GEORGIE SANK GRATEFULLY into Laurie's visitor's chair. "I'm glad you were free to see me this morning, Laurie. Stan wants us to make some decisions on interior finishes so he can place orders and keep the renovation moving. I would like oak hardwood flooring throughout. Would that be good?"

"Certainly, Georgie," Laurie replied. "Flooring's a good place to start. So many design decisions flow from there. As we move forward, we also want to consider your lifestyle and creating a dwelling with universal access features allowing you and Angus to remain there as you age."

"Oh, absolutely, Laurie. I have friends who use wheelchairs, and we could never entertain them at the house. We could get them in if we put out a temporary ramp, but they couldn't stay too long or drink too much. Our only bathroom has a narrow door. It was always a pain."

"We'll take care of all that. Wide halls, wide doors, easy opening, and safe access to everything. OK?"

"Oh yes. Let's make it as barrier-free as possible. I'm very aware we're all temporarily able-bodied. I'm certainly feeling my age today," Georgie sighed.

Laurie turned to pick up a large sheet of paper on her drafting table. "I wanted to talk to you about the site, Georgie. I know the story of how in the 1960's your in-laws cleared the site and built that iconic house. I've always wondered how they acquired the lot in the first place. It borders on the Acadia Forest and the University guards their Wapane'kati Acadian Forest like it is sacred ground."

"Yeah, they do now, but in the mid-1800's things were a little more fluid. My mother-in-law is the great-grand-daughter of an Acadia University president. The story goes that he got a gift of a plot of land on the edge of the old Acadia farm that's now the Acadia Forest. My mother-in-law often worries about the kind of gift it was. She suspects it may have been self-gifted."

"I think some of that still goes on today–in some places," Laurie replied with a wink.

"Yeah, privilege still has its privileges, doesn't it? Anyway, when the destitute draft-dodger and the privileged presidential descendant got together, they cleared the land and built the house. Fortunately, they had the foresight to build it in the middle of the plot so there's a good buffer from the established neighbours to the east."

"Yes, the house is nicely situated on the plot with the Acadia woodland across the street. Perhaps you would like to reflect the forest setting in the design."

"Oh yes. I want the house to blend into the environment. It's always looked so incongruous and out of place. Ever since it was built, people have seen it as a bit of a joke. I want it to be taken seriously from now on."

"Very wise. You may need to judiciously cut a few trees to prevent some potential foundation problems. You should talk to Stan about that right away. I've marked my suggestions on this plot plan."

An hour later, Georgie left all happy renovation thoughts behind and drove to talk with Angus. A sad lament filled the car.

"There were ninety and nine who safely lay,
In the shelter of the fold,
But one was out on the hills away,
Far off from the gates of gold."

THE COVEN WAS meeting at Tim's again. "So, what did he say about the poster?" Judy asked as she stuffed a large bite of apple fritter in her mouth.

"He drives me crazy. He just looked at it and handed it back. Then he left the house. He only says about three words a day. I have to trap him on his way in and out." Helen took a vicious bite from her cream cheese laden bagel and chewed furiously.

Irene grinned at Helen and sipped her coffee. "Not working out like you planned, eh? Well, the man never did turn me on. I like a man who pays attention, you know?"

"I think the poster is great," Judy said. "Lots of people are asking me about it, but some of them think it's advertising for a concert. Irene, you'd better get your protest group organized or this could all go sideways."

"I've been thinking about this. You know, I originally thought we'd march in front of the house, but now I'm not sure that's a good idea. The house is kind of isolated at the top of the hill and Skyway Drive isn't all that busy. I think we'd make more impact if we tied up Main Street," Irene remarked with a twinkle in her eye.

"Oh, God, yes. I love it," Helen grinned. "You are one fine shit disturber."

"Right back at ya, darlin'. Another thing..."

"Hold on you two." Judy interrupted. "Don't forget I'm part of this team. I've got the Historical Society riled up. We've called a special meeting for this Thursday evening. If Miss Goody-two-shoes shows up, she'll get an ear full."

"The mayor's no help. He told me all the permits are in order and the Town is relieved that the house will be brought up to code." Helen drew her finger across her throat. "Just wait until he runs for mayor again, the worthless jerk."

Irene burst into laughter. "You never voted for him anyway. I don't think he'll miss you too much. Let's get down to business. Helen, do you think you can get Angus to talk at the protest? We need to show the crowd he's on our side."

"When's it going to be? I'll need some time. He's a slippery one."

"Judy and I are planning for Friday at 4pm. We'll gather at the Waterfront Park for speeches, march up Front Street, then down Main Street to Town Hall. I've got a student lined up to take anyone who wants to go up University to the top of the hill to look at the house."

"Yeah, that steep hill will turn a lot of people off. I don't want to hike that far myself," Judy said.

"Don't worry. Tying up Main Street for an hour will get our point across." Irene laughed.

"Did you get a permit for the parade?" Helen asked.

"Permit? Nah. It'll be over before the Town can call out the cops on us. We'll make more impact surprising everyone." Irene stood up and went to the counter to refill her coffee.

Judy and Helen stared silently at each other for a moment.

"I'll be surprised if she doesn't end up in jail one of these days," Judy muttered. She doesn't give a damn about anything."

"Well, we've known her for forty years. She's always been that way. People don't change. They just get older." Helen thoughtfully licked the cream cheese off her fingers and considered Angus. "Maybe that guy will never smarten up, but I'm gonna shake him up and see what falls out of that brain of his."

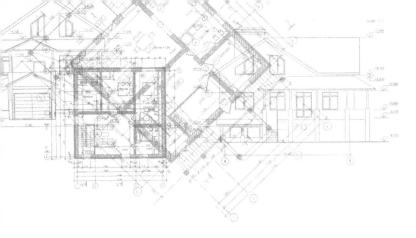

Thirty-Three

A NGUS STARED AT his computer screen. As soon as he returned to his office, he had googled *menopause symptoms at age 50*. He was astounded to read, *"How long does menopause last in a 50-year-old woman? The menopausal transition most often begins between ages 45 and 55. It usually lasts about seven years but can be as long as 14 years."*

Seven to fourteen years? He shut down the computer and leaned back in his chair to consider this new information. It was hard to concentrate. He was so tired. He stayed at the office as late as possible every night and left Helen's house as early as possible every morning. He managed to sneak in and out of her house without a confrontation most days but lately she was getting harder to dodge.

Seven to fourteen years? He wanted the old Georgie back now. He couldn't stand much more of this. Seven to fourteen years? He stared in silent resentment at the blank computer screen.

Georgie stood in the office doorway and watched him for a moment. He looked older and very tired. How could one change so much in one week?" A penny for your thoughts, Angus," she said as she entered and sat in his visitor's chair.

"Georgie!" Angus stood up abruptly and moved quickly to her side. "You've no idea how worried I am about you. Are you OK? I've been reading about menopause. You have to take care of yourself. Have you been to a doctor?"

This is more like it, Georgie thought as she felt a wave of affection for his concern. She leaned forward to give him a brief kiss on the cheek. "How are you, Angus? Everything OK?"

"Do you know menopause can last seven to fourteen years?"

"You're looking tired, Angus. Not sleeping well?"

"Seven to fourteen years! That's way too long for a midlife crisis."

Affection was rapidly giving way to agitation. "Oh, are you having a midlife crisis, Angus?"

"Georgie, it's you who've had a crisis and changed–not me. I still love my home."

Agitation became extreme. How dare he talk about loving his house and not her? "Too true, Angus, but I'm not having a midlife crisis. I'm having a midlife awakening. I'm paying attention to what I want for the first time in my life. Listen carefully, Angus. I want a safe, beautiful home for my family. I want grandchildren. I want a husband who is a wide-awake partner."

"I want to go home. I haven't been able to think about anything since you changed everything. I can't wait seven to fourteen years!"

"Well, you can't go home until the work is finished. It will be finished by September."

"Work? Don't you mean destruction? Helen tells me you've already torn down Dad's garage."

"Ah, yes, Helen. Have you seen that vicious poster she's put-up all-over town?"

"She showed it to me, but no one will pay any attention to it. Dad with a rifle? Ridiculous! Everyone knows he's a draft-dodging pacifist."

"Angus, Helen is planning trouble. You have to get out of there. Poor Emily is so embarrassed, and you should be too. Honestly! Your first wife's sister? It's the talk of the town."

"I tell you I can't wait for seven to fourteen years. I haven't even been able to think about the Erlichman problem since menopause hit you. Have you seen a doctor, Georgie? They've made lots of medical advances and by now they may have a treatment that speeds up menopause and takes care of a midlife crisis. That would be good."

"No, Angus, I haven't seen a doctor, but perhaps you should. A little medication might help you cope with your own midlife crisis of not getting your own way."

"Georgie!"

"Angus! Get out of Helen's house. And wake up before it's too late."

"THIS IS A week from hell and it's only half over. Did you hear about Aunt Helen's latest move?" Emily tore out her messy ponytail and vigorously scratched her head. "They're all crazy. I can't figure anyone out."

"Yeah, it's gross. A protest march on Friday. I'm finding it hard to keep up," Carrie agreed.

The two friends were at the conference table in Walker Real Estate waiting for the boss to arrive. "Mum's never late for our Wednesday morning staff meeting. Something must be up."

"Please God, it's nothing to do with my family," Emily said.

"Hey, not everything's about you, you know. By the way, how is the curly-headed wonder boy?" Carrie asked as she fluffed up her own curly locks.

Emily was saved from answering by the pinging on her phone announcing a text message. "Wow, it's from my Nana. She's not a regular texter. Hope nothing's wrong."

Emily opened her phone, read the text and stared vacantly toward the conference room door.

"Hey, tell me! Are they OK? Emily!"

"Oh sorry, Carrie. Didn't mean to frighten you. I just don't know how many more surprises I can absorb. Nana and Poppa were planning a trip to California this summer, but Nana's just texted me, 'See you by Friday at the latest.' What's going on? Does Dad know about this? Does Georgie? God, I'm confused. I don't even know where they are."

"Somewhere on the road between here and Alabama, I guess. Your life gets more interesting every day. Wait 'til Mum hears about this!"

"Hears about what?" Anne asked from the open door. "Sorry, I'm late. Now, what's going on here?"

"Emily just got a text from her Nana who said, 'See you by Friday.' Isn't that weird?" Carrie said.

"Oh. Good. But it would be better if they got here before Friday. Still, you can't always get what you want—as the song goes."

"You knew they were coming home? So, Stepma must

know too. Does dad know? On my God, does Aunt Helen know?" Emily gathered her long hair in a high ponytail and used several rubber bands to hold it tightly in place. "Oh, shit, my head hurts! I'm going crazy just like the rest of my family."

"It's OK, Emily, Georgie knows and told me, but no one else. It's a good thing, really. They were outraged that Helen used one of your grandfather's old publicity photos and photo-shopped it. They wanted to come back and help calm things down."

"Oh, Anne, you don't know my Poppa. He's truly a BB Gun. He will be firing off in all directions and no one will escape without a wound or two. He hasn't a calm bone in his body."

"Hey, that's right. I used to wonder how your dad could be related to him. They're like, you know, completely Arctic opposites," Carrie said.

Anne burst into laughter and Emily allowed herself a small smile in the midst of her worry. "I think you mean 'polar opposites', Carrie. But you nailed it. BB Gun's a pistol, as they say in Alabama, and my dad's a real dud."

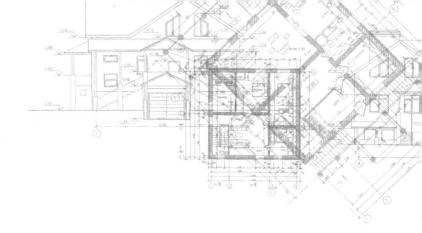

Thirty-Four

G EORGIE LEFT WOLFVILLE and drove to the Look-Off
to meet Owen. She was singing again. This time it
wasn't a hymn.

"I've been cheated, been mistreated, When will I be loved…"

She pulled into the parking area and slowly got out of the
car. Owen hadn't arrived yet. She was all alone. Perhaps she
would be alone forever. Monday's long-awaited conversation with Angus had not turned out as planned. She lost her
temper and never mentioned the Grand Pre motel. It was
already Wednesday, and she hadn't heard from him. Emily
said he was still at Helen's house.

She moved to the edge of the cliff and shouted into the
void. "Stupid, stubborn, self-centered, mindless man!"

"Sounds like a husband to me," a voice from behind
her remarked.

"Owen! I am so happy to see you. How are you? Is your

family still mad at you? Mine is."

"Oh, yes. Still mad. I'm still uncompromising. Still a stupid, stubborn, self-centered, mindless man, I guess."

"Oh dear. That was a bit much, wasn't it? I'm just angry about a 'conversation' with my husband. I wouldn't say there was a meeting of minds and certainly no meeting of hearts. Where has all the love gone?"

"Love's a tricky thing to figure out, and even harder to practice. You know the term 'tough love'? I never liked that concept, especially when applied to children, but right now I think my love for my family has turned from accepting to tough. It's hard on all of us but the love is still there."

"Would you like to talk about it? Don't they say talking to a stranger is sometimes easier than talking to loved ones?"

Owen looked thoughtful for a moment then took Georgie's hand. "Let's call ourselves Good Samaritans, who found each other by the side of the road, rather than strangers."

"Kindred spirits, too, I think," Georgie smiled and squeezed Owen's calloused hand. "Tell me your story."

"I'm a farmer. I've farmed on my family farm all my life, first as the youngest son and then as the owner of our farm in Port Williams that's been in our family for generations. I married a wonderful woman who also loved the farm, and we had two sturdy boys. I always hoped one of them would take over the farm, but both became city people. One now lives in Halifax and one in Calgary. They have good careers and families of their own and have no interest in the farm except for its immediate sale and division of the proceeds."

"Oh dear."

"Exactly. I'm sixty now and our family trouble began over

a year ago when my wife, Ruth, died. Since then, the boys are pressuring me to retire and sell the farm, preferably to a developer. I've told them I'm in good health except for a gammy knee and I have no intentions of retiring for at least another ten years. Farmers don't retire, you know. They just change their boots for slippers and then supervise." Owen laughed heartily. "At least that's what my father did."

"Owen, if your sons have moved away and you're a widower, how do you manage?"

"It's not getting easier, but I have a loyal group of farm hands who've been with me for years. In the summer we hire temporary foreign workers. It's not ideal, but then farming is never easy."

"You've told your sons you aren't selling or retiring for another ten years? Why ten years?"

"Well, see, Georgie, I have faith, and I made a promise. I have to wait and trust that love will win out in the end."

THE FIRST NIGHT of Church Camp was over. "I never knew air mattresses could be so invigorating," Emily grinned and stretched out to rumple Ross's already rumpled hair. "Bounce up, Ross, and nuke me some instant coffee. I love camping!"

"Yeah, they say you never forget your first night at camp." Ross kissed Emily's bare shoulder and rolled off the mattress. The floor was cold. They were in the church basement. It was finished in standard church basement style with cheap tile flooring, dropped ceiling and fake panelled walls. They had decided to set up their temporary camp here because it had a rudimentary kitchen, and the only bathroom.

"You were right again, honey. This basement doesn't smell musty or damp. It's only underground on two sides and this row of windows gives lots of light. Hey, there's a great view of my new parking lot."

"Also, a great view of a naked, very slow, coffee provider. Hustle! Laurie's coming this morning to give us some reno ideas. Then, I have a day full of crazies. I'm having lunch with Aunt Helen to try one more time to get her to back off. I'm also having dinner with dad. I can't decide whether to tell either of them that Nana and Poppa are on their way home. Oh yeah, and I have to fit some work in there somewhere. It's a good thing my boss is a family friend, or I'd be in worse trouble."

"It's your fascinating family, hon and your decision, but I wouldn't mention your grandparent's plans to those two. I think shock and awe are their due."

"Good point. Serves them right. After all, they shit in their own beds."

"Too true. By the way, did you see the house yesterday? It's all jacked up and there's a small excavator in the basement. Impressive."

"Nah, I don't go up there anymore. I'm afraid a neighbour will flag me down. I'll wait until Stepma is finished and Dad has regained his senses. I'm off to the bathroom. You know, this basement is OK." She looked carefully around. "It kind of reminds me of home."

LAURIE ARRIVED MID-MORNING for her consultation. By lunch time Emily left the safety of Hantsport and drove fretfully into the war zone. Wolfville - heavily mined, but nuclear free. She stopped into the office and told Anne her plans. "I feel I have to watch my every step, or I might blow something up. Poppa and Nana may arrive any minute, but I don't want to warn dad or Aunt Helen. Do you think I should?"

"Well, it's your decision, Emily, but they haven't contacted Angus, have they?"

"I don't think so. Dad couldn't keep that news to himself."

"So, I'm thinking they're counting on a surprise."

"Hey. You're right. I wouldn't want to ruin their plans. Thanks, Boss." Emily kissed Anne on the cheek and left for her lunch with her aunt.

She entered Paddy's Brewpub and spotted Aunt Helen immediately. Helen had decided they would lunch in public this time. She was in the window seat.

"Oh, hi Emily. It's busy in here today. Let's order right away. Their County Cork Club is excellent."

Emily sat down and studied her aunt. She was looking tired and somewhat anxious. That was unusual. "Everything OK, Auntie? You're looking a bit stressed."

"You would be too if you had as much on your mind as I do. If you'd been around more, you would know your father is being very difficult. I'm not sure what to do with him."

"What are you talking about? He's hardly ever at your house. How is he being difficult, for God's sake? What do you want to do with him? He shouldn't even be there. I've told you that before."

Helen took a tissue out of her purse and dabbed her eyes. "That's just mean, Emily. I took him in when he had nowhere to go. I've put up with his shifty ways for almost two weeks. All I want him to do is come to the rally on Friday and say a few words in support of the people who are trying to help him."

"My God, Aunt Helen. Are you still planning on that

ridiculous protest? I've told you I want this renovation and so do my grandparents. You and Dad are the only ones who seem to have your tails in a knot. I don't understand why you even care."

"Well, I want Angus to be happy even if your stepmother doesn't. Is that so hard to understand? After all, he was my brother-in-law and you both were part of my family before that woman wrecked your lives."

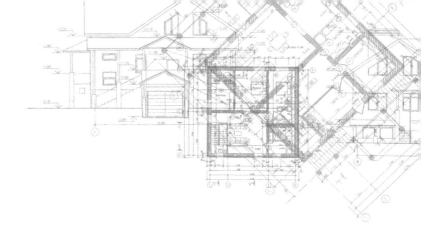

Thirty-Five

L IFE WASN'T GETTING any easier, but Georgie was still sticking to her plan. Early Friday morning she received a text announcing the arrival of the Rescue Squad. She sped to Tideways and joyfully embraced her in-laws.

"Oh, I'm so thankful you're here. You must be tired after all that driving."

"Not a bit," Miriam declared. "Our little van has a bed in the back. We drive until we get tired then find a Walmart parking lot. We can rest there until we feel like driving again. BB marked every Walmart on our North America roadmap before we left. Clever man."

William Robert, aka BillyBob, and BB Gun, smiled broadly at Miriam, winked at Georgie and said, "You bet, sweetums."

Miriam rose promptly to the bait. "Just you stop that silly talk, BB. Can't you see our Georgie is upset? How are you dear, and where is that son of ours?"

"Oh Miriam, I'm so worried about him, and I'm so grateful you're here, He won't listen to Emily or me. He's still in Helen's house. It's been almost two weeks."

"Well, I'm surprised, Miriam said. "I didn't care much for Helen, and he never seemed to either. That family was never very trustworthy. She tried to hang around right after Julie died, but we soon put a stop to that. Then she got mixed up with that Gaspereau man and we didn't see much of her for years. What is he thinking?"

"Never could see past the nose on his face. Been the same all his life," BB pronounced. "Doesn't think at all 'cept how to get what he wants. I hate to say it, but that boy is plumb spoiled rotten."

"It breaks my heart what he's doing to you and Emily, Miriam said. "We'll go get him this afternoon and bring him back here with us. If BB can't talk some sense into him, then I'll have to turn him over my knee. I should have done it years ago."

Miriam's comment brought a smile to Georgie's tense face and earned a knee slapping laugh from BB. Georgie filled them in on the house plans, the afternoon's planned protest rally, and her last fruitless conversation with Angus.

BB was left to unload the van while Georgie took Miriam to Hantsport to stock up on essentials for the weekend. Miriam explained, "I'll go to Wolfville on Monday to do a more complete shop, but I don't want to show my face there until we're ready to pick up Angus. "

Shopping completed, Georgie showed Miriam the Hantsport church Emily's new beau had bought and allowed herself to share her dreams about Emily and Ross and future grandchildren.

Miriam smiled sadly at the thought of her dear grand-daughter starting her family. "Oh, I hope she has a girl first," she said. "Boys are so hard to understand, and they know how to break a mother's heart."

Georgie stayed to have a cup of tea and a sandwich with her in-laws then went to hide at Anne's. She decided she would stay there until all surprises and protests were over.

She suddenly remembered one of her father's proverbs.

A wise son brings joy to his father, but a foolish son brings grief to his mother.

Poor foolish Angus. He had hurt both his mother and father. How many more people would he hurt before this was over? Still, the original hurt was hers. She had caused all this misery. Selfish. Selfish. Selfish.

ANGUS HAD NOT escaped this morning. Helen was waiting for him as he came down the stairs with his shoes and his briefcase in his hands.

"Angus, I want an answer right now. You need to be at Waterfront Park at 4pm today. Can we count on you or not?"

"Helen, I can't think in the morning. Come by the office at noon today and we can talk then." He put on his shoes, picked up his briefcase, gently moved Helen out of his way and left.

"You better step-up Angus or I'll kick your sorry ass out of here," a frustrated Helen shouted at his departing back.

Angus headed up town to Joe's but suddenly turned back. He didn't want to talk to perky servers or intrusive profes-sors. He decided to forego breakfast. He was having dinner with Em tonight that would be enough food to keep him going. He was too tired and too miserable to eat anyway.

He turned back toward the university and walked slowly down Main Street. Several passing students nodded and smiled at him. He didn't notice. Nearing his office, he realized that his head was filled with anxiety and foreboding. How could a man survive seven to fourteen years of menopause? He needed peace to work. This was no way to accomplish significant research. He needed calm to think, He could not wait seven to fourteen years, and neither could Erlichman. Someone else would solve that problem if he didn't get his mind back to his real work. Mathematics had saved him when Julie died in childbirth. Mathematics had preserved his sanity all these years. There was nothing more important than his academic research. He was sure of that.

'Sylvia met him at his office door. "Good morning, professor. I had a phone message from Dr. Erlichman this morning. He would like your opinion on an email he sent you last week. Have you checked your email lately? I know things have been a bit unsettled for you."

"Oh, yes. Thanks, Sylvia. I'll check it right away. Is there any coffee around by any chance? I missed breakfast this morning."

"Oh, my goodness. You need your breakfast. I'll find you something." Sylvia hurried away. A grateful Angus sank into his office chair, stared vacantly at his blank computer screen, and waited for his breakfast to appear.

Sylvia returned quickly with a large mug of coffee and a plate with a doughnut and an orange. "It's all I could find, but at least it's something," she said. "You need to look after yourself. Did you check that email?"

"Thank you, Sylvia. I appreciate your kindness. By the way, you're a woman. You must have experienced menopause.

How long did it last for you?"

"Well, that's shocking question coming from you. I didn't think you even knew about menopause," Sylvia said.

"I'm just starting to learn. It's not a good thing, you know."

"Yes, I know. You get your mind back on your work and look at that email. We don't want those Toronto people to think we don't have the internet down here."

HELEN'S MORNING WAS not improving. Irene and Judy were late for their meeting at Tim's. She was on her second double-double and practically choking on impatience when they finally arrived.

"What the hell kept you two?" she asked.

"Well, Miss Snippety-boots, we were busy. We've posted notice of the rally at the park but haven't mentioned the march. That will be a last-minute surprise." Judy chuckled and slapped Irene on the back." And old Irene here has just signed up another speaker."

"Go get some coffee while I tell Helen the news." Irene looked smug as she described the line-up for speakers at the Rally. "Judy's heritage people will speak and this morning I got a radical tree-hugger on board. He's furious that Stan's crew has cut down three old trees on the property. He's as mad as hell about 'the destruction of the Acadian Forest.' He's going to be awesome!"

"Yeah, we're all set. So, what have you done, Helen? Is Angus going to show up?" Judy demanded as she delivered their coffee.

"I caught him this morning, but he wouldn't answer. He wants me to see him at his office at noon," Helen said with a heavy sigh.

"Well, you'd better get him. Just stay there and drag him over with you. He's such a wimp he won't put up a fight," Judy said.

"You don't know him, Judy. He acts like a wimp when he doesn't care about things, but he's stubborn as a mule when he wants something."

"Typical man stuff. They don't care about much except what they want," Irene took a long drink of coffee and looked off into the distance. "Did I ever tell you how I finally got rid of that worthless man of mine?"

"God Almighty, Irene. You've told us that story a hundred times. I could tell it better than you by now," Judy said.

"I got the local reporter from the paper to cover the rally, but the radio wasn't interested. They'll be sorry when they hear about the march down Main Street," Helen said.

Irene nodded. "We can get people to call in to the station's morning program tomorrow and complain. That's always an attention-getter. Has anyone gone by the house recently? We should have some pics to show people just what's going on up there."

"Of course, I've gone by, Irene. I go up every day and take lots of pictures. It annoys the hell out of Stan. I tell him I'm documenting everything for the court case." Helen's cackle made several heads turn in their direction. She gave them the evil eye until they turned away.

"Bet that's making old Stan sweat. You go girl!" Judy finished her coffee and got up to go. "Gotta run. I'm picking up a bunch of placards. Helen, you drag that worthless Angus with you or else. See ya later."

"I don't feel good about this," Helen said. "I haven't been able to make him do anything in the past two weeks. He's a very strange man."

"They're all strange. Helen. Just cry a little if you have to. Sometimes that works if you don't use it too often."

"Well thanks for the voice of experience, Irene. I haven't cried over a man for a long time, and I don't intend to start now. I'll think of something."

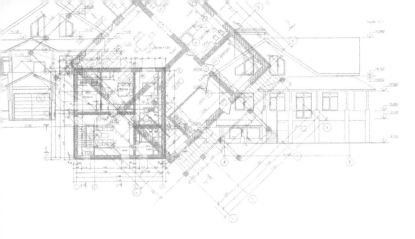

Thirty-Six

GEORGIE DECIDED TO talk to Stan before she went to back to Anne's. He would probably be worried about Helen's pals and the rally this afternoon. She would let him know the Rescue Squad had arrived.

The lot looked different. She stood on the street searching for the change. She suddenly realized that two huge maples that extended over the roofline in the back were gone. On the west there was only a stump where a huge pine had once crowded the entire side of the house. Stan had moved quickly on Laurie's recommendation and now the house looked naked and exposed.

Stan waved to her from the basement entrance. "Georgie, come see your new concrete basement." She walked slowly up the drive and joined Stan. "It looks more like a concrete floor," she said.

Stan smiled an indulgent smile at the ignorance of the general population to the details of the building trade. "Well, we started at the bottom, and we have the footings in now. We'll soon have the new sills in and then we'll lower the house and start on the second storey and roofline changes. We're moving along nicely."

"Yes, I see. I'm a little unnerved to see the big trees gone."

"Well, I never like to cut down an old tree, but those three were damaging the foundation and had to go. The new roofline and the new deck on the west side will make up for the loss. And you'll get a lot of light in those new windows you're putting in. It's all good."

"I know. I'm the one who insisted on change and now I'm crying over the milk I spilled. Don't mind me. Actually, Stan, I came by to let you know that Angus's parents have arrived and will be talking to him and to Helen today. You shouldn't have to worry about what Helen's up to anymore. I think they'll spike her guns."

"Well, that's great news. Helen keeps coming up here and taking pictures and making vague threats. She's always been a real shit-disturber. I expect old BB Gun can take care of her. He's a force to be reckoned with, that one."

Georgie drove slowly back to Anne's prepared to await developments from her bunker. She pounded the steering wheel with a strong marching beat and burst into song.

"Onward Christian soldiers..."

The song ended abruptly. What had she done? She had launched fateful events that had turned sleepy, complacent Wolfville into a war zone. This was all her fault. She couldn't hide behind the lines. She would have to go to the front. She stopped the car and took out her phone. She couldn't face this alone.

IT WAS HIGH noon when Helen stepped into Angus's office with her guns loaded and extra ammunition in her backpack. She didn't like this office. It was full of books and magazines with no pictures on the covers. There was only one small window, and the windowsill was always piled high with stacks of papers and files. He did have a visitor's chair, but you had to move junk off it before you could sit. The man lived in a paper lined cave.

She sat and fired the first shot. "Well, Angus. Here I am. Are you coming to the rally this afternoon? You'd better show up or else."

There was no return fire. Angus looked up from his computer screen and stared at Helen for a moment. "Helen? What are you doing here? I haven't time to talk now. I'm responding to an important email. It will certainly take all day and then I'm having dinner with Em." He paused and stared thoughtfully at an increasingly irate Helen. "I wonder if Em could meet earlier for dinner. I'm exceptionally hungry." Helen rose from her chair to take a close shot. She came around his desk to lean over his shoulder and put her phone in front of his face. "Just look at what that woman has done to your home. I was there this morning and they've cut down all the trees and are getting ready to tear off the roof. Angus, you have to come and help us put a stop to this before it's too late!"

Angus focused on the phone in total shock and disbelief. Helen put a sympathetic hand on his shoulder. "See, Angus. I was telling you the truth. You can't trust that woman. These aren't little cosmetic changes. She and Stan are destroying the only home you've ever known."

Angus took the phone from her hand and studied it

carefully. "This can't be my house. You must have doctored this with one of those photoshop things. Georgie wouldn't do this. It's just not possible."

Helen took back the phone and abandoned her handgun for a well-placed grenade. "Take a look at this, then, and get your head out of the sand."

She handed the phone back to Angus who reluctantly looked at the new photo. His face turned a very gratifying shade of deep red. Helen smiled in satisfaction and pulled the pin. "I took that pic of the two of them yesterday. They were standing in front of the house laughing at it. You can see them clearly."

The grenade detonated with noise and fury. "Son of a bitch! Who does he think he is? That's my home. That's my sick wife! Damn him to hell!"

A smiling Helen took back her phone and put it safely in her pocket. "I'll come by at 3:00 to take you to the rally."

IT WAS A workday and Emily was in the office, but not of the office as her Stepma would put it. She couldn't concentrate. She pushed the paperwork around on her desk and wondered again how she could manage to live through the day. "I can't decide if I want to die or kill someone," she announced.

Carrie laughed. "That's a very stark choice. Really, can't you think of something besides dying? What about giving birth?"

"Don't you start. How in God's name can you think of bringing a child into my crazy family? Georgie is tearing the place apart. Dad is in a massive sulk. Aunt Helen is stirring up the whole town and I'm stuck in the middle. If it weren't for Ross, I'd consider moving to Australia."

"Brave talk for someone who was living with her parents

until a few weeks ago. Relax. Your grandparents will fix everything. You need to get your mind back on your own business."

"Business. Yeah, you're right for a change. Say, have you noticed how all our new Wolfville listings are about twenty percent higher than usual? I can't find anything reasonable for my first-time buyers."

"You bet. This is the looming affordable housing crisis Mum was talking about last week. She said everyone sees it coming, but no one is doing anything about it."

"Typical. Fortunately, Hantsport didn't get the memo. I got the church at a really good price for Ross." Emily's worried frown was slowly replaced with a dreamy smile and a lusty sigh.

"Carrie laughed and went to the door. "Keep thinking those creative thoughts and get some work done. It's almost 1:30 and we're leaving for the rally at 3:30. We don't want to miss a minute of Armageddon."

"This better be 'the last battle' or I'll leave town. I can't stand much more of this." Emily moved a stack of paperwork closer and studied it. "I can't work, Carrie. I'm going to look at the church. Wanna come?"

The two friends left for the demilitarized zone and arrived in peaceful Hantsport to find the church parking lot full of trucks and a huge dumpster. "What the hell? I didn't think Ross was going to start renovation until next month." Emily parked the car and looked around for someone in charge.

A man came out of the basement door with an armload of debris and made his way to the dumpster. Emily called out, "Hey, what's going on? I'm Ross's real estate agent. Can we come in?"

"You can ask Ross. He's inside. I'll get him." The dusty worker walked away, and a few minutes later Ross swept Emily into a warm hug. "Hon, you can't come in the basement right now. We're tearing out just about everything, but we could go upstairs. I moved our camping gear up there and we could have a microwave cup of tea."

Carrie smiled broadly and made for the front entrance. "Too bad I missed the site of the first church camp. I heard a little about it though. It sounded very uplifting."

Ross grinned at Emily and gave her another squeeze. "So, you two talk a lot, eh?"

"Never mind, nosey. What's going on here? I thought you weren't starting until next month."

They entered the church to find the afternoon sun pouring through the stained-glass window. Carrie stopped short. "Oh wow. You told me about this, but I didn't realize how beautiful it is. This is spectacular."

"Take a pew, ladies and I'll make some tea. The guys can carry on without me. We're just stripping everything and then we'll rebuild a nice little basement apartment."

"That makes a lot of sense," Carrie said. "That way you'll have a good place to live when your friend Bruce wants his condo back."

"Exactly. I plan to make a good side-of-the-hill apartment down there. All mod-cons and tons of style a-la-Laurie. You know, it's all Emily's fault that I've started tearing things apart."

"Me? Oh my God. It's the family curse come to get you. What did I do?"

Ross winked at Carrie and sat down beside Emily. "Well, sweetheart, the first time we camped in the basement you said it reminded you a lot of home. That got me moving."

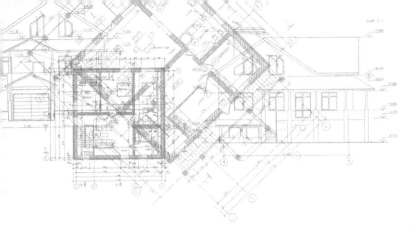

Thirty-Seven

I T WAS HARD to hide at Tideways. The van was very visible and soon the doorbell was ringing, and welcome hugs and treats were being dispensed. Questions were being asked. Explanations were demanded. Several visitors had photos on their phone of the poster of BB Gun.

Everyone had questions about Angus and the rally. Miriam offered cups of tea and accepted sympathy. BB, seemingly overcome with need to explain the inexplicable, began to talk slower and slower. His Southern drawl became more pronounced as he fell back on the speech patterns of his youth.

"Well, bless your heart, Dot. We don't know why they all went crazy, but we're here now and we'll sort it all out."

"Now, just hold your horses, there Keith. That boy of mine might be willful but he ain't sinful. There's nothing going on between him and that Helen."

"What in the Sam Hill are you talking about? I didn't make that stupid poster. Whoever did it will be sweatin' like a sinner in church when I get hold of them."

"Poor little Georgie is just trying fix up her home and the whole damn town has stuck their nose in her business. Well, I'm telling you, that dog won't hunt and we're gonna put a stop to this nonsense this afternoon."

Finally, the well-wishers and the avid seekers of grist for the rumour mill left and two sobered and worried seniors were alone.

"This is worse than I thought," Miriam said as she loaded the dishwasher and put away food. "What has that boy done?"

"We should have whipped his sorry ass when he was seventeen and got mixed up with that Carter girl."

"The good Lord didn't give him time to learn anything then. The next thing he knew she was gone, and he was right back depending on us. He's had his head in a book ever since," Miriam said.

"Yeah. I don't think he's thought of anything but himself since that girl died. He thinks everyone's job is to make his life easy. We didn't do right by him."

"Well BB, we have to make things right now, Let's go get him before he does something that makes things a whole lot worse."

A loud pounding on the door interrupted their plans. BB opened it to find Keith had come back.

"Now don't start asking questions again, Keith. We gotta get to town and pick up that boy of ours."

"I've got news. BB. We just got a call from Irene. You remember her? Anyway, she invited us to join a march down Main Street after the rally this afternoon. She's planning to tie up the whole damn town."

HELEN ARRIVED AT Waterfront Park to find her friends sitting on a bench enjoying an afternoon coffee break. "I thought I'd stop by before I pick up Angus to see if you need anything."

"Well, La-di-effing-da, look who's here at last. Me and Irene have been here all day."

"Leave her alone Judy. If she's going to pick up Angus, she's done her job. How'd you get him to change his mind?" Irene asked.

"I threw old Stan under the bus. I never saw Angus mad before, but he sure is fiery when he wakes up. He thinks something's going on between Stan and Georgie." Helen's loud laugh echoed through the park.

"OK, that's a good one, Miss Goody-two-shoes and Stan the man all alone in the woods at the top of the hill. She's probably there all day every day. She hasn't worked a day in her life since she got married." Judy said.

"That's true," Helen agreed. "She just flits around town 'doing good' and pretending she's looking after my family. Angus is finally seeing what's she's really like."

"With a little help from you, Helen," Irene pointed out with a smile. "See, we've set up a good sound system here so Angus can curse old Stan loud enough to be heard in Kentville."

"Yeah, everything's all set. Irene just made a few phone calls to tell friends about the march on the q t. There's a lot of interest. This should be a real good time." Judy chuckled.

"It's a great day for it too" Helen said as she looked around the sunny park. There was a broad deck with a wide railing allowing visitors to gaze over the famous nuclear free Wolfville Harbour.

"Yeah, if you don't mind looking at bunch of mud. The damn tide is out again," Judy complained.

"Just look off at a distance and think of those New England sailors who found this spot in the 1700's. They didn't mind the mud," Irene said.

Helen walked to the edge of the deck and looked out to sea. So, OK, it was really out to the Minas Basin, but you could see the dykes and imagine the water that stretched from this muddy shore all the way to the United States. Foreign wars had been fought over this land. When England routed the French, they cleared the land of the Acadians and opened the door to settlement by New England Planters. Helen knew all that from school, but she was surprised by some of the information on the large public information sign. "Hey, it says here that Wolfville Harbour was once known as the smallest registered port in the world. Crazy!"

She turned to gaze over the park again and imagined it filled with irate protesters. "I'm off to fetch Angus. People should be arriving any time now. I wonder if Stan will show up. That would be fun."

ANGUS FELT LIKE crying. He angrily reminded himself that grown men didn't cry like eighteen-year-old boys when terrible things happened. When Julie died leaving Emily and him alone, he had cried for days. His parents had insisted that he stay at Acadia and finish his degree. They were so wise. For years mathematics had focused his mind and given him peace. Mathematics had saved him.

Mathematics was failing him now. The cool abstract logic of the Erlichman problem was replaced with turmoil and fury. "What kind of a man would take advantage of a menopausal woman?" he shouted at his abandoned computer screen.

Shouting didn't help. His fists clenched and unclenched. He suddenly had a vision of them clenching around Stan's predatory neck. He sprang from his chair and left the office remembering one of his father's songs. Yes, he was *hell-bent on destruction* and the sooner the better. He marched smartly up University Avenue toward home and a confrontation with Stan.

Unfortunately, it was a steep climb, and he wasn't twenty anymore. His pace slowed, but he didn't need a lift for God's sake. A car was following him, and someone was shouting at him to get in the car. He ignored them.

The car surged ahead and pulled to the curb. The passenger door opened to reveal his mother who pointed an accusing finger at him as she shouted again, Angus! Get in this car now!"

Anger and frustration melted away to be replaced by sweet relief. His parents had come home. They would talk to Georgie. All would be well. He moved to the car and embraced his mother giving her a noisy kiss on her cheek. "Mum! Dad! You came home." He slid the side door of the van open and got in with a welcoming smile. "I guess you heard Georgie isn't well. I don't know what to do. I'm so glad you're here."

"Well, son. You've made a right mess. Your mother has a few things to say to you, but we don't have much time. I have a meeting to go to in a few minutes. I'm taking you and your mother back to Tideways so you can have a good talk." BB pulled the van into a driveway and turned back down University Avenue.

"Wait, Dad. I was on my way to the house. I need to talk to Stan. He's been taking advantage of Georgie and I need to have it out with him."

"You need to talk to your mother, boy. And that's what you're gonna do. It's time you had a good listen to a few home truths."

Angus gave up and maintained an injured silence on the drive to Tideways. His parents were also silent. Miriam was holding a tissue to her eyes and occasionally sniffing. BB's knuckles were white as he gripped the steering wheel. He pulled into their designated parking spot at Tideways and turned to speak sharply to Angus.

"Boy, your mother better be happy when I get back or your ass is grass."

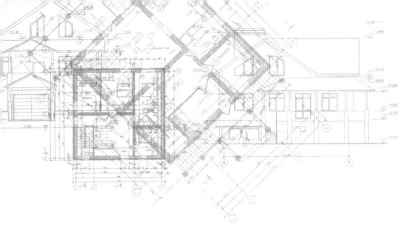

Thirty-Eight

E MILY AND CARRIE sped down the Avonport Hill on their way back to Wolfville and Friday afternoon's appointment with Armageddon. Carrie was channeling R.E.M.'s classic hit and singing at the top of her voice.

"It's the end of the world as we know it and I feel fine..."

"Thank God, you only know the chorus to that song," Emily snarled. "Give it a rest. This is my Stepma's confrontation with the forces of evil, led by a member of my family while my dad goes AWOL. I feel sick."

"Yeah. Sorry. It just felt like the right song for the moment. At least your grandparents aren't MIA. They got back in time."

"Oh, great. Thanks, for reminding me. Things could get worse. BB isn't the kind of guy to call a truce. He's more likely to call in his friends and launch a counter-offensive. Carrie, I think I'm going to upchuck again."

Emily lowered the driver's widow, pulled the car to the side of the highway and threw up. "I hate this stress. It's killing me. Open the dash. I keep wipes in there."

Carrie passed the wipes and stared thoughtfully at Emily. "Stress, eh? I guess stress might do it. You did say "again" didn't you?"

"OK. OK. Don't even go there. It never happens in the morning, it's always the afternoon or evening after I stress about the family all day. It's not that!"

"That can happen when you aren't expecting it. You've never been able to take the pill, have you?"

"No, but we're always careful and use condoms. It's not THAT!"

"You scoot over. I'll drive. You have to take care of yourself until I get to a pharmacy and buy you a pregnancy test. Move! I love this. Stress, eh?"

A gleeful, still smiling Carrie pulled into a parking space at the Shoppers Drug Mart and rushed inside. She returned clutching an oblong box in her hand and waved it at Emily. "Let's drive to the office and walk to the park from there. When the rally is over, we can go back and use this little gizmo. I'm so excited."

Emily nodded in agreement and tucked the box in the glove box. "I'll do it just to prove you wrong, you idiot. I told you I'm not sick in the morning. Let's go and get this rally torture over with. Not much wonder I'm vomiting."

THE PARK WAS not overwhelmed with protesters, but there were enough to surround the pavilion. A few protest signs were waving slowly back and forth. A young man with a bushy beard was addressing the crowd. He held a mike in his hand and sometimes spoke into it so that his voice echoed through the park, but more often he forgot, waved his arms, and lost his amplified voice.

Carrie laughed. "See, Em. Amateur hour. Nothing to stress about. Oh, there's Georgie. Let's go give her our support. The good news can wait until later."

"Shut up, Carrie. Hey, she has someone with her. Who's that?" Emily was sure she had never met the older man who was leaning on a cane. "I don't see Helen or Dad here. Maybe it won't be as bad as I thought."

They made their way to the fringe of the crowd where Georgie was standing with the stranger. She looked anxious but resolute. Emily gave her a hug. "I thought you weren't coming, but I'm glad you're here. I hate this whole mess."

"Me too, but I couldn't let you face this alone. Emily, let me introduce you to Owen Vaughan from Port Williams. We met at the Look-Off and he's become a good friend. Owen, this is Emily, my beautiful stepdaughter."

Emily and Owen shook hands and assessed each other. Carrie was busy assessing the crowd.

"Well, this little protest doesn't look too stressful," she said. "At least not enough to cause anyone to throw up. The speaker could use some public speaking coaching. He keeps waving the mike and losing his audience."

Owen smiled and remarked. "He's protesting the destruction of the Acadian Forest because Georgie allowed the cutting of three trees on her lot. He's passionate but completely ineffective. The crowd isn't engaged."

Emily grabbed Carrie's arm and held on tight. "Oh hell. Here comes Aunt Helen and she looks mad enough to start a war." What in God's name is she wearing?"

Carrie struck a pose and held an imaginary mike to her mouth, as she gave an impromptu runway commentary on Helen's Armageddon fashion.

"Our model is showcasing the latest in end-of-the-world ready-to-wear. Dressed appropriately in black, her out-of-date palazzo pants allow for plenty of violent movement and her vintage bell-sleeved cardigan emphasizes her dramatic gestures as she seizes the mike from the hands of the hopeless."

"Flowing black. Where's her witch's hat?" Georgie asked.

Any reply was drowned as Helen shouted into the mike. "I'm calling on you to defend the rights of us all to live in peace in our own homes. Not only have innocent lives been destroyed by this unwarranted renovation but an historic home is being threatened. This home is the pride of Wolfville. It's part of our unique heritage of providing shelter for others, no matter where they come from or what they did. Together we can save BB Gun's house and his family home from the forces of evil."

There were a few cheers and a lot of protest sign waving. Irene reached out and took the mike. "Thank you, Helen. We know the willful actions of one person have threatened your precious family. Professor Angus MacLean planned to be here today but is too upset to speak about this situation. Let's help him and preserve this historic house. The Town needs to take action. Let's march together down Front Street to Main Street and on to Town Hall. Our voices need to be heard!"

SEVERAL HOURS LATER, Carrie was still laughing as she reported to her parents. "And then the voice of God was heard and judgement like a mighty Southern wind blew down upon them. Too bad I don't read the Bible. I could make up a real good Armageddon story."

"You're doing OK now, but it's time for some facts. What happened?" Terry asked. "Anne and I didn't get there until it was all over and there was nothing to see but a young guy with a bushy beard cleaning up and wanting to talk about protecting our sacred environment. Where did everyone go?"

Carrie grinned an evil grin. 'Oh, they all ran away like frightened sheep and goats. It was so funny. BB arrived and just reached out and took the mike out of Irene's hand and the crowd went wild as they say."

"Ah, he got there in time, I'm so glad," Anne said. "Georgie will be so thankful to know that."

"Oh, Georgie was there. BB told the crowd that he was proud of Georgie and all the family was grateful for her timely action to repair and protect the family home."

"Oh, I'm so glad he did that. She's been feeling so guilty," Anne said.

"Yeah, he was so cute and so clever. He reminded everyone of his reputation as a scrounger and said he had built that house on a wing and a prayer and it was only through the good Lord's kindness that it was still standing today."

"Good point," Terry agreed.

"Then came the best part. Oh, I wish you could have been there! A van pulled up and two old guys got out and joined him. He said, 'I want to thank you kind folks for coming out today thinking you were supporting my family, but you've been hoodwinked. My family is one hundred percent behind this renovation. And so are these gents who used to sing with me in the old days. You-all remember BB Gun and the Pistols?'

"Oh my God, it was hilarious. You could feel the shift in the crowd. They were expecting something and they got it."

"His old band? How did he pull that off? Terry asked.

"I don't know but it was fantastic. You know what they did? They sang that old country tune, *This Ole House*. You know the one." Carrie sang a bit of the chorus which was, as usual, all she could remember.

"Ain't a-gonna need this house no longer, She's a-gettin' ready to meet the saints…"

"The whole park was swinging and singing along at the end. People were yelling and cheering and throwing their protest signs down to clap. It was kickass! Then he said, 'You-all go home now and leave my family in peace.' Helen came rushing up and he shook his finger at her and said into the mike, 'You too little lady. You've seriously misled all these kind folks.' Oh, it was sweet."

"I always knew he was a clever man but that was brilliant. I guess that's where Angus gets his smarts," Terry said.

"Speaking of Angus. Where was he during all this?" Anne asked.

"BB told us later that he was with Miriam at Tideways. Oh, I didn't tell you. Georgie was there with a new friend, Owen Vaughan from Port Williams. She's always picking up new 'friends' who need help. There must be a story there."

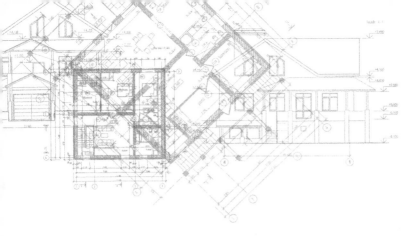

Thirty-Nine

E MILY WAS HIDING out. Her cell rang again. She had ignored the first call and the second, but this time glanced at the caller. It was her Nana. "Emily, dear, we need your help. Your father is going to stay here with us and we need you to pick up his things at Helen's and bring them here. Can you do that today?"

"Oh, sure, Nana. I'm at the office now just organizing a few things but I'll pick up his stuff. How is he?"

"He's just fine, dear. We've had a good talk."

"Oh, well, if he's been talking, that's progress. I'm glad he's staying with you. I'll get his gear."

"One more thing, dear. BB and I are holding a family meeting here Monday evening at 7:00. We need the weekend to settle in."

"I'll be there, Nana. I'll go get Dad's stuff and drop it off on my way to Hantsport to see Ross."

"Oh yes, do bring your young man with you on Monday.

Georgie tells me he's almost part of the family. Bye, dear."

Emily put down her phone and thought of Ross. He's a bigger part of the family than he knows, she thought. Her brain was whirling out-of-control. She ordered it to function. *Get organized and stop dreaming!* OK. First, Aunt Helen's, maybe she won't be home, then Tideways to drop off his stuff, maybe I won't have to talk to Dad, then Hantsport, maybe Ross will be happy. She grabbed a big tote bag and left for the witch's den. She smiled as she remembered Aunt Helen's rally costume. She truly did look witchy.

At Helen's front door she rang the bell then used her key to enter. Shit! The three of them were in the living room. They were drowning their sorrow-big time. Aunt Helen looked up from her beer. "Oh, it's only you. I was expecting your father, the cowardly creep. What do you want?"

"Dad asked me to pick up his stuff. He's staying at Tideways with Poppa and Nana. I'll just pack him up. No need for you to leave your friends."

"Helen deserves a real apology from that jerk, Judy said. "He was supposed to show up and support us at the rally today."

"Well, I'll get to work. Should only take me a few minutes." Emily went quickly upstairs and threw up in the bathroom. Family matters were getting more and more demanding.

Thirty minutes later she came back downstairs and deposited Angus's suitcase and a stuffed tote bag by the front door. "That's it," she called into the living room's beer laden atmosphere. "Thanks, Aunt Helen, I'll talk to you later." There was no reply.

Emily loaded the car and drove carefully to Tideways.

What was Ross doing now? He hadn't come to the rally, but then she had told him not to. Sometimes it was hard to know what you really wanted.

She parked and walked slowly to her grandparents' apartment. She left everything in the car. Dad could come out and carry his own damn things in. She was still annoyed at him, but she was going to be cool and in control.

She knocked on the door and her Nana opened it and her welcoming arms. Emily burst into tears and hugged her fiercely." Oh, Nana, I'm so happy to see you."

"Well, goodness, child. I'm glad to see you too. Come in. Come in and dry those tears. Your father is going to do better. Everything will be alright. Hush now."

"Angus rose from the couch and came to pat Emily on the back. "Your stuff is in the car, Dad. Can you get it? I'm on my way to Hantsport to meet with Ross."

Angus left without a word and Emily gratefully accepted a tissue and a glass of water. "Sorry, Nana. It's been a stressful day. Where's Poppa? He was on fire at the rally."

BB came out of the bedroom. "I'm right here, Dumplin'. I did good, didn't I? The boys helped, of course. It was like old times. I really worked that crowd."

"You sure did Poppa. I love you both so much." To her horror she burst into tears again. She quickly left to use the bathroom and vomit as quietly as possible. When she came out her three loved ones were standing in the living room looking anxious.

"Sorry about that," she said. All this stress is finally getting to me. Gotta run. See you Monday evening. Love you. Bye."

THE ABORTED RALLY was over and the end of the world was

postponed again. Owen and Georgie walked slowly down Front Street to retrieve their cars from the Chimney Swift parking lot. Georgie said a silent prayer of thanks for the power of music, and the witch-destroying charm of her clever father-in-law.

"Thanks for coming with me, Owen. I was really dreading what Helen and her friends were planning, and yet I couldn't stay away."

"No problem, Georgie. I rather enjoyed myself. It was a blast from the past to see BB Gun again. He hasn't lost his charisma. I don't think you have to worry about public protest movements anymore."

"Yeah, I think BB put all the rumours that the family was opposed to the renovation to rest. Helen may give up, but she's never been my biggest worry."

"Ah, yes. Your husband. He wasn't there today. That should give you some peace. At least he wasn't helping those women stir up the town."

"BB told me he picked Angus up and took him and his mother to Tideways to have a good talk. BB and Miriam have organized a family conference on Monday. I'm dreading it. Angus still might not talk to me. It feels like one crisis after another."

As they passed the rear entrance to Rosie's restaurant, Owen paused. "If you don't need to rush away, let's go in here and have a bite of supper. I'll share some of my family woes."

They settled into a comfortable booth and placed their orders. Owen looked thoughtful for a moment. "I don't know quite where to begin, but remember I told you I made a promise. Ruth made me promise I wouldn't sell right away. I consider it a sacred promise and my two sons consider it expendable. From their point of view my wife was dying and therefore nothing she said has any merit."

"Ah, you made a promise to your dying wife." Georgie nodded encouragingly.

"And a promise to her beloved nephew. When Ruth found out she had cancer, my son in Calgary decided to bring his family home for an extended visit in the summer. He invited my brother Jesse's son, Evan, to come with them. Evan had just turned eighteen and he and my wife fell in love. It's the only way to describe it. They just fell in love."

"Oh, dear. Was that a good thing?"

Owen smiled. "Sure was. It was wonderful to see that instant soul connection. Anyway, Evan also fell in love with the farm. Before he went home, he said he wanted to take over the farm. Ruth told him he had to finish university because farmers needed a good education these days."

"That's certainly true," Georgie agreed.

'Yes, well, that's the root of the problem. You see, Ruth made me promise not to sell the farm until Evan was ready to take it over. She didn't tell me I had to wait ten years. I decided that on my own. I want to give Evan enough time to figure out what he really wants. My boys are furious with me, but I'm going to stick to my guns. They don't need the money, but I need to give that boy a chance."

"Does Evan know all this?"

"No. No. Neither do my boys. It's none of their business why I'm waiting. I don't want to have them angry at Evan. It's bad enough they want to strangle me." Owen sighed deeply then dug into his pan-fried haddock.

"I can see that is a heavy cross to bear. Is Evan still determined to be a farmer?"

"Oh yes. He's here again to spend the summer with me. He's a fine young man. For Ruth's sake, I'm going to put my faith in him and hope it will all work out. If he changes his mind or something else happens then there's no harm done, except that my greedy boys have to wait for their pot of gold."

"Ah, money. It does cause a lot of problems."

"But it can fix some too, don't forget."

"I wish I could be sure that I've fixed things and not completely broken everything."

"Don't lose faith, Georgie. Sometimes we have to wait patiently while our loved ones work through what they've broken all on their own."

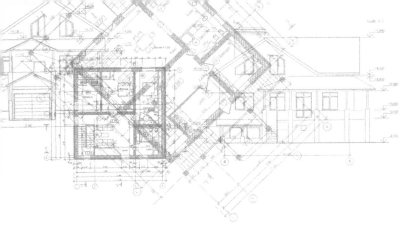

Forty

ALL WAS QUIET in the Hantsport church parking lot. Only Ross's Honda remained, parked far away from an overflowing dumpster. Emily sat in her car and stared at the building. It was a peaceful scene if you didn't count the evidence of destruction sitting by the basement door. Sometimes things just had to be torn apart before they could be put back together. The trick was to patch up the cracks and strengthen the walls while you were at it.

She got out of the car and entered the basement. Ross was sitting on a stack of insulation and talking on his phone. He looked relaxed and happy.

"Hey, thanks for the report, Carrie. Emily just arrived. Did you want to talk to her? No? OK. See ya."

He rose and enveloped Emily in a very welcoming hug. "That was Carrie. She called asking if you were here yet and then didn't want to talk to you. I'll never understand that girl."

Emily disengaged herself and looked seriously at Ross. "You said, 'thanks for the report.' What was she reporting?"

"The rally. The one you didn't want me to go to. Remember? Carrie said it was awesome."

"A once in a lifetime experience, I hope. Poppa saved the day. He was like an avenging angel. Aunt Helen went home and got drunk with her friends. I hope she has a wicked hangover and learned her lesson."

"Carrie said your dad has moved to Tideways. He's still not with Georgie, but at least he's left the witch's den. That's a good thing. Let's go upstairs and watch the sunset."

Emily looked around at all the construction debris. "Yes, let's go. I don't think this is a good place for me at the moment."

`Ross looked at her carefully. "You do look pale, hon. Is all this stress getting to you? You need some peace and comfort. A family can be hell on the nerves."

"You have no idea," Emily said as they went up the narrow staircase to the sanctuary. "I love this church but while you're working on the basement perhaps you could do something about these steep stairs. I don't think they're safe for a family home."

"You sit and relax, and I'll fire up the microwave for some tea." Ross pulled a Styrofoam cup from a package and poured water from a jug. A vague unease hit Emily's stomach.

"No tea, thanks. I think I remember reading somewhere that there are chemicals released into Styrofoam cups of tea. I need to be careful. I'll just have a cup of cold water."

"Sorry, princess. I didn't bring any china cups to the camp. Water it is."

Emily burst into tears. "There's no need to be snarky and

call me stupid names. You should be happy I'm taking care of myself."

Ross sat beside Emily and pulled her onto his lap. "Emily honey. I'm sorry. I was only teasing. Of course, I'm happy you're taking care of yourself. Let me take care of you too. What's wrong?"

Emily's reaction to these loving words was to cry harder. Ross patted her on the back and waited for the storm to pass. It took some time.

Suddenly, Emily scrambled out of his lap and moved quickly to run down the basement stairs. "Emily! Don't leave. Let's talk about whatever this is." Ross went after her to see her run for the bathroom instead of the exit door. He stood there for a moment and then heard the unmistakable sound of retching. He sat down abruptly on his stacked insulation. Putting one and one together and getting three, he suddenly laughed out loud. "Life! It just keeps on giving. Wait until Georgie hears about this. It better have curly hair."

ANGUS DID NOT appreciate the Tideways 'settling in'. Early Saturday morning he asked BB to drive him to the office so he could work. BB flatly refused and told him to mind his manners and help his mother. Miriam had a list.

"I'm so glad you're here to help, Angus. I don't like BB to climb the stepladder anymore."

Angus looked bewildered. "Stepladder? What would you need that for?"

"Why, to reach to the top of the cupboards and dust everything and take things out of the top shelves to clean that I can't reach. We keep the ladder in our storage unit. Here's the key, dear."

Angus made his way to the storage unit. Several people stopped him on the way there and back. Everyone wanted to talk. He didn't. Over the years he had trained people at the university to leave him to his thoughts. They knew he had better things on his mind than discussing the weather or listening to their stories. These Tideways people just kept on talking. It was exhausting.

By lunch time, Angus was certain his parents were determined to deaden his body as well as his brain. He was exhausted and his calves were complaining at being mis-treated as he went up and down the damnable stepladder. He began to plan for early release. "Dad, I put the stepladder back in the storage unit. I finished dusting the top of the cupboards and Mum and I cleaned all the light fixtures. I replaced some bulbs. I think that's enough cleaning for one day. Mum is pretty tired."

His father and mother exchanged a look. BB took up the challenge. "Well, it's good that you noticed that, son. We men have to look after our women. Miriam, why don't you have a little nap while Angus and I do that shopping you were worrying about? We'll go to one of those big grocery stores in New Minas. We'll leave now and give you some peace."

Angus got into the van trying not to look too much like a sulky teenager while his father drove to Kentville and talked non-stop. "We'll drop in to see the boys before we shop. They really came through for me yesterday. You can't find better friends than old friends. Remind me of some of your old friends. I don't think I've seen you hanging around with anyone for a few years now. There was that guy you played high school basketball with. You know the one I mean. He had enormous feet and kept falling over them. God bless me, he was a funny guy. Miriam loved him. Where is he now?"

"Angus felt a twinge of unease. His mother had also brought up his lack of contact with his old friends. "I don't know, Dad. He didn't go to university and I kind of lost touch. I think he works for the Town now. I see him around sometimes."

"It's not good to lose touch with old friends. In fact, I suspect you've lost touch with just about everybody, including your family. I'm worried about you, boy. You're fifty years old and you're making a real mess of your life."

"Well, thanks, Dad. I thought you and Mum were proud of me, but I see now that my intellectual accomplishments don't mean a damn thing to you."

"Sarcasm don't work on me, sonny. Sure, we're proud you've earned the admiration of the ten people in the world who understand what you do. You take care of them real good. But how are you taking care of the people who truly love you? You've abandoned Georgie because she wants something you don't. You've tied your daughter to a place she doesn't want to live because you don't want any change. You're a spoiled son of a bitch and that's the truth."

Angus did not immediately reply. He considered his father's words carefully. After a few moments he reached a conclusion. "You're wrong, Dad. There are only four or five scholars who truly understand and appreciate the elegance of my mathematical reasoning."

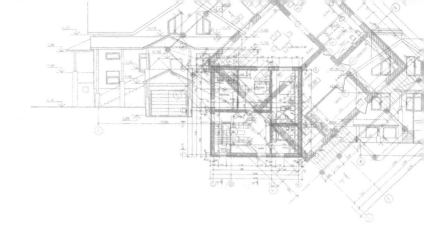

Forty-One

As soon as BB and Angus left, Miriam called Georgie. "It's worse than I thought, dear. Angus doesn't seem to have a sweet clue about his role in all of this."

"Oh Miriam. I'm so scared. I thought I was doing the right thing, and he would come to see I was right but..."

"Now, don't you blame yourself. It's our fault. BB and I let him go his own way after Julie died. He was so shocked and had no idea how to take care of baby Emily. He just stuck his head in a book, and we let him keep it there."

"And then, he married the world's dumbest do-gooder," Georgie said. "I thought all I had to do was look after him, and he would love me forever. Now he hates me."

"No. No. Don't think that. He's just never learned that learning isn't enough. BB and I never asked him to do anything but study. We thought it made him happy, but it just made him stupid." Miriam sniffed and had to stop talking for a moment. Georgie waited.

"We had a long talk yesterday. He doesn't blame you. He thinks you're sick. I hate to say it about my own son but he's dumb as a rock, and just as hardheaded. We need to talk about how to soften him up."

The conversation was a long one. When it was over, Georgie sought out Anne in the den. Anne was reading a novel.

"Hey, don't you know that sticking your nose in a book can lead to rampant stupidity."

"No worries. It's only women's lit. It has no effect on the intellect. You're talking about non-fiction, particularly mathematics."

"Yeah, you're right. I've just been an hour on the phone with Miriam. We're having a family meeting on Monday, and we were plotting how to crack the skull of a hardheaded idiot."

"I think Terry has a sledgehammer you could borrow."

"Thanks, but I'd better not take it. Miriam says BB is mad enough to use it. They've talked it over and decided to re-parent their son."

"Re-parent?"

"Yup. That's what she called it. They blame themselves for letting him avoid everyday life after Julie died. They've decided to keep him with them this summer and re-parent him. They're keeping him busy helping them, and not letting him escape to the university."

"Wow! That's a lot to take on at their age. He'll be as relentless as a two-year old. I predict temper-tantrums. Poor Miriam."

"She told me he doesn't blame me. He blames my menopause. We're going to use that idea as a virtual sledgehammer.

You know, Angus wasn't always so spaced-out. He was sweet-fully attentive early in our marriage when Emily was fight-ing me tooth and nail. Then, as Emily became less hostile, and I accepted I wasn't going to get the home I wanted, life became calm, and Angus checked out. And I let him."

"Oh yeah, I remember. I thought marriage had changed you both, but then you went back to being the Town Volunteer and Angus reverted to Absent Minded Professor. Maybe you can recapture the dependent, weepy Georgie that kept him awake for a few years. I remember hearing the sex was good then too." Anne laughed and picked up her book.

THE FAMILY WAS gathered at Tideways. There was tea and cake, but no one ate or drank. Emily and Ross sat side by side on the couch. Angus and BB had pulled kitchen chairs into the living room. Miriam and Georgie were perched on the edge of an ancient love seat in front of the window. BB cleared his throat.

"My folks raised me to do good in the world and to take special care of the ones we love. I never thought a son of mine would neglect his sick wife. I'm sorry, Georgie. We raised a piss-poor husband."

"Dad!" Angus turned his eyes from his father to stare at Georgie. Miriam stood up and put her untouched tea on the kitchen table. On her way back to the living room she paused by BB's chair and put her hand on his shoulder. "Angus, we both let you down, but we can't let you continue to neglect your sick wife."

Emily gasped and clutched Ross's sleeve. "Oh my God, Stepma. Is it cancer?"

Georgie sighed heavily and mopped her face with a tissue.

"No, it's not cancer. It's menopause. I knew I had it some time ago, but it's just getting worse and worse. I don't know when it's going to strike and... Oh, never mind. No one wants to hear people talk about their illness."

Ross patted Emily's knee and smiled at Georgie. "I know I'm new to this family, but I have a long-term interest. I want you to know that Emily and I will support you through this any way we can."

"Now, there's a real man," BB announced and smiled broadly at Ross. "Welcome to the family, boy."

Georgie gratefully drank a glass of ice water Miriam brought to her. "The hot flashes are the worst. I never know when they'll strike. I've had to cancel a lot of my volunteer activities."

"Oh, hey, Stepma. That's terrible. I know how much people depend on you."

"No worries." BB said. "Miriam and I have worked out a solution. We're here until September and we'll all help Georgie through her time of travail." BB beamed with self-satisfied goodwill.

"Goodness, BB. She's not in labour. But we will help out, dear. Just let us know your needs and we'll help where we can."

Everyone looked at Angus who had been quietly staring at Georgie. After a moment he felt the unwanted attention. "I knew it was menopause causing you to change. I'm sorry, but I can't help at the moment. I'm solving a problem for the University of Toronto and I have to work."

"BB reached out and cuffed Angus on the side of his head. Angus yelped. "Pay attention here, son. Your wife is feeling sick. You step up right now. The damn University of Toronto can help itself."

Miriam began to cry. "Oh BB, don't hit the poor boy. It's all our fault. We just didn't raise him right. Georgie, I'm so sorry you got tangled up in this messed-up family. I won't blame you if you leave."

Georgie rose to give Miriam a hug. "I can't leave. I love you all so much and it's my fault Angus is useless. I never let him help me. I always wanted to be in charge and do things myself. I'm a wicked person." She burst into tears.

Emily suddenly jumped up and ran to the bathroom. The sound of retching filled the small apartment.

"Jiminy Christmas!" BB bellowed.

"ONCE YOU START being wicked it seems to come naturally. It's a lot easier than trying to be good all the time." Georgie confessed to Anne. They were sitting in Anne's kitchen enjoying a sunny June day and a huge celebratory breakfast.

"Yeah, I get it. You lied about being sick so Angus would feel guilty and help you, but in the end, it wasn't that important, was it?"

"Now, there's an interesting theological question. Does intentional wickedness matter if nobody cares? You're right. No one gave me a thought after Emily threw up and Ross announced the news."

"Oh Georgie, your first grandchild! That must have waked Angus up."

"You bet. But trust Angus to do it his way. He's terrified that Emily will die like Julie did. He's moved into total protective mode." She suddenly laughed, "Emily–One, Professor Erlichman–Zero."

"What? He can't have given up mathematics."

"Yup. He's taking the summer off and intends to devote

himself to Emily. He's awake and aware like he was when we were first married. I never realized how much I missed the old caring Angus until he reappeared before my eyes."

"So, OK. He's awake and aware of Emily, but what about you and the house?"

"We're not there yet. Miriam thinks I have to play sick a little longer until he gets over the shock of Emily's pregnancy. She thinks she can convince him to take care of me too and then time will heal all wounds."

"So, you have to stay wicked a little longer? Sounds good to me."

"Deception, even in a good cause, is not my cup of tea, but I'll do it if it brings Angus back. Actually, to be entirely truthful, it's kind of fun to indulge in a little wickedness."

Wickedness is a tricky thing. Georgie thought. She had spent a lifetime avoiding it and never learned how enticing it could be. Now, she was looking forward to playing a new wicked version of herself as a weepy, dependent, and helpless victim of a fictitious disease. What would her father think of her now? The answer was clear.

The times of ignorance God overlooked, but now he commands all people everywhere to repent.

Forty-Two

MIRIAM WAS FRUSTRATED as only a mother can be. "I swear that son of mine will be the death of me. I talk and talk and talk to him and he just smiles and doesn't hear a word I say."

"Well, you won't let me cuff him, so I don't know what to do with him," BB said. "I'm getting a little tired of him myself. Thank the good Lord he goes up to town every day to have lunch with Emily."

"True, he's paying a lot of attention to Emily now, and that's good. We just need to get him and Georgie together again. She says the house will be finished by September. Time is passing. I'm calling her this morning and we're going to figure out phase two of our 'Helpless Georgie' plan."

"Well, if that don't beat all. Georgie? Helpless? How'd you come up with that cockamamie idea?"

"Angus thinks she's sick but he's still not helping her. We need to get them together. I woke up this morning with a great idea."

"I had a great idea too when I woke up, but you were already in the kitchen," BB leered at Miriam and gave her his best wicked grin.

"Miriam laughed. "Well, old-timer, if you can remember that great idea until tonight you might get lucky. Now, go find someone to talk to. I need to call Georgie."

Georgie arrived at Tideways within the hour. She and Miriam sat at the kitchen table and drew up a 'Help Georgie' schedule. There was an activity every day of the week.

"My land, Georgie. Have you been doing all this for years? I never knew."

"It's not so much, Miriam. I like to be busy and there's always something or someone needing a little help. Angus and I thought it best if I didn't work full-time when Emily was a teenager. By the time she settled down I was hooked on being a community volunteer."

"I think this should do the trick." Miriam said. I'll explain to Angus that you'll come by every morning to pick him up. You need help because you can't just abandon these people. He's a good man and he wants to heal the breach. He just doesn't know how."

"Oh, Miriam. I hope it works. I miss him so much. I don't want to lose him because I was so selfish." Georgie sobbed several tissues full of guilty tears.

"Goodness, child. Don't take on so. There's no reason you shouldn't have what you want and no reason for a grown man to cause such a fuss. It's time his mother put her foot down. You leave him to me."

THE CONDO WAS pregnant with multiple scenarios. Ross was

treading carefully. Emily was quietly folding and refolding the same newly laundered towel. He sat down beside her and held her hand.

"OK, I can see you're deep in thought. It looks like a very tough problem."

"Very true. I'm trying to work out how to get Aunt Helen and Georgie to end the hostilities before the baby arrives in December. And how to get Dad and Georgie back together, if I don't kill him first."

"Oh, is that all? I thought perhaps you were considering how to be a single parent. You still haven't agreed to marry me."

"Everything's a mess. I'm a mess and my family's worse. You don't want to get married to me."

"You know, honey, I do. Desperately. Not only do I want to marry you, but I want to be part of your crazy family. Just say yes, and together we'll turn this family mess into a baby paradise." He gathered Emily into a fierce hug and poured heart and soul into his kiss.

The kiss ended and all doubts ended with it. Emily realized she was crying with tears dripping off the end of her nose. She mopped her face with the handy towel and whispered, "Yes. We both say yes."

Ross was preparing to show his gratitude and had just pulled Emily to her feet when someone pounded on the door. "What the hell? He opened the door to reveal Carrie and Henri.

Carrie bounded in and swept Emily up in a twirl around the room. "I couldn't wait any longer. Henri didn't want to come but I made him. You said yes, didn't you? Of course, you did. Ross told me this afternoon he was going to get an answer tonight. I'm so happy."

Henri closed the door and shrugged apologetically at Ross. "*Vraiment*, I couldn't stop her. She's obsessed with making wedding plans. He put a large pizza box on the table and added a bottle of sparkling water. "No alcohol for the baby," he explained.

"I'm glad to see you," Ross said. "I'm starved and we need to tell Emily Carrie's plan to end all her troubles. All this stress isn't good for her or the baby."

Carrie drew Emily back to the table and sat beside her. "I can't eat a thing. Wait 'till you hear my plan to heal the feud. Ross thinks I'm brilliant."

Ross moved the fragrant pizza to the kitchen counter and brought plates and glasses to the table. "Just help yourself, Henri. Hon, do you want any?"

"I'll have some sparkling water, thanks. That was very thoughtful of you, Henri."

"For sure, I'm practicing. I'm going to be a very fine uncle."

The Condo filled with laughter and hope for the future as the four friends discussed the details of a family wedding designed to protect the unborn and bash the heads of stubborn people. All problems would be solved, and a Christmas miracle could be born into a family at peace.

THERE WAS NO peace at Tideways for Angus. Sunday mornings with Georgie were always peaceful and full of good hot food. Sunday mornings with his parents were full of demands and cold cereal. His father was talking again.

"Your mother wants you to go to church with her today. I'm playing golf."

"Church? I haven't been to church for years."

"No need to tell us that," BB said. "You're in need of a good sermon. Your mother comes from a long line of proper Baptists, and they know how to put the fear of God into you."

"Dad. I don't believe in God."

Miriam sniffed in disgust. "No need to point that out either. You'll come with me this morning and no more talk about it."

It was a very big church. It took at least twenty minutes to move to the pew where Miriam insisted on sitting near the front. Angus tried to look supportive as he gently pushed his mother along. It seemed everyone needed to ask her a question or offer sympathy for the recent family troubles.

He sank gratefully into the hard pew. "I don't think I need that sermon. Those friends of yours are scary enough."

"You be quiet and let me pray for your soul." Miriam bowed her head. Angus took the opportunity to look around. He was not surprised to see many Acadia professors and their families in this church. Acadia University was founded by Baptists and still had a Divinity School. He remembered coming here as a teenager. "*Didn't do me much good*" he thought. *I got Julie in trouble and it killed her.* The organ began to play, and he recognized an old hymn that Georgie often sang around the house. *Georgie. Where was she?*

The pastor and the choir entered and took their places. The congregation stood for the first hymn. He found himself singing with gusto. He liked singing. He liked music. He used to play with his dad years ago. His guitar still hung on the wall in the living room. Anger overtook him as he remembered he didn't have a living room anymore. Georgie had probably thrown his good guitar away.

His mother pulled at his arm. He sat down abruptly

realizing the hymn was over and he was standing alone. The pastor began to pray. It was a prayer for forgiveness for our sins. "Georgie should be here to hear this," he whispered to his mother. She rapped him on his knee with her hymn book. Hard. It hurt. It all hurt.

Was there a sermon? There must have been a sermon, but Angus missed it completely as he nursed his hurt and anger at Georgie for taking away his home. Suddenly, he was brought back to the present.

The choir had risen to sing the anthem. He had forgotten that many of the Acadia music students sang in the choir. The compelling voice of a classically trained soprano rose to the heavens. The choir joined her in a complex modern arrangement of an old hymn,

"Love lifted me. Love lifted me. When nothing else could help. Love lifted me."

Angus began to cry quietly. His mother patted him affectionately on his shoulder and handed him her handkerchief. When the service was over, they stayed in their seats while the church slowly emptied. The pastor came back down the aisle from bidding goodbye to his flock.

"Good morning, Miriam. Angus. You folks OK?"

Miriam smiled with satisfaction. "Just catching our breath. That was a truly uplifting service, Pastor Jim. Angus had forgotten how powerful the Holy Spirit can be. He just needs a moment to recover, then he's taking me to lunch."

Pastor Jim smiled and went on his way. Angus looked at his mother. "I love her, you know."

"Yes, I know. Let's go, dear. I need to tell you about your schedule this week."

Forty-Three

A NGUS WAS WAITING in the Tideways yard when his sick
and needy wife arrived on Monday morning. He got in
the car and studied her carefully. She looked beautiful. He
missed her.

She studied him in return. "Angus, you're looking tired.
Are you OK?"

"I had a sleepless night. I was thinking. Georgie, do you
know where my guitar is?"

"Your guitar? The one that hung on the wall in the living
room? The one you haven't touched in years?"

"I thought I might play it again. I used to love music."

"I think you gave up music when you got tenure. That's
when you told me that mathematics research was the most
important thing in your life."

"Hmmm. That sounds right. You didn't throw it away,
did you?"

Georgie's jaw clenched. She tightened her grip on the

steering wheel and controlled her urge to pound something—
or someone. She started the car and decided to change the
subject. *Let him stew. The insensitive moron.* "Did your mother
give you the schedule? We're going to do a wellness check
on Mrs. Rankin up on the Ridge. She's alone now that her
husband has died, and I check in with her every week. This
morning I'll introduce you and next Monday perhaps you
could do the visit yourself, if I don't feel up to it."

Angus nodded and fastened his seat belt. "I need to be
back in town by 11:30. I have lunch every day with Em. If
I don't take her out, she forgets to eat. It's not healthy for
the baby."

"You're eating lunch every day? Interesting. It's a good
thing you're a walker or you'd lose your boyish figure."
Georgie spent a few enjoyable minutes imagining a pot-
bellied Angus trying to bounce a curly-haired baby on his
nonexistent lap.

Mrs. Rankin lived in a little bungalow perched on the top
of the ridge that defined the north shoulder of the Gaspereau
Valley. The view from the road was spectacular. They paused
a moment to admire the view, then entered the small house
to find it stuffy and stuffed with furniture. She led them into
her tiny living room dominated by a large upright piano bur-
dened with an array of family photos.

Georgie made the introductions. Mrs. Rankin was astonished and gratified to have a real university professor visiting
her. "I never finished school, you know. I was so pretty my
parents lived in fear for me and arranged a marriage with a
friend of theirs when I was fourteen. He was a good, kind
man and we had a good life and twelve children. She turned
to the piano. This is my eldest, Becky. She lives out West now

and has five children herself. Now let's see. This is..."

Angus smiled and nodded and thought about babies while Mrs. Rankin introduced him to every photo on top of the piano. *Twelve pregnancies!* The mathematical chances of something going wrong were astronomical. He would need to speak about this to Em.

Georgie tapped him on the shoulder and moved to the front door. "See you next week, Mrs. Rankin. Angus will be back as well, and you can tell him about your grandchildren. He loves babies."

ANNE WAS LOSING her sense of humour. She had nurtured it carefully all these years knowing that it was the only thing that kept her from sinking into Anne Shirley's 'depths of despair'. Finding the humour in every situation had been her *modus operandi* since she had read Anne of Green Gables long ago. Today it wasn't working.

"Carrie! You're out of your mind. I won't help you with this. Friendships are at stake here. Leave me out of this."

"Mum! You have to help. You know everything. We just need a clue about why those two don't like each other. You must know. Emily is frantic to get this feud patched up before the baby's born. We have a great plan, all we need is some first-hand inside information. What's the scoop?"

"It's not my story to tell. If Emily wants to fix this, then she needs to talk to Georgie and Helen herself. I've spent years trying to stay out of it. I'm not getting in the middle now."

"Oh Mum. She's tried talking to them a hundred times. They won't talk. Helen just snipes and Georgie sighs. You have to help."

"Tell me this great plan of yours. I'm beginning to think

I'll have to do something or you two will blow up this whole damn family—nuclear-free zone or not."

"We're planning the wedding for Saturday, August 4th. We've reserved Churchill House for the rehearsal dinner on Thursday the 2nd. You know it. It's part of the Hantsport Memorial Community Centre and they're going to cater for us. It's a beautiful historic house standing in the middle of a park. Emily loves it."

"Yes, of course I know it. They do a fantastic Haunted House there every year on Halloween. Your event sounds almost as scary."

"We've got a plan. Sometime during the rehearsal dinner, Emily will start crying and demand that Helen and Georgie settle their differences for the sake of the baby. Ross will take them upstairs while BB and his boys play some loud music to cover up the upstairs conversation. Emily swears she'll keep them there until they break. We've given them a day between then and the wedding to let emotions settle. We've thought of everything except how to make them talk."

Anne looked thoughtful. "It might work. I don't think those two have been in a room together for any length of time since elementary school. But, Carrie, there's a lifetime of hurt and misunderstanding between them. This won't be easy."

"Aw, Mum. Give us a clue. We're all sick of worrying about Helen's next move. What happened to them?"

"I can't tell you that, but let me think about this for awhile. Getting those two together in a highly emotional situation with a pregnant Emily, whom they both love, just might work. Go away now, brat, and let me think. Tell Emily I'll help if I can."

Anne picked up her book and tried to read. The fictional problems of the main character were not as compelling as those of her real-life best friend. Poor Georgie. Would she and Helen finally talk to each other and gain some understanding of the effect they'd had on each other's lives? Perhaps.

What could she tell the kids that would help them end the feud? She certainly wasn't going to mention Santa Claus. No one but Georgie could tell that unique story. Perhaps she should warn Ross to find a closet door to hide behind. She suddenly smiled. It seemed her sense of humour wasn't entirely gone. Maybe she could find a way to nudge along a better future for world peace and grandchildren.

ROSS HAD AN appointment with Laurie. He'd made the appointment the moment he realized Emily was pregnant. He wanted to fast-track the renovation of the upper floor of his church.

Laurie was sympathetic and positive. "It's a big project but it's also a very worthwhile investment. The housing market is really tightening up and to find comparable square footage these days would cost you much more. That is, if you don't go overboard and buy a gold toilet."

"I'm a money man. I only buy gold bricks," Ross assured her with a laugh. "I 'd like to have this project done by December. Do you think that's realistic?"

"That gives you five months. It should work out if you get a contractor now and have your materials ordered as soon as possible. This means you need decisions on the basic plan and the interior finishes within the next month. I'll give you my suggestions for the floor plan today. Once you approve that we can discuss finishes."

"I've got a great local hardware store in Hantsport. They're helping me with the basement work. I bet they can suggest some local contractors. Let's make this happen."

He walked thoughtfully back to his office. A money man indeed. He was just getting started in this new job. Emily had offered to help but she had taken a leave of absence and worked on commission. *Time to apply for a couple more credit cards – perhaps four.*

It was almost quitting time when Georgie timidly knocked on his door. "Have you got a minute, Ross? I want to ask you something."

"Hi Georgie. Glad to see you. How's the Helpless Georgie plan working out from your point of view? Emily gets a report from her dad over every nutritious lunch."

"It's been two weeks now and I hardly have to do anything but drive. Angus seems to be rediscovering human need. I don't think he's thought about non-university people since he got tenure. He's amazed that people live in sub-standard conditions with inadequate assistance. Sometimes I despair of the mindlessness of privileged people."

"Yeah, I know what you mean. It usually takes a disaster to wake us up to the rest of the world."

"Well, yes. But I didn't come here to talk about Angus. I want to consult you about my money. Do I have any left?"

"Georgie! I send you reports every month. Don't you read them? Of course, you have money left. Stan tells me you'll need about two hundred thousand to finish the project. It's essentially a re-build not a simple renovation. The whole project should cost you a bit less than four hundred thou. In the meantime, the market is strong, and your fund is still earning money. You'll have lots left for another project."

"Good! That's why I'm here. I went to lunch with Angus and Emily yesterday. Emily was worrying about bringing a baby home to your basement apartment. She said you talked to Laurie and have plans for finishing the upstairs. I want to help. After all, I'm the one who tore down her apartment and made her homeless. Would a hundred thousand help get the church finished by December and ease her stress?"

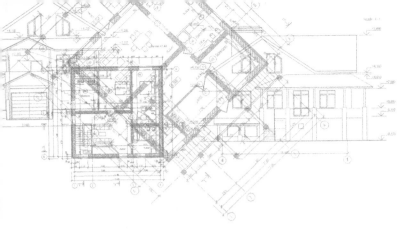

Forty-Four

SOMETIMES HUSBANDS WERE very useful. Anne put her chilly feet on Terry's warm calves and sighed with contentment. They were lying in bed enjoying the unusual comfort of a Sunday morning without an appointment or commitment. Anne sighed again and asked for the umpteenth time. "What should I tell them?"

"The same thing I've been telling you for a week. Say nothing!" Terry moved his legs and wondered again about the mystery of female biology and perpetual cold feet.

"I've thought of that myself, Terry. But if I don't give the kids a clue about how to start, I don't think their plan will work. Those two have been freezing each other out for years. They're experts at it now."

The cold feet were slowly creeping back to his side of the bed. Terry gave up. "I'll make some pancakes and a huge pot of coffee. You make some eggs, and we'll crack this problem over breakfast. You've been worrying about this long enough.

Oh, where's Georgie this morning?"

"No worries. She took Angus out to brunch. "That man is hilarious. He won't talk to her about anything important, but he whines about the inconvenience of living without her. Apparently, his mother doesn't do Angus approved meals." Anne laughed and hugged Terry. "Poor baby. He doesn't know how to cook like my clever husband."

'I like cooking gourmet food for you. Where did you hide the pancake mix?" Anne laughed again and wished with all her heart that Georgie would win back the love and care of an attentive husband.

She smiled appreciatively as she ate her scrambled eggs and 'gourmet' pancakes smothered in butter and real maple syrup. She raised her coffee cup to Terry. "Superior breakfast, Chef. My compliments. Now what do I tell them?"

Terry stuffed the last of his pancake in his mouth and chewed slowly and carefully. "I've chewed over this question," he said. "And I think you tell the kids you can't help them. Just tell them to demand that Helen and Georgie stop this shit before they ruin an innocent little kid's life like they're ruining Emily's. Guilt 'em. That's all you can do."

Anne considered his words carefully. He was right. It wasn't her fight. She would reveal no secrets. No confidences would be betrayed. Just an appeal to recognize the impact their behaviour was having on Emily. It might work. "Thanks, love. I might have to reword a bit of that advice but it's pretty good. I won't have to explain the past and I won't have to tell any secrets."

The Sunday peace was shattered by the ringing of the landline. Terry answered. It was a very short conversation. "That was Carrie," he reported. "They're coming over. I'm going for a walk. Have fun."

Carrie arrived with Henri in tow. Henri noted the pancake mix, searched the cupboard for cinnamon and took a package of frozen blueberries from the freezer. Anne sat at the counter sipping Terry's excellent coffee and watched her guests wolf down a stack of blueberry pancakes.

These two had been together now for two long years. Henri would graduate from Acadia with his Education Degree next May and planned to teach French. A June wedding? A grandchild in July? It was a fine family tradition! Anne smiled to herself remembering her own hasty, shotgun wedding.

She brought herself back to the problem at hand. "So, OK. Your father and I have discussed your plot to get Georgie and Helen sorted out. I can't tell you anything about the past. We think you should pour on the guilt about them making Emily miserable. She could threaten to keep the baby away from both of them, if they don't kiss and make up. Georgie is very susceptible to guilt. They both love Emily. It should work."

ROSS WAS HAVING a unique money experience. He didn't know what to do with a large amount of it. He wasn't used to worrying about money. He was used to manipulating it. A whole week had passed since Georgie offered to support the church renovation with a 100K of her personal funds. Funds he was managing. Bloody hell! What a mess.

He wanted that money to create a safe new home for Emily and the baby. He didn't want that money which would call into question his personal integrity and probably cost him his job. He didn't want to burden Emily with the problem, and he didn't know anyone he could talk to about it.

Fortunately, Emily was totally preoccupied with the on-going loving attention of her father, and Carrie's constant consultations about the plot to solve the family feud. The wedding was almost an after-thought to the rehearsal dinner where he was expected to be the ringmaster at a three-ring circus.

His personal monetary reserves were pretty well maxed out, but he was now the owner of a well-appointed one-bedroom apartment with all mod-cons. It was good enough for temporary housing, but he didn't want to bring the baby there.

He passed an indecisive and unprofitable day until finally it was quitting time. As usual, he went directly to Hantsport to check up on the day's renovation progress. The apartment was almost ready. Today, he was stopping at Tideways to pick up BB and Miriam who asked if they could come see the church.

Miriam was in awe. "Ross, the western sun through this stained-glass window is heavenly. Whatever you do here, you have to feature this window."

BB looked around with a more practical eye and sat on a convenient pew. "Man, if I'd had access to these pews when I was building, we wouldn't have had to buy any furniture. What do you plan on doing with them?'

"Never you mind, BB. Forget furniture and tell Ross what we're thinking." Miriam said.

BB sighed and rose to do his duty. "Ross, our little Emily is upset about a lot of things right now, but she's real happy with you, and so are we." BB took a cheque out of his wallet and handed it to Ross. "We'd like to see you get this church fixed up before December. This should help you get started."

Ross took the cheque and sat suddenly on a pew. "BB, I can't take this. Oh my God, this is overwhelming. It's probably most of your retirement fund."

"Ha! Don't you worry about us," Miriam said. "BB hasn't spent a dime since he married me. I manage our money and we can afford this easily. You stop your fussing and make a good home for our Emily and the baby." She smiled at a shaken Ross and patted his shoulder. "We were going to leave it to Emily anyway. Think of it as an early inheritance."

"Listen to me, boy. You cash that cheque. Money is no damn good unless you spend it." BB sat again and rubbed the worn pew. This is fine wood. You could make some great stuff out of it. I might be able to give you a few ideas."

Ross stood up and hugged them both. "This is Emily's money. I'll talk to her about it tonight and let you know what she says. It's her decision, but whatever she decides I want you to know I'll take care of them both as long as I live." He rubbed his eyes with the heels of his hands and turned to look at the window high on the back wall. "A person could start to believe in miracles here," he said.

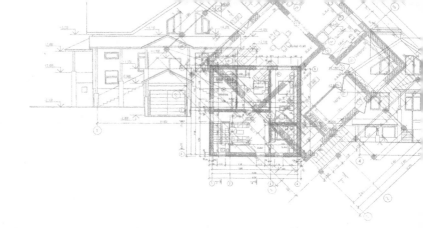

Forty-Five

G EORGIE HAD HAD enough. It was her third week of playing helpless and the effect on Angus was totally unrewarding. It was clear he was enjoying himself immensely. He had taken over most of the visits while helpless, over-heated Georgie sat in the car. He couldn't stop talking about his good works. He was driving her crazy.

Today was Thursday, and he was tutoring Al Miles. He came back to the car with a bounce in his step she hadn't seen for a decade. *The jerk.*

"Georgie, I swear that young man never had a chance in life, but we're going to change that. He has a hard time reading but his math instincts are terrific."

"A lot of people don't get a chance, Angus. You shouldn't be surprised that there are people in the world outside the privileged life of the university."

"You know, he might just make it to university. I can keep tutoring him even after this summer is over." Angus smiled a sweet, satisfied smile that almost drove Georgie off the road. She pulled to the curb and turned to face him.

"Angus! Get real! When you go back to Acadia you will sink into your bolt hole and the only person you'll be talking to will be that man in Toronto." Her face was bright red, and Angus could feel the heat radiating from her body.

He reached out and patted her shoulder. There was heat coming through her shirt. "Georgie, please be calm. You're making menopause worse. I can feel the heat from here."

It's damn near time you felt some heat. You-you-you Philistine!"

Angus carefully removed his arm and leaned against the passenger door. Georgie sobbed quietly while her husband was lost in thought.

"I've never been called such a name before, Georgie. I don't think it really applies. As I understand the term, it refers to people who have no interest in intellectual thought. I know you are sick but..."

"I'm sick of this whole situation, Angus," Georgie interrupted. I thought you loved me, but it's clear you love that damn house more than me. You won't talk to me about it. You won't even go with me to look at it. You won't talk about how we're going to live after this summer is over. You are a passive-aggressive son of a bitch."

Angus clutched the door handle and considered jumping from the car as Georgie pulled from the curb and make a hair-raising U-turn. She was driving while she was still crying. She had called him a vulgar name and she had cursed – twice. Menopause had her in its grip and she had him in the suicide seat.

"Georgie, please stop. This is dangerous. Where are

you going?"

"I'm taking you to the house. You're going to look at it and see how tall and straight it is now. You're going to finally admit that I saved it from sliding down University Avenue. You're going to get over this crazy obsession or else."

OWEN AND EVAN were celebrating a family victory. They decided to dine out. Owen sent a text to Georgie.

Problems overcome. Meet at the Pub at 6 tonight.

"I hope she can join us Evan. She's got a lot of family problems of her own, but I'm sure she'll enjoy knowing that families can eventually come through." They settled into a comfortable booth and ordered a celebratory beer.

Georgie arrived shortly after 6:00. "Owen. Evan. How good of you to text me. I needed that text more than you know. Tell me all you've overcome!"

Evan was literally bouncing on his seat. "I'm staying here from now on. My mum and dad agreed that I can finish my degree at Dal and that I can live with Uncle Owen and help him out this winter. I'm pumped!"

Owen laughed, "Yeah, we're both pumped. I've been liberated from being a horrible person. My sons are happy that Evan wants to eventually take over the farm. They told me they didn't want the money from the sale. They were just worried about me. Sometimes, we make unfair assumptions about people. I wronged those good boys of mine."

Georgie was thoughtful as she enjoyed the effusive outpouring of future plans from Evan and the quiet pride of his obviously happy uncle. Her own future was far from certain. It seemed she was now the only Horrible Person left on the

Look-Off. She couldn't stop the quiet tears that threatened to dampen the joy of Owen's victory.

Owen noticed her distress. "Oh, Georgie, forgive us for being so insensitive. We're so relieved to have restored good relations with the family we're acting like all family problems have been solved. I'm so sorry."

"Oh, please don't apologize, Owen. I'm truly embarrassed to be raining on your parade. I'm so happy for you both. I'm crying happy tears, I think."

"Yeah, that's it, Georgie. Fake it 'till you make it. That's what I always do." Evan reached over and held her hand for a moment. "Maybe you should have a beer, too."

Georgie liked an occasional beer, but certainly not in public. She made a quick decision. "Thanks, Evan. I'll have whatever you're having. I'm not an educated beer drinker." *I'm the talk of the Town already, Mother, so give it a rest!*

Dinner over, Georgie drove cautiously to her temporary home. Anne was in the kitchen, "Anne, I'm going to hell."

"Glad to hear it. I don't want to live without you in this world or the next."

As Anne hugged her, Georgie let go of every bit of pent-up misery. She cried out her frustration with Angus and her fear for herself. "He doesn't love me. I'm a horrible person. Oh Anne, what am I going to do?"

"Blow your nose. Is that beer I smell on your breath? Where have you been? You're not drinking alone, are you? Oh my God, did you drink in public? Holy crap. Did you just break a mother rule?"

"Menopause will do that to you," Georgie quipped as she used most of the box of tissues on the kitchen island. "I had a beer at the Pub with Owen and Evan. They're so happy it made me miserable. I'm going to hell."

THE CONDO WAS peaceful. Deep contentment lay over the lovers like a weighted blanket. Emily was almost asleep when Ross's voice broke the silence.

"Who passes on the hair gene? Is that the man or the woman? Expectations have been raised. I don't want to fail."

"I think they're born bald. Relax. We can always do a home perm if the kid doesn't come up to scratch."

"You are the woman of my dreams. Did I ever mention that I love you dearly? Seriously, I love you from here to Hantsport. How do you feel about gifts?"

"If you are going to keep asking questions, I want to be fed. What do we have to go with chocolate ice cream?"

Ross obediently got up and looked in the fridge. Salsa? Bacon? Oh, wait. Here's a bottle of blue cheese dressing. I'll make you a sundae."

"It would serve you right if I threw up all over you. I'll have chocolate ice cream from the carton and later some crackers and cheese."

Ross laughed and handed over the ice cream and a table-spoon. He sat at the table and studied the love of his life.

"Sweetheart, one more question. Would you like to finish the upstairs of the church before the baby is born?"

"It would be the best of all possible worlds, but we both know there's no money. We have to wait. We'll be OK in the basement for awhile."

"Maybe we don't have to wait. Your crazy family is coming to the rescue. BB and Miriam gave me a cheque today and Georgie offered to give more. If you accept, we can renovate the upstairs right now. Would you feel OK taking their money?"

Emily scooped out a gigantic spoon of ice cream and smiled at Ross as she waved it about. "Speaking for the women of the world I have to ask. Why are they talking to you about this? You've already made your deposit. I'm the one holding valuables in the vault."

Ross winced. "Ouch! They thought you were overburdened with Angus and the feud and didn't want to add to your stress."

"Oh stress. I'm determined to give it up until December. I've decided that good things are going to happen from now on. Stepma and Helen are going to reach a peaceful détente at the rehearsal dinner. Dad will be overcome with emotion at our wedding and propose again to Stepma. She will finish the house and at the big reveal in September dad will see the error of his ways and devote himself to making everyone happy instead of smarter. There is just so much to look forward to."

"Yeah, there will be a wedding. But, after the rehearsal dinner, do you think we'll have any wedding guests left?"

"Who cares? I've decided to trust in the universe. Didn't someone say things always work out for the best?"

"Yeah, that was my grandmother. She was often wrong."

Emily licked the empty spoon. "I don't see the problem about the money. Let them do their thing. They wouldn't offer it if they couldn't afford it. Nana is a life-long saver and granddaughter protector. Stepma always wants to get rid of her money. Let's take the money and run."

"If I took the money, I would have to run. These gifts have to come to you, and you decide how to spend the money. Here's your cheque from BB and Miriam. Georgie offered more." Ross slid the cheque over the table to Emily. She glanced down at it and dropped her spoon.

"Ross. This is for 90K. Georgie offered more? We can do up the church big time. Why aren't you ordering drywall? I've had enough ice cream. Pass over the crackers and cheese."

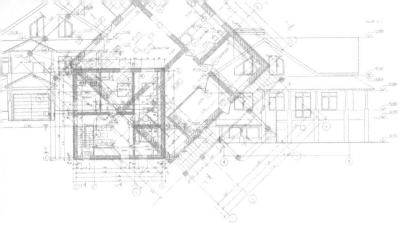

Forty-Six

IT WAS REHEARSAL Dinner time. The beat of BB Gun and the Pistols playing below in the Churchill House dining room seemed to come through the soles of Carrie's feet, but she didn't feel like dancing. When she'd come up with this confrontation plot, she was certain there would be a positive outcome. Now she was doubtful the divide could be conquered.

Emily was doing her best. She was crying and pleading with the two silent combatants. "You're breaking my heart. I don't understand why you hate each other. I love you both, but you don't love me and my baby enough to talk to each other and stop all this tension."

"Emily, honey, I don't hate anyone. Not even Helen."

"Yeah, that's it. Butter wouldn't melt in your mouth, but you say hateful things anyway. You've always been like that." Helen smirked at Georgie and put her arm around Emily.

Carrie saw an opening and leapt in. "She's always been

like that? Even when you were in school together?" Helen took the bait. "You bet. One day she was your friend and the next you were chopped liver. I should know. She did it to me."

"Sometimes, the only way to protect yourself is to stay away from dangerous people. That's especially true when you are a helpless child," Georgie replied calmly.

"Wow! That's a good one. What kind of a dangerous person was I in grade four? That's when you ditched me without any reason. You wouldn't even walk home with me anymore."

"I had to protect myself. I couldn't trust you." Georgie said with a small sad smile. "Some children can be thoughtless and destroy things without thinking."

"Oh, so now I destroy things. What the hell's the matter with you? You sanctimonious bitch."

Ross was about to say something, but Emily laid a restraining hand on his arm. "Let them have at it," she whispered. "This is good."

"Yes, Helen. You destroy things. You destroyed my happy childhood. You destroyed my trust in my parents, and I've never felt really sure of anything since." Georgie broke down in tears while Helen and the audience looked stunned.

Helen's bluster was gone and replaced by genuine confusion. "What in God's name did I do to cause all that shit? I was only a kid."

"You took me behind the cloakroom door and told me there was no Santa Claus," Georgie wailed.

Helen burst out laughing. "That's it. That's why you dumped me? For God's sake Georgie. Everyone was laughing at you. You were the only kid who still talked about Santa

257

Claus like he was real."

"He was real to me. He was important in my life and you took him away. And you didn't care."

"Get a grip. Whoever heard of Santa Claus ruining a life? Jeez! Look at what you did to me. You stopped talking to me. You wouldn't walk home with me. You just froze me out of your life and I had no idea why."

Carrie was totally unaffected by the emotions in the room. "OK, you two. These true confessions from grade four are all very entertaining but you're both well past your childhood. It's time you stopped all this bickering and acted like expectant family members creating a positive environment for our new baby. You owe it to Emily and the kidlet to stop this right now."

Emily dried her eyes, rose, and took Helen and Georgie by the hands. "Carrie's right. I'm so sorry you were both hurt so long ago. I hope it makes you understand how important childhood is. I want my kid to come into a peaceful family. So, give each other a hug and snap out of it. We have a wedding and a baby coming and I want a happy family. Understand?"

IT WAS THE day before the wedding. Miriam was looking forward to the unusual ceremony in the Memorial Garden at Churchill House. The children were having a civil wedding with a Justice of the Peace presiding. They had written their own vows. Thank heavens Carrie had taken charge of the music, so BB's only role would be as a non-performing guest.

This morning, she had commanded Angus to accompany her to Halifax. Her excuse was to look for an appropriate hat for the wedding, but in truth she wanted a private talk with her troublesome and troubled son.

"Angus, dear. It's time to make some important decisions. You need to move home. Georgie says the house is right on schedule and will be ready by September. Have you seen it yet?"

"Yeah, she drove me by it. She wanted me to go in but I refused. It's not my house."

"Angus. Don't be ridiculous. Of course it's your house. She's doing all this for you."

"No, she isn't, Mum. I don't understand her at all. I was happy. Emily was happy. I thought she was happy. She never complained about anything. Then she got menopause and that legacy and she just - just went crazy."

"Angus! She didn't go crazy. She decided to stand up for herself. She told you when she first moved in that she wanted to make changes, but you and Emily wouldn't let her."

"She agreed not to change things, Mum. She promised!"

"Good God, son. So, she promised. Did you think she would never change her mind while she watched the house fall apart? While she watched Emily grow up and want to move away? While she watched you do whatever you wanted never paying a bit of attention to her?"

"She didn't want my attention. She always wanted to do things herself. She liked being busy, doing good works and helping other people. I thought she wanted me to leave her alone to do her own thing. I thought we had an understanding."

"Well, perhaps you did at one point, but Angus, that was almost twenty years ago. Emily grew up. The house needed serious repair. You got tenure and focused on your career, Georgie needed more from you. And you, my dear, were absent."

"Tenure was a life-changing milestone for me. Georgie reminded me recently that when I got tenure, I told her mathematics research was the most important thing in my life."

"Oh no, Angus. You didn't!"

"Well, certainly, I did. Getting tenure is recognition that your intellectual contribution is critical to the community of scholars. She understood that."

'I wonder. It seems to me neither of you understood anything." Miriam gave up and concentrated on her driving. She had no idea where to look for a hat. Did anyone in Nova Scotia sell hats these days? Should she have ordered one online from England? The 101 Highway ended, and they drove into the Bedford commercial hub.

"We'll start in the Bedford Mall," Miriam told him. "There are some very nice stores here and there should be a hat or two. You can sit and have a coffee while I shop. Use your time to think about where your life is going."

Angus sat gratefully at a small table and prepared to wait as long as necessary for his annoying mother. He ordered a roast lamb sandwich from Pete's and munched it happily.

Georgie used to cook his favourite dishes for him. He suddenly recalled the Beef Wellington he never got to finish at the January birthday party. Georgie was strange all that evening. It must have been the start of menopause. His throat tightened and the lamb suddenly tasted like cardboard. Would there be another birthday party? What if she never cooked for him again?

He rose quickly from the table and threw the remains of his sandwich away. He bought a large coffee wishing he had a bottle of Scotch to go with it. He was tired of living without Georgie. True, she was suffering from menopause, but he couldn't let that ruin their lives. He had to find a way to get her back and let her take care of him again.

Finally, his mother appeared beside him. "I hate shopping, she announced. "Let's go home."

Arriving at the van his mother passed him her keys. "You drive home, Angus. I'm exhausted and hatless. What a day!"

"Mum, I haven't driven in years. I always forget where I'm going, and I scare everyone. You have to drive."

"Oh pooh! That was before you had some real-life experiences this summer looking after Emily and helping Georgie. I've been watching you and you're beginning to smarten up. Drive the darn van. I'm tired."

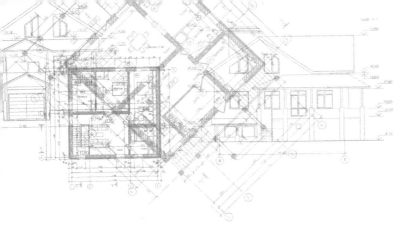

Forty-Seven

H ELEN LOOKED AROUND Anne's spacious kitchen, "Well, this is a step up from your kitchen, Georgie. This is great."

"I'm glad you like it, Helen," Anne said. "I wanted us to get together before the wedding to see if there's anything more that needs to be said between you two. I know we all want to make Emily happy."

Georgie was finding it hard to concentrate on the wedding. Guilt had her in its mighty grip. "Helen, I've been awake most of the night thinking about how badly I treated you. I'm so sorry. I can't believe how thoughtless and hurtful I was. I was just thinking about myself. Selfish. Selfish. Selfish. Have you really forgiven me?"

"Well, I'm tryin'. Don't they say forgive and forget. I think I can forget all that kid stuff but you're still freezing me out of the only family I have left."

"Helen, that's not true. I've never stood between you and

Emily. You get together with her all the time."

"Yeah, at my house. I want to be included in the family birthday parties. You've been having them for years and you never invited me once. That hurts."

Georgie began to cry. Anne pushed the box of tissues toward her and grinned at Helen. "Helen, you would have spit on her birthday cake if she'd invited you. You were always doing your best to make her life miserable. 'Fess up! You did some bad things too."

"Don't blame Helen," Georgie sobbed. This is all my fault. I'm a horrible person. Ask Angus. Ask anyone. I'm going to hell."

"Anne laughed out loud. "Helen, let me introduce you to Georgie, the Martyr. She enjoys blaming herself for everything. I've been listening to this crap for years. Her parents ruined her, but I was hoping that she'd started to smarten up."

"I thought her parents were Mr. and Mrs. Perfect. They always gave me the willies. How'd they ruin her?"

"Well, they told her she wasn't worthwhile unless she was doing something for others. That lesson sunk in and now she doesn't believe it's OK to want something for herself," Anne explained.

"That can't be true. She wanted Angus and got him and Emily too."

"Oh Helen, give it up! Angus went after her, not the other way around. You never had a chance with Angus and you know it."

"Helen grinned. "Yeah, well, I got to know him a bit more this summer, and I've decided she's welcome to him."

Georgie was still crying. Helen reached over and patted her shoulder. "I'll 'fess up to one more thing, Georgie. I agree with you about the house. It was a wreck and needed to be fixed. I went by last week and it looks fine. I even told Stan he was doing a good job. You should have seen his face!"

"He won't go in the house. He won't even look at it", Georgie wailed. "What am I going to do? I can't live without him. I can't." She gave up trying to be upright and dropped her head down on her folded arms and sobbed her heart out on the island counter.

"Anne was unimpressed. "Don't worry, Helen. She'll recover in a minute and want to save the whole damn world all by herself again. She never learns."

"Shit! No man's worth all that crying. Snap out of it, Georgie. If he means so much to you just go get him. Men aren't that hard to figure out."

ROSS WAS HAPPY. Today was his wedding day. Yesterday, he had gone to Halifax to visit a barber who specialized in making curly headed men look like mature, sober adults who got married and raised a child. It was almost successful.

His best buddy, Bruce, had flown in for the weekend just to offer support.

"Dude! You should have asked for a messy man bun. You look weird with short hair."

"Thanks, Pal. Your man bun looks super paired with your full beard. Do people get confused looking at you?"

"Ha! Not in my part of Northern Ontario where men are men and barbers are non-existent. Speaking of confusion are you sure you're doing the right thing?"

"Yeah, I am. I'm betting my life on this one. You'll see. She never got an engagement ring, but I found a great wedding band. Don't lose it! I've got to get dressed. And I don't want to hear any north woods comments on my wedding attire."

Ross dressed quickly in his wedding finery. They were getting married in a garden. Emily had decided to wear a flowered sundress and he was wearing a flowered short-sleeved shirt and jeans. Bruce raised an eyebrow but restricted himself to supportive silence.

They arrived at Churchill House early. Carrie had been busy. The garden was full of baskets of flowers and carefully arranged white folding chairs. The day was fine. The setting was beautiful. Family and friends were gathering. Emily would soon be here. Ross smiled. All was right in his world.

Angus and Georgie were seated side by side, Ross and Bruce stood by the Justice of the Peace. Emily and Helen, her matron of honour, took their places. Carrie's hired string trio played soothing music from the verandah. The ceremony began.

Angus was only aware of Georgie. He concentrated on sending her telepathic entreaties to notice him. He reached over and took her hand.

Georgie was trying to pay attention to the ceremony but was only aware of Angus. She concentrated on sending him telepathic entreaties to notice her. It worked. She squeezed his in return.

The Justice of the Peace announced, "You may exchange your vows." Ross's strong voice captured Angus's attention.

I promise to love and protect you as long as I live. If we disagree, I promise to never give up working with you to find what makes us both happy. You are the most important thing in my life.

Angus felt those words go straight into his inattentive,

unthinking, and selfish heart. He was a fool!

Emily's voice rang through the garden. Georgie was so proud of her. The sullen teenager was now a loving, caring mother-to-be. Her words were heartfelt.

I promise to love and protect you as long as I live. If we disagree, I promise to tell you what I need and honour what you need. You are the most important thing in my life. I promise I will never put my needs above yours. We will build our life together.

Georgie dropped Angus's hand to mop her eyes which were now brimming with tears. Emily's words touched that last cold corner of her heart that refused to trust that love was real and would not betray her. She loved Angus. It was time she acted like it.

Forty-Eight

The wedding was a thing of beauty and a joy forever, Anne thought as she and Carrie lingered behind to thank the Churchill House people for their excellent service.

Carrie was more ebullient than usual. She danced from room to room thanking everyone, saying effusive goodbyes to people she had just met, as though they were long-lost friends. She finally danced up to Anne and announced she was ready to go home.

"I sent Henri home hours ago. Can I come home with you for awhile? I just want to talk and talk. I'm so happy."

"Sure, kiddo. Come along. I'm pretty happy myself and Terry bought a fridge full of champagne."

"You married a good one, Mother. I'm going to do the same. Henri will make a great husband. He can speak French and do lots of other clever things."

"Yes, I know, dear. Let's go home and get drunk on Terry's cache. Did you notice Georgie and Angus? They looked like teenagers again. Perhaps they've learned a lesson or two."

Terry was waiting for them. Henri hadn't gone back to the apartment. He'd arrived at Terry's and the two of them were now seriously happy on good spirits. Terry hugged his daughter. "Honey, you did a great job. That was a terrific wedding. Did you happen to notice Georgie and Angus? They looked like they had just rediscovered sex. It was hilarious!" Terry roared with laughter. "I bet Georgie won't be home tonight!"

"That's a thought. She went back to Tideways with BB, Miriam and Angus. I'd say a small prayer if I knew any," Anne giggled.

"Pour me a glass of the good stuff, Dad, and I'll give you another real laugh," Carrie said.

"While you were watching Georgie and Angus, Helen was making her own move. She and Owen were yukking it up all evening. I never saw her charming side before. It was pretty impressive. I think Owen might have been smitten."

"Or he could have been drunk," Terry offered. "It's hard to imagine Helen being charming."

"*Eh bien*, it was an excellent wedding. Everyone was happy. The families were calm, and BB did not try to rock and roll."

"Good point, Henri," Carrie said. "I had a hard time convincing BB that he didn't need to play at the wedding. He was all set to shake the walls of that old mansion."

"How are your studies going, Henri?" Anne asked innocently. "Still on track to graduate in May?"

"Oh yes. All is well at Acadia. Everyone tells me I will find a job easily, but not to accept anything in Halifax. Apparently, it is almost impossible to find a reasonable place to live in the city these days. Everyone is talking about it."

"Yup. That's the affordable housing crisis that has been creeping up on us for a few years now. Governments have stopped investing in public housing, co-op and non-profit housing starts are way down. Rents are going through the roof. All we need is some national crisis we haven't planned for, and we'll all be in a real mess." Terry sat suddenly and propped his chin up with his hand. "I think I'm drunk. That's the longest speech I've made in years."

"Well, I found it very sobering. Let's talk about weddings again," Anne said. "Who's next?"

"Very subtle Mum. I'm taking Henri home now, so he doesn't say anything he'll be sorry about tomorrow."

"*Non! Non!* I could never be sorry. Let's plan a wedding, *L'amour de ma vie.* You know, we don't have to wait until May."

"That's just what I was thinking," Anne raised her champagne glass to Henri. "Let me tell you about a very interesting family tradition concerning weddings and children."

Terry roared with laughter while Carrie pointed a finger at her mother. "Yeah, I understand your wedding was just in time."

"YOU KNOW THAT wedding reminded me of the sixties." BB sighed with nostalgia for the good old days. "Those two kids and the bush man who stood up with Ross would have made real good hippies. It was a blast from the past."

"Miriam smiled and rose from her favourite chair. "It was so simple and so real. Our dear little Emily is in good hands. I'm going to bed. Come on, old man, you need to settle down."

Angus and Georgie were seated side-by-side on the uncomfortable day bed that Angus knew well. "I'm going to run Georgie home. See you later," Angus said.

"Don't hurry back, dear. I'm sure you have lots to talk about," Miriam grabbed BB's hand and headed for the bedroom.

Angus pulled an apprehensive Georgie to her feet. "Angus, it's only three blocks. I can walk or I can call Anne. I'm sure she's still up."

"No need. It's too dark to walk. I'll take the van. I'm driving again. I drove Mum back from Halifax, and she was so relaxed she fell asleep. I think I'm going to buy a car. I remember I like driving."

Georgie fastened her seat belt and was not a bit surprised when Angus turned left instead of right as he reached Main Street. "Angus, Anne's house is to the right. You're going the wrong way!"

"Not anymore, Georgie. I've been going the wrong way for a few years now. We need to talk and I'm taking you to a convenient private parking lot. We're going to stay as long as it takes for me to convince you that you're the most important thing in my life."

Georgie was silent until they pulled into Ross's church parking lot and Angus turned off the engine. He took her hand and kissed it. "I love you, you know. I only hope you still love me."

'Oh Angus, I have loved you forever and have so much to apologize for. I've treated you so badly. I didn't try to explain how important a safe home was to me, and I didn't think about your needs. I just wanted my own way. I wanted to do everything all by myself. I'm such a horrible person. I'm so sorry."

Angus leaned over the awkward space between them and

kissed her deeply. "Don't apologize. I have a better idea. This van has a bunk in the back."

Sometime later Angus roused himself enough to speak. "Can life start again when you're fifty? I feel like a new man."

Georgie kissed him again and laughed. "You certainly do. But I loved the old one too. He just hasn't been around for awhile."

"I know, Georgie. I was lost for a time there. You know, I probably needed to be shocked out of my rut. You did good."

"Oh, no Angus. I wanted my own way more than anything else. My father would disown me."

"Well, he was a good man, but I always thought he was too hard on you. It's OK to want good things for yourself."

Georgie sighed. "When I heard Emily say that Ross was the most important thing in her life it went right to my heart. I think I've been annoyed at you for years for saying math research was the most important thing to you. And then, I did the very same thing. I made having the house I wanted the most important thing to me."

"Ah, yes, the house. I don't like it, Georgie. It doesn't look like home, but I'll move in if it makes you happy."

"Ah yes, the house. It's going to be beautiful, but it's my house. It will always be my house. I want to live in our house. A house we both love. What are we going to do?"

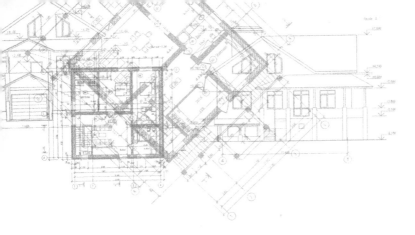

Forty-Nine

THE NEWLYWEDS' THREE-DAY honeymoon was over and White Point Beach was only a pleasant memory. Ross and Emily were back in the condo which was obviously too small to contain the energy of a non-stop dancing Carrie and an abnormally chatty Henri.

"Carrie! Slow down. I'm six sentences behind you already," Emily declared.

"I'm trying to tell you. Your wedding caused all kinds of good things. And you've been away for three whole days. You need to catch up!"

"Ok, but one thing at a time, please," Ross pleaded.

Carrie held up one finger and started to count. "One. Georgie moved out. Two. She never came home after the wedding. Three. Angus is driving again. Four. The two of them are shacked up at the Grand Pre Motel. Five. Get this! Mum says they asked her to find them a house to live in." Carrie stopped for breath while Emily and Ross tried to catch theirs.

"Man, those old people move fast once they get going," Ross said.

"*C'est vrai,*" Henri held up one finger and began to count. One. Anne and Terry want a grandchild. Two. They decided Carrie and I will get married. Three. We're planning a wedding. Four. Anne wants babies very soon. Five. We agree."

"Oh, you two, stop now," Emily said. "This is too damn much. Dad is driving? Another wedding? I can't believe my ears. Tell me Aunt Helen is tying the knot and my amazement will be complete."

"Ah ha! You might get that wish too," Carrie said." Did you know your Aunt Helen could be charming? Maybe they teach charm at witch's school so you can sneak up on people. Anyway, she and Owen have been seen at the Pub since you've been gone. The town is buzzing."

Ross was looking thoughtful. "Anne is looking for a house for them? I wonder what brought that on. Georgie has been fixated on the old house for months."

"Don't know, but Mum says they're both happy about it. Time will tell, I guess. Let's go out to eat. I'm starved and I need lots of calories to keep up with Henri these days. Now that he's trying so hard to please Mum." Carrie twirled around the table and kissed Henri with enthusiasm. The newlyweds rolled their eyes.

Ross pulled his wife to her feet. "Let's eat with these two and then check on the church. The apartment should be finished by now."

"I thought you were moving into the upstairs," Henri said. "Has Carrie missed *un peu de* gossip?"

"Oh, they're working on it. It's seems there's some kind

of trouble in China and some supplies are late getting here. You can't buy everything local or even in Canada these days."

"We'll be fine in the apartment for awhile," Emily said. "Hantsport's interesting. You can walk everywhere. And everyone seems to have a dog. Ross! We never discussed dogs."

"Ross held up one finger and began to count. One. I like dogs. Two. They always have names. Three. Babies need names too. Four. I like Rosina. Five. Rosco works too."

"On my God," I hope those are your dog names, Emily said with feeling.

ANGUS WAS IN the math building for the first time in weeks. It felt like a lifetime ago. Sylvia was very pleased to see him. "Oh, Prof MacLean, we've missed you around here. How are you?"

"Wonderful, thanks, Sylvia. Can you set up a meeting with John? I'll only have time for one class this semester. I'm involved in a number of community things. I'm not going to be here as much this year."

"I've heard there've been a lot of changes in your life." Sylvia allowed herself a small jab at the so-called intellectual elite. "It seems you've learned a lot over the summer."

"You bet. I suppose you heard I'm driving again." Angus laughed heartily. "Mum got me started and then I remembered I like it. I don't even mind getting lost once in awhile."

"Don't worry. You seem to be on the right track now."

"Sylvia. I'm a changed man. I'm paying attention to where I'm going from now on. Let me know when John can see me. I bought a cell phone too. Here's my number."

A changed man, indeed, Sylvia thought as he left the

office. A cell phone! And he didn't even ask about Professor Erlichman. Perhaps there's hope for all of us, if women can stand up for themselves and demand that their men pay attention.

Angus walked to the parked van and drove to Tideways. He was grinning like a mad man. *The right track, eh? I still get lost sometimes but my family always sets me straight.* He drove down Main Street waving to every student he saw. "Georgie," he said out loud. "I'm having fun!" He gave the idea some careful thought. Perhaps the last time he was totally carefree and full of fun was when he was seventeen before Julie unleashed repressed hormones. His short life with Julie was clouded with the enormity of expecting a child and worrying about her health. When Emily was born and Julie died, he became focused on making himself a worthy father and a success at university. Even his early marriage years with Georgie were not carefree as he tried to navigate the treacherous waters between her and Emily. Then he got tenure and essentially left Georgie on her own. *No more*, he vowed.

He pulled smartly into a parking spot and noticed that Georgie had already arrived. Her beat-up little purple Soul was parked there. He needed to buy her a new safe car.

He entered his parents' apartment and found them drinking tea and eating muffins. Georgie rose and gave him a welcome kiss. "I went to Just Us Coffee and bought muffins and then I stopped at the Tangled Garden and bought some of their wonderful preserves. Just try this Rose Honey, Angus. It tastes like summer."

BB was lifting a muffin dripping with red jam to his mouth but paused to instruct his son. "Try this Radiant Raspberry jam and remind yourself what real food tastes like. That Beverley at the Tangled Garden can cook. Bless her heart."

Angus leaned down to kiss his mother. "We'll buy you a hundred bottles for the road, Dad. It's a long way to California."

Miriam smiled and poured Angus some tea. "We've been talking about Georgie's latest wild idea, Angus. It's truly inspirational. And it takes care of a secret little guilt I've felt for a very long time."

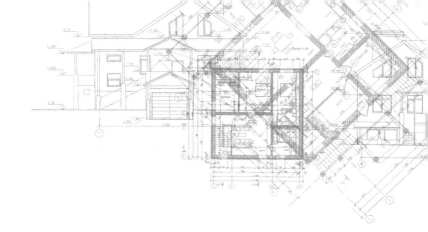

Fifty

S EPTEMBER WAS ALMOST over. Georgie was driving back
from Wheaton's in Berwick where she had purchased
two incredibly delicious coconut cakes. She couldn't bake
anything herself as she and Angus were still at the Grand Pre
motel. She sped back toward Wolfville and a celebration at
Anne's. Another celebration. She rejoiced that the unhappy,
grief-filled months since the fateful January birthday party
were over. She smiled as she realized it was now nine months
later. It had been a miserable gestation period but there was
new birth everywhere. *It seems there is a power working for
good in the world whether I behave badly or not. I'm surrounded by miracles.*

She pulled into Anne's driveway and parked behind BB's
van. *My husband–the safe driver.* A miracle indeed.

Everyone would be here tonight. It was a going-away
party for BB and Miriam. It was an engagement party for
Carrie and Henri. It was a new apartment celebration for

Ross and Emily, and it was a new home announcement for Angus and Georgie. Helen and Owen would be here too, but they hadn't made any miraculous announcements–yet.

Terry opened the door and took a cake box from her hand. "Come in. Come in. Just us four here yet. Angus and I are talking real estate over Scotch in the den. Anne is fussing in the kitchen. All is right with the world."

Anne was indeed fussing. "Georgie, where in the hell have you been? Oh cakes. Berwick. Right! Get your ass in here. Terry, go back to the den. We have things to do."

Georgie stepped forward and enveloped Anne in a long, calming and life-affirming hug. "I love you more than you'll ever know, Anne. Thank you for finding us a house with a double oven. Soon you will have a huge sesame roasted cauliflower casserole."

Anne sniffed a bit and stepped over to the fridge. She removed a bottle of club soda and filled two champagne glasses. She handed one to Georgie and said, "If ever a party called for a ritual beginning this is it. I've adapted our birthday toast." She handed Georgie an index card neatly printed with familiar words. They raised their glasses and read together.

Friends together, Friends forever, Friends without end, Love brought us grandchildren and family peace, Amen.

"OK, so it doesn't rhyme," Anne said. "It's from the heart, and mind and soul. Oh, Lord. I'm so happy. We're writing our own romance novel."

FINALLY, ALL THE family was present. Miriam looked at the precious people gathered around the dining table and said a small private prayer of thanksgiving. Her boy was safe at last. Safe from his own self-protective ways. Dear Georgie had saved him. She smiled a loving, grateful smile at Georgie across the table.

Georgie took it as a signal that Miriam was ready to speak "Quiet, everyone. Miriam wants to make an announcement."

Miriam paused for a moment then took BB's hand and held it as she began to talk. "Tomorrow, the MacLean family is going to right an historical wrong. BB didn't know when we built our house that the land had come to my family by suspected shady dealings. His honour wouldn't have let him build there, so I didn't tell him until years later. Now, Georgie and Angus have made it possible to put things right. You tell them Angus."

"Georgie and I have decided to deed the house and land back to Acadia. Mum has always thought the lot belonged to them. We're asking that the house be called, 'The MacLean House' and be a place to house visiting scholars and researchers."

Helen looked at Emily. "Hey, did you agree to this, Honey? That was your home too. Don't let them shortchange you."

"Emily put down her Club Soda and smiled serenely. "Oh, I agreed, Aunt Helen. I already got my legacy and we're building a home of our own. All is well."

Anne spoke up quickly to fend off more Helen questions. "Speaking of moving, I've just found a new home for Angus and Georgie. They saw it today and put in an offer. It's ideally situated between Hantsport and Wolfville. Easy access to work and grandchildren. Call Walker Real Estate for all your housing needs!"

Everyone laughed and the happy mood was restored

as generous slices of coconut cake were consumed. Terry proudly served his North Mountain coffee and the last of his cache of champagne.

Georgie let Angus answer the curious questions about the new house. It was a recently built brick home in Avonport on the Bluff Road. They both felt a connection with it when they walked in. Angus would have a generous office with a view of the water and Georgie would have a bright, modern kitchen with a double oven. She could see the water too from the large window above her new kitchen sink. She wanted her father to know she was finally happy and at peace. *The new house is heaven on earth, Father,* she told him. He answered immediately.

Do not lay up treasures on earth....

Georgie suddenly laughed out loud just as BB was asking if the living room was big enough to hold a concert. Several startled heads turned her way. "Oh sorry, everyone. My father is always in my head, and he just reminded me not to get too attached to earthly treasures. It made me laugh because he obviously hasn't been keeping up with me. I've learned my lesson. A house is not the most important thing in life."

Helen couldn't let that pass. "Yeah, well, I know I wouldn't want to be stuck in a motel for the next two months waiting for closing. That sucks. Anne should have made a better deal."

Georgie laughed again. "Helen, for years I've searched for a house to keep me safe. I've finally learned the only safety is to trust in love."

Anne raised her glass to Georgie. "Way to go, enlightened one. Tomorrow, I'm filing your application for membership in the, Do It Yourself Happy Ending Society. And your father can finally rest in peace."

Printed in the USA
CPSIA information can be obtained
at www.ICGtesting.com
LVHW041609300824
789714LV00001B/66